SHAWNTELLE MADISON

D1715742

Copyright © 2013 Shawntelle Madison
eBook ISBN-13: 978-0-9887985-0-2
Paperback ISBN-13: 978-1494765767
Paperback ISBN-10: 1494765764

Cover design: Shawntelle Madison
Edited by Jennifer Jakes and Abigail M.
Stock Image: Dreamstime © Masta4650

ACKNOWLEDGMENTS

Every book has a history. A beginning of sorts. And this book had been written long before Natalya and my Coveted series. Tessa and Rob's story actually helped create the universe for the Coveted books, so it seemed fitting that their tale should get a chance to hop into the hands of readers.

I have so many people to thank for helping me with this book. To Sarah Bromley and Cole Gibsen for being there from the beginning, at the moment when I found my writing voice. To my Magic & Mayhem Writer sisters for assistance in making sure the cover for Rob and Tessa's story shined. Thanks Amanda Bonilla, Amanda Carlson, Nadia Lee, and Sandy Williams! (Jeannie Lin gets major props for helping me find Rob!)

Jennifer Jakes, you're such a wonderful friend and editor! You're amazing!

Additional thanks goes to Nadia Lee, Lori Washington, and Jessica Scott for their guidance on a few important points in the story and to Amanda Bonilla for reading a few scenes for me.

The opening of this book has been read by so many people including critique partners Amanda Berry, Jeannie Lin, Kristi Lea, and Dawn Blankenship. Thanks, ladies!

I have to mention Jim McCarthy, my literary agent. Jim read a previous version of Tessa and Rob's story and somehow saw a rough gem waiting to become something more. Thanks for believing in me, Jim!

To anyone I didn't mention, thank you for being there to support me. I'm grateful to have you in my life.

Chapter 1

Dating Tip #24: Witches hate warlocks who want to jump into bed after the first date. Just because you can pull a rabbit out of your hat doesn't mean you can pull something magical out of your pants.

From behind the desk in her matchmaking agency office, Tessa Dandridge thought she'd heard it all until her client blurted, *"My last date had National Geographic boobs."*

She leaned forward, praying she had a serious expression. "Liam, you're a five hundred year-old warlock. You can't be picky when it comes to witches. I understand some women tend to decline and often use glamour to portray themselves as something they're not, but you shouldn't close yourself off from perfectly fine dates."

"Tessa, after all these years, I feel like I've obtained a status that should attract younger witches who aren't hags — no offense, ladies." He glanced to where Tessa's assistant, Danielle, took notes.

In her line of work, too many warlocks used the wand between their legs to do all the thinking. "Don't talk that way about the women I represent. The simple fact is that you won't be able to relate well to most of the younger women in my club. They have a lifestyle that you don't follow anymore. I think you'd be better suited to an older witch."

Liam shook his head and stroked his salt-and-pepper-colored beard. The wealth and power he'd accumulated in the magical community hadn't attracted any quality women—women who didn't need an enchantment spell to remain in his presence. The young ones found him disgusting and the older ones weren't going to put up with his superficial crap. Of course, she couldn't tell him that…

With enthusiasm she added, "Now, trust my professional judgment. Danielle will arrange a party in a week for you to meet eligible women. You'll love who I have for you."

Liam had approached her agency a few days ago claiming he was tired of the old-school witch matchmakers who weren't hip enough to find a woman worthy of his status. He was full of it—and she didn't mean all-power magic either. He was out for sex, plain and simple. And if she didn't need the income so badly, she'd have sent him packing.

"Why can't I just help you pick out the women you intend to invite?" he asked. "Then I'd be sure to find one I like."

"If you connect with someone, then you're free to go out on a personal date. But, you're not allowed to cast any spells on her and I expect the date to be platonic. If you both have a good time, you can continue on your own from there."

He frowned. "If you could just sprinkle in a few younger ones—"

Tessa cut him off. "Be sure to stay open-minded over the next couple of days."

He tapped his finger on top of her desk. "About this no sex thing…I see no reason why two adults can't have a good time together if the feeling is right."

"Because I run a matchmaker service. If you're looking for a call girl, there are plenty of them around town. I make marriages, not one-night stands."

Deep furrows lined his forehead. He rose, gripping an old oak cane between long fingers. With a curt nod, he shimmered and disappeared into mist. She'd won, for now anyway.

Danielle rose and removed a piece of lint from her tweed skirt suit. Tessa had dragged her best friend from Northwestern University in Chicago to New York City to join in this venture. Over the years, she had been the optimistic, perky side to the business. From her blonde pixie haircut to her short, dainty frame, Danielle exuded sunshine. "Two or three witches we have on file fit Liam perfectly."

Days like these made her long for weekends. "Thanks, Dani."

She nodded and left. Most likely to take care of something Tessa always forgot to do.

Time to focus on what the day would bring. The glare of the morning sun peeking over the New York City skyline reflected against her iPhone as she confirmed her full schedule. It looked like she would have enough time to run an errand or two before a lunch with an important client. So, with a skip in her step, she left the office to enjoy a bit of the day before she had to head back to the office.

Spring had arrived in New York City, and the streets buzzed with pedestrians flowing down the streets. April sunshine wasn't too hot or cold, the perfect time to enjoy the city. Tessa hailed a cab to the curb. A sexy businessman in a tailored suit emerged and grinned. His emerald-green eyes glanced at her legs and ran up her skirt. Before settling on her hazel-colored eyes, his gaze lingered on her chest. If Tessa didn't have a limited amount of time to get things done, a brief conversation might've been in order. Her gaze drifted to his ring finger. Not married. But he wasn't supernatural either, so she smiled and tried to enter the cab, only to find out she wasn't the only one eager to reach her destination.

An older woman dressed in a dark red coat swept in like a vulture on a kill and slid into the seat.

"Whoa!" Tessa said.

One would expect the cab driver, or even the gentleman in the suit, to say something, but the woman gave Tessa a rude gesture, grabbed the door, then slammed it shut. Everyone left her standing on the curb gaping.

Just another day in NYC.

The man in the suit shrugged and offered a half-assed apology, then walked away. Wow. Good thing she didn't do matchmaking for herself.

She glanced at her iPhone. Since she didn't have much time left, she'd have to walk until she caught another cab. The exercise wouldn't kill her.

The first stoplight she reached took forever so she checked her cell for any new messages. She got through a few before a strange sensation stirred her stomach. It was that feeling of being watched. A long shadow extended toward hers, showing the profile of someone tall and lean. Long legs. Wide shoulders. Even though he stood a few feet behind her, she could practically sense his heated gaze as it traveled from her high heels up to her calves. Caressed her inner thighs then rested on her ass.

She shifted her weight while the light remained red. Enough time had passed for him to take in her favorite black skirt which showed off her hips. His gaze then tickled the nape of her neck beneath her shoulder-length brown hair. For a moment, she was self-conscious that he could see through her and take in the opening of her shirt.

The desire to lick her dry lips intensified, and the urge to turn around to see the man grew stronger. Was he attractive? Would she be horrified to know he was checking his phone instead of checking *her* out?

Hell, wasn't she usually spot-on with this kind of thing?

She slowly turned around to see a gorgeous Asian man staring at her. Most of the time—like earlier—she would've glanced at his ring finger, but her gaze left his to linger on muscular legs wrapped in jeans before moving up to his intimidating chest. His shadow hadn't lied. Matter of fact, it had held quite a bit back from her. This dark-haired guy was hot as hell and had bedroom eyes to boot.

A buzzer sounded, the light turned green, and a few pedestrians began to walk across. For a second, she wasn't sure what to do. Yeah, a shocker. Most men just spoke up and tried to strike up a conversation. This one simply walked around her and strolled across the street and this time, Tessa took in *his* backside. She would've watched the view even longer if she hadn't stared so long the light changed to yellow. She prepared to dart across but gave up since she didn't want a free ticket to the emergency room.

Now separated from him by a busy street, Tessa lost the mystery man as he disappeared down the street into a parking garage.

Rob Shin rarely used his magic in public—especially for something as childish as messing with stoplights—but he couldn't help himself.

He was practically on the clock with a time limit imposed by his employer: Repossess the vehicle at the 12th Street parking garage by noon. No pit stops, no coffee breaks, and most certainly, he shouldn't have held up all those humans so he could undress that witch with his eyes. He made a beeline for the elevator. He could practically hear his boss busting his chops. "You keep messing around and sooner or later, the wrong person will see you doing that shit, Rob. If you really want to get paid, play by my rules."

There really weren't many rules to be honest. Just one in particular for his line of business: *Don't get caught.*

He couldn't afford to break the rules right now. Not with others he had to be financially responsible for.

His target, a Honda Coupe Civic, sat between two other smaller cars. Everything was squeezed in nice and tight, but he had more than enough room to work. He opened his worn satchel and reached into the folds.

A whisper, followed by an old man's chuckle, emerged from the satchel. "I've never seen you do that in public before, *Doryeonim.* What was so special about that one?"

Rob sighed. "Oh hush and pass me what I need, Harabeuji."

Magic brushed against his hand like layers of electrified silk. Between the layers, his hand encountered wands, bolt cutters, and other tools. So many toys to play with — the tools of the trade for a warlock who needed to collect on the debt of others.

The restless spirit woven into the old leather bag harrumphed. "You don't see me casting spells to charm the Gucci bags off 5th Street."

Rob chuckled. "Every man has his weakness. Mine happens to involve beautiful women with long legs. You have no room to talk. You almost convinced me to let you spend the night in a leather outlet."

"The craftsmanship in that place was impeccable. Almost as fine as what you'd find in a *Goryeo* marketplace. Have I ever told you about the time I armed my handler with a grand ice staff? He stood proud against ten fire demons!"

Rob couldn't help but shake his head with a smile. Harabeuji had constant tales from medieval Korea to tell him, but he had work to do. First things first, he needed to disable the spell protecting the vehicle. A pretty powerful one, but he'd faced stronger ones before. After that, the hardest thing he'd have to face was the parking brake. He tried to focus on the mission at hand, but frowned when he smelled perfume. The scent was probably from the car beside this one.

The feminine perfume filled his nostrils and then settled into his tightening groin. He couldn't help but think about the woman he had on the street. Damn, she was beautiful. She'd satisfied his curiosity easily enough when she peered at him.

Rob had been too long without a woman.

He should remedy that when he got some spare time which, unfortunately, he didn't have much of. Just one month of medical leave and then he'd have to report back to base.

His commanding officer had been kind, yet firm. "You're too good of a SEAL to stay down for long, Shin. Don't get too comfortable."

He returned his attention to the task at hand. Finish the mission and get paid.

Chapter 2

Dating Tip #13: Ogres have a face only a mother could love. But simply because you're not the best looking broomstick in the closet doesn't mean you can't put your best foot forward. Treat a woman right and she'll fall for the fine qualities you possess inside.

Not long after running her errands, Tessa headed to lunch with her high profile client, Archibald Cramer. The guy was a serious head-case. In a few weeks, she would hold his fourth party. When she'd interviewed him nine months ago, Tessa sensed an oncoming train wreck. At first he had wanted a regular run-of-the-mill witch. Tessa had held back a grin at the time. Was that even possible?

"They're all boring," Cramer had said with a snort during the first dinner party she'd arranged for him.

The whole process reached the point where Tessa needed multiple recruiting events over several months. The second party had blonde witches, while the third included hippie witches from Canada. She'd all but given up on that party, but to her delight, six witches clad in sundresses and overalls, spouting free love, had hitchhiked here from Quebec. The fourth recruiting session had plagued her with his most outrageous request yet: witches who had witnessed the Salem witch trials. At the time she remembered trying to keep a straight face — that didn't last very long.

With most clients, Tessa would've told them they were casting spells from the wrong end of their wands. But this man offered an opportunity her agency needed to break into an exclusive circle of clients and generate major income. So she replied with her standard response. "I can think of a few successful ladies who would fit your requirements."

Most of these successful ladies only exist in your imagination.

He'd paid his past invoices, but he'd made it clear he wouldn't toss out the big bucks unless the right women showed up for his next party. The growing pile of bills filled her with worry. A few months ago, she'd secured her first business loan at the local bank. After that, she'd contacted the dwarves for a low-interest loan. Now that things had thinned out considerably, she'd scraped the bottom of the cauldron pot and got some cash from warlock loan sharks so she could continue to operate her business. She was far too ashamed to ask her parents for money.

One big payoff was all she needed to catch up.

After arriving fifteen minutes late to the elegant Porterhouse Restaurant in the Upper West Side—thanks to an accident—she spotted Cramer in the far corner of the dining room. Loud business conversations filled the room as she walked past the white linen-covered tables to reach him. She slid into the leather seat, and a waiter offered to place her napkin.

The older, black-haired warlock looked up from his meal and snorted. "You're late."

Cramer was a bear of a man, filling space both physically and mystically. A protective bubble of magic formed a haze around his shoulders like volcanic ash, bobbing and weaving as he ate his food. The telltale scent of cinnamon hit her nose. No matter where he went, dark magic followed him like an obedient pet.

"Sorry about that, Mr. Cramer."

The waiter came by with a salad and a glass of white wine.

"I ordered your usual when I grew tired of waiting," he grumbled.

On the inside Tessa cringed, but her face was all smiles and apologies. Why show the client how petrified she was? To gather confidence, she beat her fear into submission with a heavy rock and met his hard stare.

His bushy eyebrows rose. "So far, I've been disappointed with the women you've found for me. Not that any of them weren't decent witches, but none of them seemed a perfect fit."

He stabbed into his rib eye and took a generous bite.

"Now, you know as well as I do, Mr. Cramer, that finding love, real love, is a difficult journey that takes time…and patience." *And realistic expectations.*

"After the first party, I was hopeful and patient. But this round and round, with a bunch of boring old biddies — I want to get this over with so I might move on with her in my life. I expect you to pull out all the stops or else your business may not fare well with the Supernatural Business Bureau."

His last comment was as sharp as his knife slicing through his bleeding lunch. Tessa's heart skittered and the cucumber she swallowed nearly lodged in her throat. *Keep smiling, even if you're choking.*

Just like the Business Bureau for humans, the Supernatural Business Bureau was important for supernatural business owners. You couldn't be some witch selling random grow-hair spells on the street like the olden days. You needed credibility and the Supernatural Business Bureau offered that.

They dined in silence for a few minutes. Two werewolves entered the dining room. Instead of following the maître'd, they gave a wide berth around their table to reach their seats. The attractive couple scowled in Cramer's ·direction. From her werewolf clients, Tessa had learned powerful warlocks and witches reeked of earthy magic. Whether this was a pleasant scent or not, she never asked, but from the look on their faces, Cramer wasn't the cleanest shirt drying on the rack.

Men like Cramer swung around their staffs like proud peacocks, and at least among witches in the magical community, he knew he was hot stuff. Based on this expectation, he made obnoxious demands on Tessa's agency.

He finished his glass of scotch in a single gulp. "Look, Miss Dandridge, I know I've been a difficult client. But I believe in your abilities. If you can get ole Ebenezer Clarke married, then you've got a fighting chance in my regard."

The waiter swooped in with a fresh drink like he'd been waiting for the exact moment Cramer emptied his cup.

Her client continued to speak. "I'll be traveling for the next few weeks in the fifth dimension performing a great incantation with some associates. I expect to hear from you when I return. If all goes well, I'll confer glowing recommendations to my colleagues in the Supernatural Council."

Tessa hid her pleasure with a short smile. "Why, thank you."

Inside she flipped across the dining room floor—heels, skirt and all. Getting your name mentioned in the Supernatural Council was like making it big in Hollywood. No more waiting tables hoping for the big break, just red carpet events and rubbing shoulders with the rich and famous. Well, the rich and famous who raised the dead and howled at the moon. Her crossed legs twitched nervously, but she managed to sip her white wine and smile during the appropriate moments as the lunch concluded.

They parted ways outside the restaurant, and Tessa tried to stay optimistic, even with his dire warning nipping at her heels. After several months of courting a member of the Supernatural Council, she couldn't afford to lose this opportunity. All of her time and investment had to result in a positive outcome so she could get more clients.

Now that she'd temporarily placated him, her next step was to catch a cab to the parking garage. She had a long trip to Jersey to meet with yet another client. This was one of those particular moments she wished she could teleport places, but instead, like every other young witch, Tessa used the car her family bought her or hiked in high heels. She could've bought a staff or some other magically imbued object to travel in style, but the majority of her money was tied to her business.

After a short cab ride, she reached the garage and headed for her parking spot. Her fingers dove into the bottom of her purse for the keys. Using magic to travel long distances offered advantages, but it didn't replace the normalcy of traveling like a regular person. A city girl like Tessa loved hopping into a car, turning on the radio, and singing off-key to her favorite sappy love song. As she rounded the corner, she finally located her keys and stopped abruptly in front of her parking space.

Her *empty* parking space.

Chapter 3

Dating Tip #6: Wood nymphs are easy to piss off. I don't recommend a bonfire dinner by the beach. You may be using her sister's home as kindling.

As Tessa stared at the empty parking space, hundreds of scenarios ran through her head: was her car stolen, did she park somewhere else, or maybe someone towed it away?

The scent of cinnamon hung in the air, wafting from the position where her Honda Civic Coupe should've been parked. A spell had been cast.

"Sssssshit! Shit! Shit!" Cursing loudly would've been much preferred under the circumstances, but a loud hiss worked instead.

The smell of cinnamon and a missing car meant only one thing: Her car had been repossessed. And tucked inside a locked box in her back seat had been one of the lifelines for her business: a magical object called a Smythe Scroll.

Thanks to a sizable part of the trust fund

from her grandmother, Tessa had been able to purchase the old magical parchment. The scroll was indispensable for anyone who needed to contact magical creatures who preferred to live in the Dark Ages. If you needed to contact crazy Uncle Elmer who lived in a cave outside of Vancouver, then a Smythe Scroll offered mystical instant messaging. Tessa's only method of contacting Cramer was gone.

She seethed as she paced around the vacant space. The fast and hard clicks of her heels echoed through the garage. Getting angry wouldn't solve the problem, but it would damn well make her feel better. She'd hired someone to cast a pretty powerful spell to keep the curious and other minor spellcasters away.

Their magic had failed. Big time.

This whole situation never should've happened. She was usually on point for these kinds of things.

Tessa checked to see if any curious eyes lurked about. A lone car pulled out of a parking spot. She waited for it to leave before examining the signature of the spell. With a delicate dabble in the magical residue, she pulled out a stark cream-colored notice:

ATTENTION: YOUR PROPERTY HAS
BEEN REPOSSESSED

Based on the orders from our client, HOLDSTEAD FINANCIAL GROUP, your vehicle has been repossessed. Please contact the Municipal Supernatural Court for information regarding associated repossession fees, towing charges, and Limbo storage fees.

Contact them my ass! She imagined the ridiculously long line at the courthouse, especially since magical red tape was much worse than the regular red type.

Standing around and mumbling to herself seemed like a viable option, but Tessa called Danielle instead.

"What's up?" she chirped. "I bet the meeting with Cramer went better than you expected."

"Oh, the meeting went fine until I discovered afterwards that my car is missing."

"You're kidding?"

"I wish. It's been repo'd! Look, can you find out for me the name of the repo company used by Holdstead Financial Group for recollections?" Tessa rested her free hand on her hip and tried to think about anything else other than her career taking a death-dive off the nearest building.

"Sure, you know I love a challenge."

Tessa walked to the garage elevator. "Thanks, Danielle. I need a stiff drink."

The rapid clicks of keystrokes echoed through the phone. Danielle moved quickly.

Her assistant joked, "You're in New York, why do you need a car?"

"I left the Smythe Scroll in the back seat."

She groaned—a rare noise from her. "Ouch."

"My thoughts exactly! Call the client in Jersey and tell him I need to reschedule today's meeting for later this week." At least one of her clients picked up a regular phone.

"No problem. Go get your drink."

After a few drinks—which hadn't helped Tessa forget her troubles—she got a text message from Danielle. It included her destination. After a quick cab ride, she found it quickly.

Not long after, she found what she wanted. Nestled between a Nigerian restaurant and Hair for the Modern Woman Salon, she spotted Clive's Magical Repossession. It was a hole-in-the-wall establishment in the Park Slope area of Brooklyn. She'd never visited Park Slope before. A plastic red and white sign with etchings of glamour marked the office to humans as Clive's Recovery.

Tessa swung open the door to the shop and entered the stuffy office. A white-haired warlock stood behind a worn pine counter keeping busy with piles of paper. The files shifted from pile-to-pile as one hand dragged and dropped, while another signed contracts with a bright red pen.

She stepped forward. "I'm sorry to interrupt you, but your company repo'd my car a few hours ago."

The man squinted at her and the progress of the papers halted in mid-air. "Your name?" he wheezed.

"Tessa Dandridge. I have a Honda Civic."

His right eyebrow rose, then he scratched his nose. "Ehh, I sent Rob on the Holdstead job this morning." The papers commenced marching again as he continued. "He went to fetch some stuff from the storage room, but he'll be back in a few minutes. He can get you the paperwork so you can head down to the Municipal Supernatural Court."

"Head to court?" She shook her head and opened her purse. "I've heard too many stories from family members about spending a few years waiting in line to pay fees. Can't I write you a check and then you can give me back my car—"

"Nope! Have a seat, please, and wait for Rob." His returned his gaze to his paperwork.

Tessa closed her purse and bit her lower lip. While she waited, she took in the office, looking for a place to sit. She spied a single seat in the corner with a horrible mustard-colored pattern that gave her flashbacks to the seventies. An old TV with its antenna covered in aluminum foil sat on a dirty end table. Folks still did that, even with digital TV reception available?

On the TV a scantily clad young woman bounded across the stage to wallop her balding overweight lover in the face. The show was a rerun of the Jerry Springer program. Visitor entertainment, perhaps? From the corner of her eye, she caught the old warlock steal a glance at the TV. Apparently, the owner of Clive's Magical Repossession enjoyed watching people lose their common sense on national television.

What kind of boss allowed working conditions like this? With a frown, Tessa strolled across the worn carpet to the water dispenser. The water was the cleanest thing in the room. After grabbing a fingerful of dust, she confirmed the paper cups had likely been used by the first settlers to New York. Using a tissue from her purse, she cleaned it.

She poured in a few drops and nearly dropped her cup as a tall glass of witch's brew walked through the door behind the counter. After placing his overflowing box of items onto a free spot on the floor, their eyes met and a moment of recognition hit.

She'd seen this guy before.

His backside, anyway.

Tessa faked a sip from her cup, but her eyes rebelled and traveled where a lady shouldn't be openly gaping — at all.

He shifted from one leg to another. "Can I help you?"

Did he catch her staring this time? She fingered her bracelet and spouted a mantra in her head, *"Desperation isn't attractive unless it has on a shorter skirt."*

Tessa's inner business maven jumped in. "Hi, my name's Tessa Dandridge." She reached to shake his hand. He didn't take it. "That kind gentleman behind the counter told me I should talk to you in regards to the Honda Civic your company repossessed recently."

His stony face never twitched as she pulled back her hand. He finally spoke after a brief moment. "I'll get the paperwork. The Municipal Supernatural Building is located—"

"Look, you seem like a nice guy." Tessa pasted her most brilliant smile on her face in the hopes of winning him with kindness. "I know how the Municipal Supernatural System works. I don't have the time to wait in line before I get the car back. How about I write you a check for the debt right now and you can pass it along to the company so I can retrieve my car?"

A devilish smirk broke out on his face as he ran his fingers through his black hair. A few messy strands rested over his ears and forehead. As his tattooed arm came back down, the biceps clenched. Tessa blinked a few times to distract herself. A part of her imagined him as a tasty steak sizzling on the grill. And she wanted to take a bite.

"Even *if* I wanted to fetch your car, I can't. It's in Limbo."

"Well, if you put it there, I'm sure you can just…" She gestured with a swirl of her hand. "…pull that puppy right out."

"Limbo doesn't work that way. I have the power to add items, but in random places. Now as to a quick retrieval, you're at the mercy of the dwarves at the Supernatural Municipal Building. They ultimately control access to Limbo." He crossed his arms, daring her to reply.

"I see, well, if you could hand me—" She barely uttered a word before the older man behind the counter directed a pile of papers in her direction.

Thoroughly dismissed by two repo men. Now that was a first.

As Tessa watched his retreating back, she tried to buck up and go over a mental list of the positive points in her life — other than the missing scroll. She had friends. She had a place to live. And her business burned through money like crazy. Positive thinking wasn't her strong point this evening.

Those warlocks who'd brushed her off didn't help her mood either. Maybe she should've emphasized how dire the situation was. Either way, hadn't the guy behind the counter checked her out earlier? Wouldn't he want to be a gentleman and offer a lady a hand?

Entering the cab, she brooded. Her grandmother wouldn't have had these kinds of problems. Yet, with confidence, her Grandma Kilburn had pushed her into the world of matchmaking three years ago.

She could hear her now. The memories from her graduation dinner never faded. "Straighten up in your seat, Tessa," her grandmother had said. "Surviving in the real world isn't an exact science, you know."

The day after her college graduation, Tessa enjoyed dinner with her family, all the while ignoring the stench of burnt lamb her mother had prepared to hopefully impress Grandma.

No matter how much her mom tried, even the best-casted spells on the pots and fine china couldn't cover the sad truth that her mom couldn't cook.

Her mom refused a caterer, hell-bent on staying in the good graces of Grandma Kilburn by cooking the meal herself.

A huge grin spread across Aunt Lenore's face as she pushed her plate of pumpkin cookies toward Grandma's matriarchal seat at the head of the table. Tessa's other four aunts and mother lined the sides of the fifteen-person dining room table set with Tiffany china. They cowered like advisers from an ancient Chinese emperor's court awaiting the next royal decree.

"Daisy, why do you wear that awful sweater all the time? You'll never find a good man wearing something so matronly," Grandma scolded. Her transparent graying form stirred. Not good to rub a rich ghost the wrong way.

As usual, Aunt Daisy would smile as if Grandma had told a great joke and reply, "Oh, Mom. I haven't met the right guy yet." She straightened the neckline of the over-sized forest-green sweater as she used the fork in her right hand to stab her salad.

Aunt Daisy worked with a tax firm that rubbed elbows with Chicago's supernatural elite, but based on the fashion choices Daisy made from day-to-day, Tessa would have to agree that her aunt plunged headfirst into spinsterhood.

Tessa might've inherited money from

Grandma's undead will, but she sure as hell hadn't inherited her barbed tongue.

"Gertrude." Grandma turned to Tessa's mom. "Why ever don't you have a graduation cake for Tessa? I'm too dead to eat, but I don't see why everyone else has to suffer from your cooking."

"Well, I—"

"You act as if you never planned an event before." Grandma Kilburn addressed Tessa's father. She kept everyone on their toes. "Jacob, have the cook run out to the store and fetch my granddaughter a cake."

Her dad nodded with a smile, but Tessa tried to be the peacemaker. "Grandma, I don't need a cake. There's plenty of food and Aunt Lenore made your favorite cookies."

"All right, if you're happy, that's all that matters."

Aunt Daisy smiled. "Tessa, are you sure you won't reconsider the business analyst position?"

During her junior year, Tessa spent a brief summer internship at her aunt's office. After graduation, her aunt expected her to work for them. She dreaded the thought of countless days of boring rows of numbers and ledgers.

Grandma's transparent form darkened as the ghost addressed Aunt Daisy. A chill spread across the room. A common occurrence when Grandma got mad. "I told you she's not joining the firm. My granddaughter's going to New York City to start a business as a matchmaker."

With her grandmother's blessing and

financial backing, Tessa set her plan in motion. At the time, she'd been so energized with the possibilities. She could help people and make a living at the same time. That type of prospect offered more scenarios for fulfillment than project specifications and business plans to create cost effectiveness. But even with her new business, she wanted—no, needed—companionship.

After a day like today, though, Tessa wondered if she'd ever find it for herself.

Chapter 4

Dating Tip #17: Never change into a werewolf on the first date. Some dates need time to adapt to Mr. Tall, Dark, and Furry.

Two days later, Tessa sprang the news to the entire agency.

"Ok, ladies, the Smythe Scroll is missing. That means we have no way to contact Cramer. I have a few weeks until Cramer told me he'd return. Are there any other clients we contact only through the scroll?"

Her morning meeting with the staff started with the most important business. Naturally, Danielle smiled in what could only be considered an oh-shit moment. "I already looked up the information. Don't worry. We need the scroll to contact seven clients."

"And how many of them need arrangements within the next couple of weeks?"

She looked down at her notes, avoiding Tessa's gaze. "Oh, all of them."

"I see… How about we go through all past correspondence and any phone logs to see if we can recover any contact information? That sounds like something for you to try, Ursula."

The intern nodded and made a note.

"Now, we need to proceed as if nothing is wrong with the agency at this point. We'll have to suck it up and use our computerized system for all clients from now on. If the client says we need to use magic to contact him, he needs to provide an emergency number in case our spell 'fails' to contact him."

They nodded in agreement.

"I think we may be able to establish some contacts through networking," Danielle suggested.

Over the past two days, Tessa had gone from angry to frustrated to determined. A lost Smythe Scroll wouldn't be the end of her business. There had to be some way to retrieve the scroll before Cramer, or any of the other six clients, wondered why her agency hadn't contacted them.

A pain bit into her stomach, but she held herself in check. Even though she couldn't shake away a single thought: All of her hard work to establish her business might've been for nothing. Maybe she should've set up shop in small-town Illinois. She snorted. Not as many bachelors, but at least the rental space costs would be manageable.

Once the meeting ended, Tessa escaped to her office for some privacy. Her assistant followed, always a hovering and protective friend.

Danielle closed the glass door behind her.

From her desk Tessa glanced at Danielle and tried to smile. Things would only get worse around here. All she was doing was shuffling money from one place to another. Hiding out until she cornered and caught the big fish that could save her business. Maybe she needed to try harder to reel in that sucker.

She traced her fingers along a piece of paper as a spark of an idea came to her. Didn't Rob dump repossessed stuff in Limbo? Couldn't she follow him around until he opened the doorway to where she needed to go? He had to be the big fish she needed to get out of trouble! She couldn't contain the crazy giggle from her lips. She'd be insane to do it, but her options were limited.

"Tessa, do you need a moment—" Danielle began.

"—I'm fine, Dani," she said. "No need to call the men with straight jackets yet."

Danielle lowered her eyebrows with suspicion, then patted Tessa's shoulder and left the room. Tessa quirked a grin. Now she had a definite plan to find her scroll. She checked her computer and blocked out a half hour in the afternoon for an important phone call. It was time to talk to a potential client.

Clive of Clive's Magical Repossessions.

Later that evening, at a quarter-past eleven,

Tessa stood outside the Nigerian restaurant in Brooklyn. She was in a prime position to catch free smells as the strong aroma of spicy scents tickled her nose each time the door opened.

When she first arrived outside of Clive's Magical Repossessions, she questioned her logic. A woman for Clive in exchange for letting her tag along on repo jobs. Great. But how the hell could a witch with French tips pull off this ruse?

Four hours ago, she'd laid out two outfits on her bedspread and thought to herself, *which one best looks like a repo chick on the hunt*? Courtesy of an hour and a half of "Repo Man: Stealing for a Living" episodes on her DVR, she'd oriented herself to the grittiness of the repo busincss. In every situation the repo men, and women, encountered irate people oblivious to the fact they neglected to make their payments. The reactions ran the gamut from the crying soccer dad to the knife-wielding pimp.

So she selected some jeans and a pair of sneakers. Then she checked herself in the mirror. There was no way she looked tough. She screamed socialite with her jewelry, makeup and hair. For good measure, she'd ditched the jewelry.

Rob left his office, and she walked up to him.

At first he was silent and stared her down with his frigid facial expression, perhaps hoping she'd turn and bolt in the opposite direction. Tessa straightened her back and took a step forward. Her head reached his chin, and she had to tilt hers upward to check out his expression. His mouth formed a hard line, and she could faintly hear him grinding his teeth. This wasn't good.

"Good evening, Rob," she managed.

"C'mon, before I change my mind." He pivoted in the opposite direction. Tessa followed and tried to keep her eyes from straying to view how finely his blue jeans fit over his ass. He had a weathered brown satchel over his shoulder that rested on his trim right hip. A black t-shirt completed his repo man ensemble.

Thanks to her call earlier with Clive, Tessa now had a new client and an opportunity to follow Rob a few times a week. Clive had forewarned her of the dangers involved, but she swatted his concerns away. She had a few offensive spells under her belt. She could handle a disgruntled dwarf or bitter valkyrie who hadn't made payments on a loaned item.

Three blocks later toward 3rd Street, Rob stopped at Starbucks. Was this their first collection point? The twenty-four hour establishment was full of magical and non-magical patrons reading books, using laptops, or eating a late-night snack.

The willowy, dark-haired nymph behind the counter giggled at him when he reached the counter. "Who's the tag-a-long, Rob? She looks scrawny."

He pursed his lips. "Don't start, Arielle. Give me a double black this time."

The nymph offered him a sly smile as her thin fingers prepared the coffee. The other patrons couldn't see her delicate hands as they flowed over the counter with magic trailing like strands of silk blowing in the wind. Dryads, like the one in front of Tessa, usually frolicked in Central or Prospect Park. To see one filling orders at a local Starbucks was a bit offsetting. Perhaps her tree had been relocated to the big city and she was making the best of it.

Rob reached into the pocket of his jeans. Tessa expected him to turn in her direction to ask what she wanted, but he paid for his drink and headed for the door. Her mouth dropped open. *What an ass.*

"Hey, I would've liked something to drink," she growled to his back. A short snort was her reply.

He reached for the handle and paused as he had a change of heart. *How kind of him.* "You got five minutes."

Tessa quickly ordered her latté and trailed after him into the street. After a block, she determined that, smoking body or not, Rob would make a horrible boyfriend for someone. The man was rude and intolerable. They weaved through pedestrians heading toward 2nd Street. She raced to keep up with his wide strides. "Can you slow down, please? Maybe we can take a cab to the next place?"

Rob came to a stop at a busy intersection. She ran into the brick wall of his wide back, her nose smashing into his hard flesh. For a moment, she caught the scent of spicy cologne.

He tilted his head in her direction, revealing his disgruntled profile. "We're almost to my jump point. It's a block away."

She grimaced. "I wouldn't have asked about this if you didn't—"

The light turned green and Rob darted into the street. She sprinted, determined to keep his pace.

When they reached 1st Street, Rob entered a diner. The patrons in green-colored booths ignored them as they walked toward the restrooms in the back. She followed close behind—until he went into the men's restroom. *Well, isn't that fabulous...*Of all the times to stop for a piss. Maybe he did this to annoy her.

She waited a bit before the door opened and a middle-aged Hispanic gentleman brushed past her with a polite, "Excuse me." As the door swung shut, Rob waited near two urinals with his hands on his hips. He frowned in her direction as if to say, *"What the hell are you doing out there?"*

He couldn't treat her this way. Tessa charged inside and raised a finger to cuss him out. He didn't wait for her. She shouldn't have been so surprised when he went into a single closed stall. At least he left the door open. As she joined him, something changed in the air. A speck of magic hummed and crawled along her skin. The cramped space smelled horrible.

So this was the jump point. How quaint! What kind of genius placed a teleportation spell in the middle of a foul bathroom?

Tessa closed the door behind her and

backed into the stall. She turned to face him, finding his hard body only a few inches away. Her raised hands rested on his chest for moment and she brought them quickly to her sides as if she had touched a flame. The enclosed space wasn't the most romantic of settings, but he exuded a strange energy. A brooding power that made her bite the inside of her cheek and look toward the stall's scratched up drab-gray walls.

Up close with the bathroom lights shining down on his head, she could make out the faint stubble on chin. The tight muscles along his shoulders.

"I've never used a jump point in a bathroom before. How do we trigger it?" she whispered. "Maybe flushing the toilet?"

He shifted closer to her. She bit her lower lip as he leaned forward—almost as if he took in the scent of her hair. "The trigger works off our bodies. The gate should open any second now."

Tessa nodded, waiting patiently. Having this man standing close, while trying to be nonchalant, was so damn hard. She'd stood next to countless men of all ages and sizes. Some of them offered wonderful conversation. Yet, here she was—in a stall—standing next to this boorish repo man, wondering what he thought about her. The hum along her skin intensified until all sounds disappeared. It had been years since she'd done this. As a teen, it had been a dare among friends to see how far the rabbit hole went down like in *Alice in*

Wonderland.

The teleporting spell triggered and, with a whoosh, they were snagged out of the bathroom and tossed into the stuffy darkness of a dusty broom closet. The smaller space shoved her toward Rob's chest. She sensed his breath on the crook of her neck, his hardened torso pressed against hers.

"Just a sec, I need to open the door," he whispered. Rob couldn't turn toward the door so his arm snaked from around her waist to reach for the knob. As he tried to open the door, he brushed against her breasts and her breath came out in a gasp. The door creaked open — far too slowly — and she squeezed past him into the hallway of an abandoned store. The faint streetlights outside of a small shop illuminated a display case in the room.

"Where are we?"

"Englewood — we're in Jersey."

From the placement of the dusty counters, this place had to have been some type of pawnshop or jewelry store. Rob peeked outside the door's window. He pulled a stone from his satchel. Using the tips of his fingers while he grasped the stone, he drew an "X" across the pane. The air around them surged to the spot like wind escaping through a tunnel. In one moment the glass was there, in the next, it flickered into a milky white form. Once Rob walked through the opaque glass to the street outside, the glass returned to its regular form. She sighed and waited for him. Not again. She didn't have some fancy rock in her pocket to convert glass to thin air. She tried a basic unlock spell on the door without success. Another spell on the long list of incantations she had to study to advance as a witch.

He appeared at the door again and smirked.

"Not funny, pal. Open the door or get me through it."

Rob stood outside the door with a pleased smile on his face. With a loud click, the door opened. Once outside, they headed east out of the business district into the residential area. At a white ranch-style house, Rob headed up the driveway before she yanked on his arm.

"Is this the place?"

"Yes, could you please not broadcast to the rest of the neighborhood what we're here for?" he hissed.

"Sorry..."

A magical presence was nearby. Something from the basement pressed against the back of her skull. Not the most pleasant feeling. Someone stored something powerful here. As to whether it was a witch, wizard, or warlock she didn't know. Was this what they sought?

Rob reached the maroon-colored side door and, with another unlock spell, he went in. Tessa hesitated before following him in. What was a respectable business owner like her doing entering a home without permission? She could wait outside for Rob to return, but what if he decided to toss the item into Limbo the second he retrieved it? He wouldn't care if she missed the opportunity either way.

The interior of the home was dim with

hardly any lights. In the darkness, the shiny counters of the kitchen gleamed as Rob's flashlight hit them. The only sound was the faint hum from the fridge.

"Isn't this illegal?"

Silence met her inquiry.

They walked through the kitchen to the basement doorway. An ornate arch above the door glistened with a warding glamour carved into the wood. Tessa's nose wrinkled as a putrid smell hit and an urge to flee strengthened. The homeowner must've coveted something in the basement and cast a spell over the space to prevent spellcasters, or even the slightly curious, from opening the door. The shadows around the door twitched and she sucked in a breath. Why was this a good idea again? With each step, the muscles in her legs tightened. Almost tight enough to become painful. Four steps from the door, she couldn't walk any farther and panic settled in her stomach.

Yet Rob continued forward, murmuring softly under his breath as he reached into his satchel to retrieve a long peacock's feather. With the feather in hand, he opened the door and descended into the pitch-black darkness of the basement.

"Rob!"

She managed to step backward before the spell released its firm grip. She turned around and gasped. A small old lady in a floral print shift stood in the middle of the kitchen staring at her.

Chapter 5

Dating Tip #3: If you are allergic to cats, then dating a witch with a familiar is not a good idea unless you are packing some serious antihistamines. Witches are cat hair magnets.

Rob had left her alone for less than a minute and that woman had already gotten into trouble. He wasn't surprised one bit. He smirked as he fetched the crown from the basement. The peacock feather in his hand gave him a very limited amount of time to make it through the deterrent spell and get back.

By the time he made it back up, Rob found Tessa facing away from him, continuing to stare blankly at a harmless elderly woman. "I'll be waiting for you outside."

Without another word, he walked around Tessa, precariously dangling the silver crown from his index finger. The small woman blocked Tessa's path to the side door. He could practically predict what she'd be thinking: *Rob, get your butt back here!*

Harabeuji chuckled, causing the bag to vibrate against his hip. "You're usually not this mischievous, *Doryeonim.*"

He should've been nicer, so his curiosity made him linger right outside the cracked door. Since he'd been here before on another collection, he knew the older woman had a simple request. While he waited, he opened the door to Limbo and quickly tossed the crown inside. Another job completed.

"Will you get me my milk, Lisa?" The elderly woman's voice emerged from the house nearby with a child-like wheeze.

He smiled. He'd fetched her milk and a sandwich last time.

Faintly, he heard the sounds of searching through the cabinets. A fridge door opening and closing. When Tessa's light footsteps approached the door, he opened it with what he hoped was a stern face. "What's taking you so long?"

She glared at him. "We decided to do our nails together while we had a nice chit-chat. I can't believe you ditched me!"

"I thought you could handle it. You wanted to be here so bad."

"Yes, I need help—but you don't just leave people like that."

She looked down at his empty hands. "Did you already open and close the gate to Limbo?"

He chuckled as he headed down the driveway. "While you were busy with your new friend, I dumped the goods."

"Can't you open it again?"

"Nope, it only opens if I have something to repo." He tried to hide his grin. "Guess you'll have to wait until next time."

The look she gave him was vicious enough to take down ten men. Even with the glare she was gorgeous. But as pretty as she was, he didn't have time to mess with debt-laden witches like this one. He had enough problems. But even if she did annoy the hell out of him, another trip with her might not be so bad.

Tessa stalked down the driveway and tried to maintain some distance from Rob. Any closer and she couldn't be held responsible for her actions. Most of them included ripping Rob's limbs from his body.

Time and time again she'd met men like him—loners, rebels without a cause, and hard core silent types whose five-word conversations were enough to drive the most patient of women heading for the hills. Then they wondered why decent women scorned them. If she ever hooked him up on a date she could hear it now: "I spent the whole time feeling like I was talking to a brick wall." Or even more straightforward, "I've had more fun taking my familiar to the groomers, and he's gay."

Rob won this time, but she planned to stick to him like those Levis he wore during his next repo mission.

They returned to the shop downtown. Rob

was silent — big surprise — as he walked ahead of her, not as fast as before. According to her watch, it was a little after one in the morning when they reached the shop. He turned to whisper in her direction as a couple walking their dog passed by. "Wait a second." He stopped her with his hand on her waist. She jolted to a stop from his firm grip.

They rounded a corner and Rob entered the shop. Tessa checked the street for cars and followed close behind. After a few seconds of adjusting to the darkness, she strode to the back of the store to see Rob waiting in the closet. Not again. She honestly didn't want to be in any enclosed space with this man, but with a shake of her head she turned to the side and angled herself into the closet. The sooner she got this over with, the better. She presented her backside to him and at the time she thought it was a great idea — until her body brushed up close against his. He shut the door and closed them into the stuffy space.

Against the crown of her head he laughed, his breath warm as he leaned in closer. *Okay, any second now please.* She could feel his broad chest against her back down to his lean legs. When something stirred and hardened against her buttocks, a whisper of mercy bubbled from her lips.

"Is this gate out of order or something?" Damn, why did her voice have to sound so hoarse? Sultry?

He tilted toward her ear, his breath eliciting a shiver. "Five, four, three..."

With an audible pop, they were thrust back into the bathroom stall at Kathy's Eatery. The toilet should've been behind her, but it was in front instead. Disoriented, she fell forward as Rob grabbed her waist to keep her from touching the seat.

Perfect timing for the stall door to swing open and have an older black guy see her bent over with Rob perched over her doggy-style.

"Not the best place to make out, people," the man said.

Last night had been the most fun Rob had experienced since he'd arrived back in New York. He'd had wild times with old friends in the past, but none of them compared to going on a repo mission and ending with him bending a hot witch over in a broken-down bathroom. Tessa probably cursed his name before she drifted off to sleep in her Midtown palace. Rob chuckled at the thought as he sat on the steps in front of his aunt and uncle's house in Brooklyn. There was hardly any traffic to distract him. Even though it was sunrise, he was wide-awake.

All kinds of debtors had crossed his path for the past couple of days. In the field he'd seen every kind of conman and swindler, but none of them were like her. Yet her car had been repossessed, just like everyone else. Which more or less made her irresponsible. Rob had never owed a debt in life. And he preferred to keep it that way.

From the day he started working, he picked up goods from repeat offenders. One of them included Dagger, an elder warlock who made his missions far too dangerous. That asshole didn't give a fuck about paying or giving back what he borrowed. Lately, the bastard had been collecting pretty powerful shit, which worried Rob to no end.

He was only one man, what difference could he make with powerful beings hiding in every dark corner?

Rob grew up in a household with a white stepmother and Korean father. His birth-mom passed away not long after he was born. During the whole time, his *abuji*, who worked day-to-day for his wage, had been bent on reminding his only son of his Asian heritage at any opportunity. "All these American warlocks don't know shit. You need to earn your way, Robert. If I have to come kick your ass to make you work harder than everyone else, I'll do it." Having someone say that to you in Korean every day when all you heard was English made it stick pretty well.

It had been five years since he'd addressed someone as father. His dad had passed away not long after he'd joined the military. Just saying the word 'dad' in Korean brought good memories instead of the bad ones.

His stepmom and dad never had the best relationship and divorced when Rob was only ten. She took such good care of him, even though she spent money faster than his dad earned it, leaving his father bitter when it came to finances. After his stepmom moved out, his father's busy work schedule never kept his old man from spending time with him on the weekends. Even with a part-time weekend job.

That was the kind of man he wanted to be.

"Stay away from women who have problems when it comes to money," he remembered his dad saying. *"I loved your stepmom more than I loved myself—I think that's why she hurt me so badly when she chose money over me."*

At times like this he missed his *abuji*.

Rob turned to see a man walking down the street. The guy, who looked innocent enough in business casual clothes, checked each of the numbers next to the homes. From the way he crept about, the man was up to no good.

Naturally once he reached Rob's place, he waved to him. "I'm looking for number 712. The Hurst family?"

Harabeuji grumbled. "He stinks like a trickster, *Doryeonim*. Should I fetch a whipping stick for a sound beating?" Thank goodness the human couldn't hear the bag spirit.

"They're my relatives. Can I help you?" Apparently, Rob wasn't the only one who was wide-awake right now.

"Just personal business with Mr. Hurst. My name's Bill. My company bought some debts they owe."

Rob stood slowly. Just another bottom feeder looking to get paid. His satchel stirred at his feet. "I'm their nephew. Any business you got with them can go through me."

The man stepped back and tried to offer a friendly smile.

Rob wasn't as amused. "Just get to the point. Show me the documents. How much?"

"The Hursts owe us $1,435 dollars. They've been overdue for the past eight months." Bill fished through his bag and produced a bunch of papers.

Rob scanned them, but he didn't need to read them all. He'd been through all the paperwork his aunt had crammed in the desk downstairs. After poring over the documents for a few hours, he'd made note of all the names and calculated every dime owed. This company was one of them.

From one of the deepest pockets in his satchel, Rob pulled out a wad of cash. After counting out what was due, he shoved the bills into the collector's outstretched hand.

"Dirty humans," Harabeuji snorted. "I wouldn't give them enough cloth to wipe the slime off their asses."

"Thank you for your payment in full, Mister?"

"Shin. *Mr.* Shin." Rob frowned. "How about you head back to the office now?"

"I'm just doing my job, Mr. Shin."

"I'm not saying you shouldn't do your job. Next time, just don't show up at the crack of dawn, Bill. There are hardworking, elderly people in this neighborhood, and I don't appreciate you coming down here like this."

Bill nodded and retreated again.

"I've seen your letters." Rob didn't want to

intimidate the guy, but he couldn't help it. "They border on harassment. So take your money and scoot on down the road."

The man was practically in the street now. "I'll take that under advisement, Mr. Shin."

Chapter 6

Dating Tip #12: If you're too embarrassed to introduce your girlfriend to your parents, family, or friends then you need to assess what others want for you. But if she's a soul-sucking succubus, the naysayers may have a point.

By eleven o'clock that evening, Tessa arrived in Brooklyn to meet Rob. This time he waited for her outside his office door. He leaned against the gray brick wall staring at the convenience store across the street. His facial expression never wavered as she approached.

"You're late," he snapped.

"I have a business to run during the day."

He snorted and turned to leave. As she trailed behind she said, "You could've left."

"I have bills to pay and, apparently, Clive's a lonely old man."

They stopped in front of the intersection to wait for the lights to turn green.

Tessa softly laughed. "Well, you could introduce him to people. I'm sure since you're such a people person you'll have plenty of friends for him to meet."

The light changed and he marched across the street, forcing her to jog to keep up.

"Where are we going this time?" she asked.

"A job."

"A job where? I don't want to use that bathroom jump point again." She shivered thinking about that horrible place.

An elderly lady using her black cane to walk her miniature schnauzer tripped and lost a hold of the leash a few feet ahead of them. Tessa expected Rob to keep walking, but in a flash he was at the woman's side helping her up.

Tessa tried to offer a hand, but he directed her away to fetch the salt-and-pepper-colored dog. "I got her. Go get the dog."

She turned around to see the schnauzer sniffing among the cars parked along the street. The royal blue leash was easy to spot as it plopped along the ground. The small dog darted from one interesting smell to another.

"Here, boy. C'mere, sweetie." The dog edged closer to the street.

"Stop!" As Tessa clamored toward the dog, it took two steps closer to the curb. She froze, watching as cars zoomed by, hoping and praying the little dog stayed put. She inched closer. Without many options, a compulsion spell seemed like the best option. The magic gathered in her mouth first, forming into an airy bite of cinnamon on her tongue as she spoke. "Calm down. No one will hurt you.

How about you come here?" The dog's ears perked up. About time her last-minute spell casting showed some promise.

Something bumped her back. Her head whipped around to see two humans closing in like a zombie horde. Smoke and booze lingered on their breath. The range of her spell went a bit too far. A couple dressed for a night of clubbing stared at her with glazed eyes. They stood shoulder-to-shoulder with their faces about a foot from hers.

Now that didn't go as planned.

"Everything's fine. Head on home," she managed.

From behind them on the sidewalk, the smiling elderly lady called her dog. Ignoring Tessa, and her kind efforts, he went obediently to his owner. Rob frowned. As the human couple marched to the west, he glanced at them, then turned to her.

Ugh! There was no way he was going to let her follow him on the job if she acted like this.

"Where are we going?"

"East River. Where no one will see when I drop kick you in."

She crossed her arms and turned away from him. As far as impressions go she didn't set the finest example, but he could cut her a break.

They jumped into a cab. "982 River Road— Roosevelt Island." Rob instructed the driver.

After a forty-minute ride to the Roosevelt Island Bridge, they reached the island. She'd never visited the area before and was pleasantly surprised by the beautiful apartment buildings along the main street. In the distance, the lights from the bridge cast a bright glow on the river.

Once they reached their destination on River Street—a brick multi-level residence--Rob paid the driver.

A tingle of power cascaded down the walls. One that Tessa had encountered before. A distant relative, who somehow avoided Grandma's wrath since she'd lost her mind in a game of cards during the Spanish Inquisition, hid herself away in farmhouse about fifty miles outside of Chicago. She wanted no intruders so she used magic to keep the curious away. Another powerful witch used a warding spell to protect this home, but this one was for warlocks only. Tessa confidently walked forward as Rob took a step back to the curb.

"You coming?" she teased.

"Yeah." Rob retrieved his trusty peacock feather and mumbled an incantation to counteract the ward spell. Power radiated from him as his first steps scraped against the sidewalk, but eventually he crossed the threshold. Quite a handy little trick he had there. Inside the lobby, a young Indian woman sat behind the concierge desk. She peeked up from her book. "Can I help you?"

"We're friends of Madame Tuliere."

The young woman checked her notes on the desk. "Mrs. Tuliere is away on business—"

Rob leaned against the counter and fixed his gaze on her. His compulsion magic bathed the counter in white. "Mrs. Tuliere has left something behind for me. *You'll let us pass to retrieve it.*"

The woman blinked. "Of course, Sir," she blurted. "Feel free to call down to the main desk if you need assistance."

"Thank you." Rob left a ten-dollar bill on the counter and headed for the elevators against the back wall and clicked the up button.

"Are we breaking and entering again?" Tessa mumbled under her breath. *As well as coercing people without their consent?*

For good measure, she tossed another ten at the poor hypnotized woman.

Rob stepped into the elevator, and she had to hurry to avoid missing the doors. In the enclosed space, he crossed his arms and faced the doors. When they opened on the fourth floor, he didn't move. She left the elevator and turned to see him standing in the same place.

"Rob, what are you doing?"

He grunted and didn't move an inch. After a few seconds the elevator beeped, annoyed with their dawdling. Tessa shot her arm out to stop the closing doors. When she pulled at him, Rob didn't budge. What the hell? Even stranger, the satchel on his hip grew warm.

"Another spell? I can't feel it." She peered down the well-lit hallway. Two red doors with large clay urns lined the hallway.

"Stop it." The words were barely understandable from his frozen lips.

"All right. All right," she said with a grin.

"Get the ring of keys out of my pocket.

Head into 4B and break the red flowerpot next to the door."

She fished her smartphone out for a quick picture. Seeing Rob like this was priceless. She posed for a quick selfie with him in the shot.

She liked this version of Rob so much better. Silent and docile. Too bad she couldn't leave him like this.

While she used her body to hold open the elevator doors, she leaned down to retrieve the key. His relaxed blue jeans hugged his lean waist. She turned her eyes away as she patted down his left pocket while trying to avoid to grazing between his legs. Empty. The right pocket of his jeans had the keys, but it was wedged deep near the middle. Damn it!

Tessa's gaze darted upwards, and she could sense his smug satisfaction. Did he know this would happen and she'd have to do this? She was tempted to click the emergency button and leave his cocky ass locked in place like this. It most certainly would've served him right.

She pursed her lips and dug her hand into his pocket. She wanted to make this as quick and as pain-free as possible on her part, but of course, she had to dig in and hunt among the pocket change and other stuff in there. Her hand grazed an ample swelling and she mumbled, "Sorry," before retrieving the key.

Rob would have to stay in the elevator while she broke the spell holding him in place. "H-head on down and by the time you come back up I should be done," she stammered with eyes cast downward. She tried to brush away the delicious thought of her intrusion, but couldn't resist mouthing out what came to mind. "Why did the keys have to be down *there*?"

Apartment 4B was the wide brick-red door on the right. A pile of newspapers sat on the drab brown doormat beckoning the homeowner back. Tessa went through the four sets of keys on the key rings before the last one worked. As the heavy door creaked open, she cringed, waiting for someone to rush into the unlit foyer. The small space had a tiny table with a red flowerpot filled with fake dark-purple flowers. A heavy scent of vanilla and clover filled the space. Beyond the foyer was a cryptic living room with billowy black shades, maroon-colored Old English furniture, and an immense grandfather clock in the corner.

Break the red flowerpot, he'd said. Not only was she entering someone's home illegally, Tessa was destroying their belongings. What a great way to build her image as a potential leader in the community. She grasped the fake flowers gingerly and placed them on the shiny marble floor. Then with a resounding whack she broke the red flowerpot against the floor. Not her best Bette Davis performance, but it would work for now.

She stepped over the broken clay pot and left the apartment to see Rob waiting by the open elevator doors. He took a step or two forward, then strode down the hallway to meet her. Once inside the apartment, he assessed her handiwork on the floor. "Better you than me."

Thanks would've been better, but she was used to his attitude.

"Let's get what we came here for so we can leave." The loud tick-tick of the grandfather clock in the corner was creepy. Every time it clicked, the sounds echoed against the walls and thudded against her forehead. She fought a compulsion to avert her eyes.

Rob strode into the living room and walked over to the grandfather clock. The ancient time-keeping device stood a few inches below the ceiling with a large face emblazoned with golden Roman numerals.

She expected him to prep the clock for removal to Limbo. Instead, he examined the edge and pried open a hidden panel to remove a 5-inch tall vase made of Tiger's Eye.

"How beautiful," she murmured. Tessa owned a few pairs of earrings made of the semi-precious stone. The streaks of gold, black, and white in this piece were far more vivid.

The vase hummed like a tuning fork. Rob grasped the urn tighter as his hand shook.

He clenched his teeth. "Active little devil."

The open space between the living room and the foyer served as a workspace for the spell to open a gate into Limbo with a popping sound. Honestly, before her repo adventures the other day, she hadn't seen Limbo before. Every young witch learned about it during her daily extracurricular studies after school. Their instructors scared them into thinking it was some demon-laden place not meant for curious eyes. Maybe it was, but now she had no choice.

Rob held a golden amulet in the air. With a swirl of his hand, light danced from the jewelry and opened a portal into Limbo. She cocked her head and gazed into the pinkish haze. She more or less expected the place to be a beautiful land full of neat stacks of items in rows as far as the eye could see. Instead, her mouth dropped at seeing pile, after pile of magical items scattered about like a trash dump.

Without any consideration whatsoever to the fragility of the object he held, Rob tossed the beautiful vase through the doorway into Limbo.

"Hey!"

"You need to move. You have five minutes." He crossed his arms, then glanced at his black watch. "Make that four minutes, fifty-two seconds."

She stepped through the gateway into the mess that was Limbo. As far as her eye could see, there were never-ending piles of junk. Magical items like wands, staffs, and brooms intermingled with kicked-in basketballs and dolls with their heads torn off. There was so much stuff she couldn't pinpoint if there was ground to step on or if a bottom to the mess even existed. She stepped over a pile of shoes, tattered pillows, and a toilet bowl (what the hell?) so she could get a better view.

"Three minutes," Rob yelled.

Tessa squinted and turned in a full circle to look around for her Honda Civic. Nothing, nothing, and nothing. A Ford Model T appeared to be the only car close by. In the distance, about a mile away, another portal opened and someone else tossed what appeared to be a leather belt into a pile. The leather belt hit a shiny, champagne-colored Honda Civic. Through squinted eyes, she recognized her license plate, barely visible by the forest-green cloak draped over the side of the hood.

"I see it!"

"You have two minutes, thirteen seconds."

She took a step forward. How the hell could she reach her scroll from a mile away across all of this junk? A tingle formed in her stomach as she tried to summon all the magic within her. She extended her hand, reaching for the water vapor in the car to push the box containing the Smythe Scroll to her hand. Not a simple feat. As an inexperienced water witch, she could manipulate water and not much else. The quiver in her belly turned into a painful twist as she pushed harder. The box rose in the vehicle. A bead of sweat formed on her brow. She sensed the light weight of the box. Felt the smooth surface of it.

Behind her, she faintly heard Rob cursing. *Almost have it...* The box floated toward her, then with a sad thud it hit the windshield.

A hand closed over Tessa's waist and yanked her backwards. In one smooth motion, Rob hoisted her over his shoulder. In three quick steps, he jumped through the gateway. Not long after, the portal vanished with a blink of light. Another opportunity gone in an instant.

"Are you out of your mind?" he growled.

Exhausted from the energy she had used to grab her stuff, she clung to his black shirt stretched tight across his shoulders. She hoped he wouldn't drop her head-first to the floor. His back muscles flexed under her fingers.

"You can put me down now."

He hoisted her off his shoulder. "You don't make the best decisions. Do you know that?"

"I almost had it, Rob. I felt it in my hands."

After leaving the repossession calling card in the air, Rob headed for the door. "You could've had it all right, while spending a few decades in Limbo."

She cringed at the thought. People had been lost in Limbo before. The unfortunate ones without the means to get out simply wandered until they croaked from starvation or lack of water.

At the doorway she stopped in front of the broken flowerpot. She motioned to Rob who was walking away. "Could you? The spell's gone."

With a frown, he turned and mumbled a spell while he snapped his fingers. The pieces jumped, and in a flurry, they rushed together to form a new pot. Tessa picked up the red pot and put the flowers back in place. After a quick glance at the grandfather clock, she closed and locked the door.

With that mission successfully completed, minus the scroll, she helped Rob repossess a magical rabbit's foot from a warlock in lower Manhattan and an imbued urn from a nymph in Central Park. By four a.m., she was exhausted and no closer to her scroll. Each trip to Limbo was a jump into a random place that was nowhere near the gateway in Madame Tuliere's apartment.

After such an easy mission gathering the vase from the witch's home, Tessa expected the next ones to go like clockwork. That wasn't the case with the warlock. His rabbit's foot was buried in his tiny backyard, and he caught Rob digging it up.

"Hey, man! What are you doing?" A short man in his white cotton pajamas peered out of his back door.

"You haven't paid your bills, Mr. Flannery. Forrester Magical Holdings is repossessing their property." Rob continued digging as Tessa took a step backwards toward the backyard entrance.

"I've paid in full. Stop that!" Mr. Flannery stumbled into the tiny backyard and tried to wrench the spade from Rob's hand. "You can call the company."

"That isn't my job." With a polite shove, Rob pushed the man back and managed to retrieve a black jewelry box from the hole in ground.

"Look, I need it to protect my home. Give a guy a break, man." He reached for his rabbit's foot as Rob pulled the amulet from his satchel. "I have a young family inside and we've had a streak of robberies."

Rob's hand fell and his face twisted in a sneer. "Don't feed me a bunch of bullshit. I'm not some punk off the street. This thing illegally generates money and you know it. Pay up so you can play up."

Flannery turned beet-red. He raised his fist.

"Try it, pal," Rob snapped. "I will knock your ass into the ground."

The angry warlock stepped back, fuming as Rob tossed the jewelry box into the open Limbo gateway. Tessa almost felt sorry for the guy.

She waited a few feet away in the shadows.

"You got four minutes, move it or lose it," Rob grumbled in her direction.

And that was just the second mission for the night.

After that unsuccessful search, along with the plucky, yet majorly pissed off Central Park wood nymph rampage, she considered tonight one of the most stressful experiences of her life.

The attack in the park flashed in her mind. That nymph was one crazy chick. Wielding a branch with an end sharpened to a point, the nymph came at him screaming and swinging. The whole situation bordered on insane.

They left Central Park, with Rob limping, onto 73rd Street. Tessa asked him if they needed to head to the emergency room, but he shrugged it off with a rare handsome grin.

"I've had worse injuries in the field. None of them from wood nymphs, though." He gently rubbed his left side.

"In the field?"

"I used to be in the military."

She wanted to pry further, but they walked for a few minutes westward in silence.

"You wanna eat before we call it a night? I'm starving," he said.

"Yeah, I could use a bite."

Rob hailed a cab and they headed over to Samuel's Deli off 74th in lower Manhattan. Samuel's was a warlock-owned establishment that offered a special dining room behind the coffee shop in the front. She'd eaten there once or twice before. The coleslaw was to die for but she refused to eat their black-magic banana cream pie. Not without a cast-iron stomach.

The decor was a bright red, black, and white 1950s-style with comfortable cushioned seats and a jukebox playing music in the corner. Her mouth watered with the delicious smells of hot cakes and burgers. Two patrons in particular, a warlock and his wife, enjoyed two tall handmade chocolate milkshakes.

Their waitress, a witch in her fifties with mousy brown hair, ambled over and greeted them. She had a welcoming smile that matched her blue blouse and floral-print skirt.

"Nice to see you back, Robert. I thought I saw you limping in. You need to stay out of trouble so you don't worry your aunt so much."

Rob offered a short smile. "I'm trying, Lindy. You know it's hard in my line of work."

"Who's you friend? She looks familiar," she asked as she handed them some menus.

He introduced them.

As she shook Lindy's warm hand, Tessa said, "I've eaten here a few times during a long lunch. You have good food."

"How nice." Lindy plucked a small twig from Tessa's hair with a grin.

"Thanks," Tessa murmured. *Oh, great.* She bet Lindy thought they were rolling around in park like a pair of hot-blooded teenagers.

"Pete has some hot chicken soup available, but I'm sure, as usual, you want a burger and fries." Lindy looked up from her notepad as Rob chuckled. "You might like the grilled chicken sandwiches, Tessa."

Normally, she tried to eat well to make sure she could fit into her business wardrobe. After her adventure tonight, she felt a treat was in order.

"I'd like the hungry lumberjack breakfast with a side of wheat toast and coffee." Before handing Lindy the menu, Tessa yawned. If she wasn't so hungry, she would've taken a nap on the table.

"You came with an appetite this morning. I'll get your orders in." Lindy left them and then passed the order through the opening into the back kitchen. The grizzled balding cook grumbled, and shortly afterward, they could hear the sizzle of a meat patty being added to the grill.

Tessa tried to think of something to say to start a conversation, but she checked her fingernails instead. Next, while avoiding Rob's face, she pulled at her bracelet to make sure the clasp was tied firmly.

Why don't I know what to say to this guy?

Lindy returned with two glasses of ice water, a coffee for Tessa, and a soda for Rob.

After Lindy left, Rob finally broke the silence. "Are you going to continue spacing off when you eat?"

"No. I'm tired, that's all," she said a bit too quickly. "Trying to stay awake."

Rob snorted. "You're a horrible liar."

She cocked her brow and she rubbed her bleary eyes. Who did this guy think he was? "You think I'm lying?"

"When you lie you look up. Pretty much like clockwork."

From his standoffish attitude, Tessa could've sworn she was just another burr in his side. The whole time he'd observed her like a fly on the wall.

"I'm really tired. As of right now I've been up for more than twenty-four hours." She took a sip of her water, shocked that he'd examined her so close. "I'm surprised I haven't walked into walls or started talking gibberish." She turned the tables on him. "How are you still alive and kicking right now?"

"Training. I honestly couldn't tell you the longest length of time I've gone without sleep." He shrugged. "A few days maybe."

"I couldn't function like that without some magical intervention."

His eyes bore into hers. "You'd be surprised what you can accomplish when your life is on the line."

Living in the Dandridge household with her mom and dad had been a comfortable existence compared to what Rob had been through. She'd never been in a *real* fight before.

The faint scars on Rob's hands and arms spoke of secrets her suburban mind couldn't understand. Hell, the Northwestern University Lacrosse team she played on couldn't be considered dangerous by his standards. And they had been some pretty vicious co-eds.

Tessa changed the subject again. "Are you from here originally?"

"Born and bred. Left a long time ago to join the Navy. Eventually, I became a SEAL."

She opened her mouth to ask him why he came back, but Lindy walked over with two plates of steaming food. Time to chow. Toothpicks held her eyes open by now, but with one bite of maple syrup-covered pancakes, her energy level rose. Across the table Rob made short work of his meal. He applied two generous gobs of mustard and ketchup on his burger. Satisfied with his handiwork, he tore into his burger with gusto. She stopped in the middle of biting into her scrambled eggs as he drowned his fries with ketchup.

"Should I toss out a life preserver for your fries?"

"No need," he said between bites. "I'll rescue them."

Fifteen minutes later, she patted her full belly. The stretchy pants she wore came in handy. Lindy gathered the empty plates and left the bill on the table. She reached for the check and a mysterious breeze blew the paper from her hand into Rob's.

"Got it," he grumbled.

She stood halfway in the seat. "I can pay for

my food."

Rob rose, left a ten-dollar bill on the table, and headed to the cash register.

While browsing the song list in the jukebox, Tessa heard Lindy whisper to Rob, "She looks nice, Rob. Is she a lady friend?" From the reflection in the glass, Tessa saw that he refused to answer, only offering the waitress a devilish grin.

Tessa tried to hide a smile. *Like she'd ever go out with a guy like him.*

After Rob paid, they hobbled back out to the busy street. At six in the morning, the city buzzed with early-morning pedestrians heading to work. They weaved around them as they stood in the middle of the sidewalk.

"I head back out in a few days. Give Clive a call if you want in."

She nodded as he turned and limped away. In a few hours, Clive would spring a bit of news on Rob. Little did he know that he'd be coming to her before she came to him. No more missed opportunities for Tessa Dandridge, thank you very much.

"Goodbye, Rob," she whispered with a grin to his back.

Chapter 7

Dating Tip #2: I cannot emphasize enough the importance of dressing for success. You may want your future dream girl to love you for what's on the inside. But, well, if your appearance hasn't changed since you led the attack on the Great Wall with Genghis Khan, then you need a visit to the local Nordstrom's.

When Tessa finished her work for the evening, she found Rob waiting for her right outside her apartment door. "Rob? What are you doing here?"

"How much do I have to pay you to get out of this security guard thing?"

"I want my scroll back. I'm not letting anyone take my ticket to Limbo away from me."

"I refuse to attend these little parties you plan to hold. What makes you think you can buy everything?"

She snorted. "If I could buy everything I'd have my scroll and a private island in the

Bahamas." She opened the door and walked in.

"What are you doing here?"

Rob grumbled and walked in without an invitation. He glanced around the living room in her miniscule SoHo apartment, taking in her furnishings. When she turned to take off her high heels, she blushed as his eyes burned into her back again.

Why did he keep doing that? Maybe he preferred to observe instead of act. To watch instead of touch…

She quickly shook her head. Didn't she tell her clients to avoid bad boyfriend material like him?

Keep moving and ignore him. By the time Tessa placed her keys on the desk in the living room, Rob made himself comfortable on the couch. A pile of unpaid bills on her desk drew her eye, so she added a thick phonebook on top. No need to advertise her problems.

"So, let me try again. Why are you here?"

"Playing security guard. Now go get dressed before I change my mind."

She chuckled.

He glanced around. "You got a nice, decent apartment."

"It's not much, but it's my place." She was about to ask him if he wanted a drink, but after he placed his shoes on the coffee table and flipped on the TV, she decided he was good to go until she changed her clothes.

He interrupted her escape. "Do you have a roommate?"

"I used to have one when I first moved

here. Now, it's me and my familiar, Kiki. She might make her appearance in a bit for attention." The cat stirred from her hiding spot in Tessa's bedroom at the sound of her name.

"You have *one* pet?" Kiki had jumped into his lap, hungry for affection. Her tail flicked like a fly-fishing pole.

She nodded. Unless she had another and was too busy to miss the elusive feline.

His eyes darted to various places in her living room. "There are nine cats in here."

Her forehead scrunched from confusion, then to frustration. "Oh, those were my familiars before Kiki. They all died."

"Died? Cats live around fifteen to twenty years. There is a roomful of ghost cats in here."

"Over the years, I've had a few problems…"

"That's not what the short-haired tabby just told me."

The madness never ended when it came to Rob. "You aren't an animal empath, are you?" Not only was he wonderful to look at, but he could communicate with Bambi as well.

"Did you really think it was a good idea to put the litter box next to your Uncle Charlie's magic hat?"

"I can't believe Little Toes told you that. It was an *accident*. Uncle Charlie left a dragon in the hat. After the cat used the litter box, he jumped into the wrong place… Why am I explaining this to you?"

She marched to her bedroom to change her clothes and slammed the door for good measure.

"You need to feed Kiki more!" he said.

As Rob sat on the couch for more than twenty minutes, he pondered as to why it took most women forever to put on a pair of jeans and a shirt. Waiting wasn't so bad, though. She had a nice enough place. He'd briefly seen her bedroom as she'd stormed in barefoot. All the while, he wondered how she undressed. Did she do it slowly, taking off her shirt then unzipping the back of her skirt? His groin stirred to life, thinking of her angry, pouty face as she unsnapped her bra.

Maybe he should check to see if she needed any help? He scooted forward on the couch.

"Is that a handmade Prada bag I see?" Harabeuji whispered.

Rob stifled his chuckle and plucked the observant satchel from the coffee table and placed it on the floor.

"Just one peek, *Doryeonim*!" the bag spirit implored.

If his father were still alive, he'd ask him how the Shin family had inherited a spirit with an expensive handbag fetish. Someone probably lost a card game of some kind…

His gaze flicked to the closed bedroom door. With a sigh, he rested against the couch. He should keep his distance. She had plenty of problems and he had a few of his own. A rib-based injury from the field plagued him tonight so he tilted to the right for comfort. Might as well get settled if she planned to take all night. Most importantly, no matter how beautiful she was, he couldn't give in. Soon enough he'd be done with her and he'd escape the witch matchmaker clinging to his side.

Eventually, she emerged and they headed downstairs.

The good news was at least he managed to escape before he fell victim to whatever killed her cats. "Where are we going?" she asked when they reached the street.

"A big job. I need to fetch a piano in Philly. Bigger-ticket items offer longer gateway times."

"That's good! Will we be gone overnight?"

"Maybe, depends on how lucky we get in the retrieval. Where are you going?" He frowned when she turned back toward her building.

"I'll be right back. I want to get my backpack with some stuff."

Rob rolled his eyes. *Good grief, it never ends.*

"No matter the century, women are all the same," Harabeuji grumbled.

Five minutes later, she returned with whatever stuff she *thought* she needed. "I'm sure this job will be easy. Most pianos I've seen can't be hidden away in nooks and crannies."

"Not exactly." He hailed a cab. "Bigger-ticket items imply more defensive measures are in place to protect the property."

As they entered the cab she had yet another question. "I thought I heard talking while I was getting dressed. Did I miss a phone call or something?"

"No phone calls." Only a handful of people knew of Harabeuji's existence and he preferred to keep it that way. Trapping a warlock's soul into cloth—a feat even Rob didn't know how to do—was hard enough, but somehow Harabeuji's powerful spirit had survived after the original leather had been altered countless times from a large pouch to a sack and now to a satchel. He refused to expose his old friend unless he trusted the other person.

"I'm curious," Tessa said, interrupting his thoughts. "How come these people never pay or just don't return the magical items they have on lease?"

Within the cramped space of the smaller cab, he could smell her sweet perfume. The feminine scent made him want to lean in a bit closer than he would've preferred a few days ago.

"Supernaturals are like regular people. They forget, they can't pay, or even worse, they borrow shit and expect not to pay for it."

She frowned as if she thought of something unpleasant. "A car, I can understand, but what kind of idiot thinks a magically imbued item wouldn't be missed?"

Rob snorted. "From the long list of collection jobs I've done this past month, apparently common sense is in low supply."

"I've noticed a shortage lately also."

As they rode south to their first jump point, Rob explained their "travel itinerary." He tried to leave out details he thought were on a need-to-know basis, especially after she began to complain yet again.

"Wouldn't a train ticket or short airplane ride work just as well?"

"Jump points are free."

"I have enough frequent flyer miles for a short trip. I'm more than willing to purchase a ticket for you in return for my time in Limbo."

"You may have money to throw around on last-minute plane tickets, but I don't. Jump points suit me just fine."

Tessa sighed. "Fine! But no bathroom stalls please."

He chuckled, the memory of holding her hips fresh in his mind. "I promise—only clean ones allowed."

The first jump point, one he rarely used, was behind the desk of a closed business south of Brooklyn in Bay Ridge. Dust and cobwebs covered the room, except for a clear path others had followed to reach the jump point. His new assistant avoided touching anything and crept behind him.

"What died in here?" she whispered as she scrunched her nose.

"Quiet!"

The tingle of magic in the jump point tickled the inside of his nose like tiny feathers. He moved the chair to the side, and they gathered behind the old metal desk. Someone had scribbled *"Clean me"* in the dust covering the paint-chipped surface.

He rather liked opportunities like this one. She tried not to touch anything—including him—but she leaned in just enough for him to make out a faint sprinkle of freckles along her nose. She'd used make up to cover the spots earlier.

The strong urge to reach out and touch her face bothered him. She was just a tag-a-long. A nuisance. But he couldn't help staring at her as they passed through the jump point.

After a few seconds, the air temperature dropped as the magic pushed them from a dusty office to frigid darkness. Tessa could hear Rob breathing as he leaned closer to her body heat. Chill crept into her bones, eliciting a shiver. The smell of frozen meat drifted to her nose. Her jeans and T-shirt wouldn't cut it for this place. Rob shifted. She gasped as he missed her shoulder and brushed against her breasts. How the hell did he keep doing that?

"Sorry," he mumbled. The freezer's loud hum made it difficult to hear him. His warm hand directed her forward.

Rob led the way as she walked behind him with her arms raised. An ugly bruise from a hit in the face with a shoulder of beef or a leg of lamb would leave her scrambling for excuses. Rob stopped, and she heard a loud click as he used magic to remove the lock on the door.

The heat from the meat-packing plant work floor hit her relieved face. A lingering stench of raw meat hid under the overpowering smell of antiseptic cleaning materials. Her nose scrunched as Rob pulled her along.

"Where are we?" she whispered.

"About a half-hour south of Boston."

She followed Rob as he weaved through the dimly lit plant until they reached the business floor. A faint hum from the air conditioning through the vents was the only sound.

"Almost there."

She could detect the next jump point around the corner. In its place was a vending machine. They approached the snack dispenser, only to halt when a troll squeezed out from the back. The little man's head reached their waists, and his knobby nose poked out from his chunky face. Even though he had magic to hide his appearance, Tessa could easily see through it to determine he was a hideous-looking fellow. Green bulbous warts covered his left cheek. When his mouth parted, short, yellowed teeth jutted out.

"That'll be four pieces of gold to use the jump point, please." He extended its palm for the cash. She'd yet to ever carry gold in any form other than jewelry.

Maybe he'd take a check? She reached for her backpack.

"I don't pay to use jump points," Rob said.

The troll smiled despite Rob's sound refusal. "Well, perhaps the good lady will pay your way."

Rob snorted. "She isn't paying you anything either."

The little man's smile faded as Rob crossed his arms. "If you want to use the jump point, you have to pay me!" he screeched.

"Why should I pay you when all I want is some candy?"

"Bullshit!" The troll harrumphed. "Look, Warlock, I've got a good deal going here. Four gold coins and you can reach seven jump points from this place. Either pay up or piss off!"

The last thing she expected to do tonight was watch Rob argue with a troll over a jump point toll fee. She'd heard from her dad and uncles all the time about trolls and goblins that squeezed a dollar out of any sucker they came across. *"Tessa, keep your pockets empty, girl. Until they process credit cards, you steer clear of them."*

That was easier said than done, though. The magical bridges of the past had been paved over with new office buildings and suburban homes. Trolls, like the entrepreneurial fellow in front of her, hustled to protect what they could. In this case, it was a jump point behind a vending machine in a meat-packing plant.

"I don't carry gold coins and my lady friend is under my protection." Before the troll could protest, Rob added, "But I'm willing to barter."

"And what have you got?" The troll tilted its head and took a step forward, eying Rob's brown satchel.

He opened the front pocket and pulled out three things: a red yo-yo, a gaudy light-purple ring, and a gum wrapper. Tessa bit her lower lip to keep her smart mouth in check. The yo-yo was the cheap plastic kind and the ring would've been more valuable if they were bartering with a four-year-old. *Way to negotiate,*

Rob!

"Is that all you got? If I wanted a wrapper I could've eaten some of the junk in this machine." The troll's nose twitched. "I sense some pretty trinkets on the lady. You're also hiding something in that powerful bag of yours. Why not show me those?"

"They're not mine to trade, Troll."

The short creature peered around Rob and glanced at Tessa's wrist. His gaze fell on her bracelet.

"What about the jewelry?" the troll asked. "That would make a fine start."

Rob glanced at Tessa. She nodded. "You'll take that and nothing more."

The troll wrinkled his nose and shifted his stance. His purple irises boiled for a second. "So be it, Warlock."

With her bracelet in hand, the short-statured road block owner moved to the side to allow them to pass.

She expected Rob to move the large machine out of the way, but instead he scanned the rows of junk food.

"What are you doing?" she asked.

"I can trigger a particular destination through the machine."

She laughed so hard it hurt. "So you can select your destination through a purchase? That's original." She peered at the row of candy bars. "Let me guess, a Butterfinger would take us to LA? A bag of Doritos to Miami?"

"No." After digging into his pocket for loose change, Rob paid for a pack of Twizzlers and Slim Jim meat snacks. His purchase triggered the jump point.

The magic didn't take long this time. They were tossed from the front of the vending machine to the space behind an old rusty car in a junkyard. Tessa gazed at the broken down vehicles and piles of worn tires. "Is this where you meant to send us?"

"Yeah. We're a short walk from the house."

Rob's idea of a *short walk* was four miles. She kept her complaints to herself. Grumbling wouldn't make the trip any shorter.

Nor would it make the junkyard guard dogs go away either. Rob had been prepared for them, though. As the mutts approached, growling with bared teeth, he tossed the Slim Jim their way. "I know you're cold and hungry," he'd said to them. "But that doesn't give you an excuse to attack people. Here's what you should do to your master the next time he remembers to feed you…"

As usual, Rob remained silent as he plodded along a few steps ahead.

The walk wasn't that bad. The rows of plowed dirt left a pleasant earthy smell, but not pleasant enough for a midnight walk in clean sneakers. Rob preferred to walk through the soft dirt, but Tessa took the long way and walked alongside the field. In the distance, rows of tall evergreens and oaks hid an old Victorian house. A light wind swayed the trees' branches. Stars in the night sky twinkled brightly, quite a contrast to the limited view in the city. She hadn't seen a field in years since moving. A sense of melancholy washed over her and brought a smile. The Midwest girl still lingered underneath.

Rob darted ahead and checked out the house. The gravel driveway was empty. A poorly kept yard showed signs of an unoccupied home. As she approached the front, a hum tickled her ears and flowed into her jaw. Rob crept up the porch's creaking wooden stairs. The wind whistled through the trees behind them. She turned to look through the shifting darkness.

Nothing shifted except the trees.

She couldn't sense any beings within the forest or the house, but her heart thundered in her chest in anticipation of the possible dangers waiting inside. A good witch was taught that sometimes powerful creatures lurked in the shadows undetected. Rob's confident stride slowed and his body stiffened. She could almost imagine him approaching the house with a machine gun in hand. Should she be scared that he was concerned?

Broken lawn chairs and an overturned urn littered the wide porch. She was in the middle of checking out a broken bird feeder when her cellphone rang in her backpack. Rob fed her dirty looks as Tessa searched frantically for her phone. She set the noisy pest to vibrate mode. To keep Rob quiet, Tessa didn't bother to check the caller ID. It wasn't like she did repo work everyday. What did he expect?

A pile of bricks from a discarded masonry project partially blocked a set of ornate oak doors. Rob finagled with the locks a few times, then with success, walked around the pail, shovel, and bricks. He placed his index finger over his lips then mouthed, "Wait here."

Tessa nodded, happy to stand outside until Rob secured the first floor. Something about this place rubbed her the wrong way. Chills on the back of her neck gave her the persistent feeling they weren't alone. After a few minutes, the door opened, and he motioned for her to come inside. The darkness beyond the door left her wary, wondering if anything malicious lingered beyond the threshold. A gust flowed through the porch, making the door bang against the wall.

In the stuffy home, cobwebs and white sheets covered the furniture. A fine layer of dust concealed portions of the oak floor. Based on the many footsteps along the floor, Rob had explored the bottom floor quickly and efficiently.

"Is it all clear?" she whispered.

He nodded.

Tessa followed him from the foyer to the great room on the right. Heavy maroon-colored curtains hung over the tall windows. Behind the covered sofas and tables, an elaborate marble fireplace and grand piano sat in the back of the room.

A few twig-shaped lumps under one of the side table covers caught her eye. Curious, she lifted the dusty fabric and peered at what lay hidden underneath. Someone had lined up wands by length across the table. She touched one, expecting a soft hum, and found nothing, almost as if it were nothing but a regular piece of wood.

"Leave them alone," Rob said. "They're tainted and useless."

Tessa replaced the cover and moved on. "It's been a long time since I've seen one. Aren't they supposed to be sent to the Warlock's Guild for disposal?" Every family had that oh-so-special someone who ended up cursing their wand due to negligent use. Angry wives cursed mistresses with death. Back in Illinois, she remembered a bitter PTA mom had blackened her staff when she tried to off another zealous mother who planned the best school functions. Certain spells shouldn't be cast and, as such, the wands were drained of magic.

"Yes, but apparently whoever owns the piano doesn't care about that," Rob replied.

Silence settled over them, but the quiet ended abruptly as a tree brushed against one of the windows. Rob's head turned to the sharp tapping, and he stopped for a moment before continuing slowly to the piano. She'd never played before, but she knew a fine instrument when she saw it. Her mother had wanted a ballerina, but Tessa danced poorly. In the end, Tessa excelled in violin throughout high school until she accidentally changed the expensive string instrument into a cheap plastic bucket.

During her lessons, her teacher would use a grand piano similar to the one in front of her. As her eyes adjusted to the dark room, she noticed the piano didn't have a sprinkle of dust.

Cobwebs abruptly ended half a foot from the legs. There should've been a cover over the piano, but somehow the fabric had been defiantly tossed to the floor. For some strange reason, her fingers itched to touch the smooth wood and read the peculiar writing carved into the sides. Columns of ancient magical glyphs only witches and warlocks could see.

"Don't touch it! The piano's cursed." His fingers caught her wrist before her curious fingers touched the top board.

"It's beautiful." The compulsion had been so strong. She had to back away to come to her senses.

"Everything around it's dead." His eyes darted to the dead space around the piano where bugs keeled over within an inch of the piano. The source of the irritating hum in her ears came from the instrument.

"This should be easy—" Her phone rang again. She ignored it as Rob fumbled in his satchel for something. The cell phone vibrated against keys and other noisy objects. She frowned and pulled the pest from the front pocket. He took a threatening step in her direction. Before he could snatch her phone away, she answered the phone. "Hello?" She scrambled toward the foyer for privacy.

"Look, I don't mind when a woman has a few kids," a male voice exclaimed. "I sired a few pups over the years. But you put me on a date with a woman who has, like, fourteen kids!"

Tessa rolled her eyes. At least she had this

unlisted client's phone number in her iPhone now. Her client, Denny, wanted an alpha female to help lead his pack. This guy went through women like a cat through catnip. This wasn't the best time for a phone call, but a few minutes and some metaphorical scratches behind his ears should hold him over until Monday.

"Denny, not every woman is perfect. If I recall, you two hit it off on your first date. You both like rock-climbing and traveling. Is the fact she has more than ten kids a deal breaker? You need to see the positives in the matter. Yes, she—"

"Could you take the call outside?" Rob hissed.

She nodded and walked toward the door.

"Is this a bad time?" Denny asked.

"Oh no, I'm working with a client on a team-building activity. You know, working on his people skills by engaging him in extracurricular activities. You can call my office about it sometime in the future."

She continued to babble on with Denny as she approached the door. As her fingers reached for the doorknob, she froze. A murky shadow slithered in front of the door.

"Oh, shit." A wraith. They were ghosts who were chained in purgatory on Earth. In some places, like this house apparently, they clung to darkness and decay, feeding on what little life remained. One of these apparitions advanced on her. Chips of paint from the old oak door fell as the opaque form of the wraith touched the wood. The nasty creature leaked death. She willed her reluctant feet to step backwards. Her mouth stammered, "Rob, R-rob—the door."

Denny called her name as she turned to the great room to see another wraith spill down one of the Roman columns on the fireplace. Another rose from behind the covered couch.

"I gotta go," she mumbled. Power tingled in her fingers, waiting to be tapped, but this wasn't the place.

Tessa shuffled away from the door into the sitting room. Hissing shadows advanced like sidewinders. A sturdy back collided with hers. "I hope you have something in the bag for wraiths. Water witch spells aren't worth shit unless they're on fire!"

Rob dug into his bag as they closed in. They flowed over the covered lamps and from under the heavy drapes. Their hissing rose to a fevered pitch.

One wraith menacingly approached her foot. Her breath caught in her throat. There wasn't any place to go. "Rob, damn it!"

From behind her, she heard the sounds of rustling, then a second later, the room burst into bright white light. The light blinded her. She covered her eyes as the wraith's painful bite seared her foot up into her ankle. Like frightened mice, the dark creatures scattered into the corners of the room. Rob left her side to drive the stragglers away, waving his knobby wood wand about like a torch, driving the more brazen wraiths into the darkness.

As a woman who'd stood in waist-deep

Midwestern snow drifts, she'd experienced the bitter cold on exposed limbs, but nothing prepared her for this. The deep ache penetrated to the bone. She clenched her teeth and caressed her throbbing ankle.

"Are you all right?" he asked.

She nodded, attempting to stand. No dice. "Ow!"

Rob sighed. "Hang tight while I take care of the piano."

Tessa plopped down on the cold marble floor while Rob opened a portal then used magic to shove the cursed piano through the enlarged opening. She peered into the salmon-pink haze, but couldn't see much beyond the piles of magical litter. The piano disappeared from view as it rolled down an embankment of junk. She grimaced as the sounds of jostled piano keys and dented wood came from the portal.

"Could you have—" She searched for the words, "been a little more gentle?"

"How about you stand here, pick up the cursed piano, and carry the damn thing *gently* into Limbo?"

She shook her head, fighting to keep her mouth shut. Rob didn't take criticism well. Another sign why he rode the crazy train alone.

"No more comments from the Privileged Princess Patrol? I thought so." Rob closed the portal and marched toward the door.

Fuming, she tried to follow, but with a single step on her ankle, the pain stabbed into her foot like a hot poker. "Damn it!" She took a deep breath and closed her eyes.

Strong arms snaked under her knees and back. Rob easily lifted her into his arms and carried her out the door. She wanted to protest, to bite off his head for his snide comments about money she didn't have. But after one deep whiff of his inciting cologne, she cradled into his hard chest and wanted to purr like one of her familiars.

"You're more trouble than you're worth," he grumbled quietly. She didn't expect him to carry her all the way to the jump point, but he did. To make her ride easier on him, Tessa moved her arm to a comfortable position around his neck. As he carried her across the field, the rocking motion pulled her closer to his neck, and for a moment, she drifted away.

She supposed it could've all been worse, but here she was getting carried by Rob to the jump point. No one had carried her this far before. Once they reached the meat-packing plant, she'd tried again to walk. Not that she wanted to walk, mind you. After Rob held her for twenty minutes, she found the rest did little good.

"I don't want you to carry me the whole way," she whispered against him.

"You can't walk on it."

"Hopping, perhaps?" She frowned. Stray wheelchairs usually weren't abandoned in meat-packing plants. She had no choice; Rob had to take her all the way back home. This guy rubbed her the wrong way at times, but she couldn't lie, this was the best ride home she'd ever had.

Chapter 8

Dating Tip #18: First dates open up the opportunity to make mistakes. It is normal to be bored and nervous, but please don't take a simple mistake out on your date with a silence spell — for life.

Monday was to be a day of possibilities. In ten minutes, Tessa's recruitment session would take place for one of her werewolf clients. Even with a minor ankle injury and the memories of the creatures that had come for them, she still hungered for the hunt. A pitiful binding spell held her ankle in check, but she'd sure as hell hobble her way through the portal to earn her prize.

Not far from her, Rob held up the wall sleeping next to Ursula's desk. His boss was a man a gal like her could appreciate. With the promise of more security guard opportunities for Rob, Clive's wallet opened up eagerly. She couldn't keep Rob like this for long, but she was optimistic she wouldn't need him once she found her scroll.

A snore from the wall drew her attention. As to how he could stand and do that—she'd have to ask him. She would've fallen over by now. Ursula snuck a peek while she tried to work on the computer. With a body like his, watching him sleep was much more interesting.

Even with Rob here, work waited for no one.

An hour later, Tessa smiled as she showed the werewolves to the elevator. The interviews went well. Rob had slept or frowned the whole time, leaving Tessa wondering what he'd given up to be here with her.

She approached him and asked what he usually did during the day.

"More repo jobs."

"I see. More missed opportunities for me."

Rob's cheek twitched and a hint of a smile appeared. "I give a rough ride. I don't think you'd last long enough."

A shiver went up the back of her thighs and settled into her stomach. After he'd said that, she should've turned away and rolled her eyes. She'd heard numerous men toss around such lines. Those guys had greasy hairlines with generous waistlines to boot. But the way Rob looked at her wasn't what she expected. His dark eyes made her want to toss any rules of civility she had out the door.

When she didn't say anything—she merely swallowed—Rob took a single step toward her.

"It's lunch time," she finally managed to murmur.

"So I'm good for the day?" His voice was

also hushed. Enough to make her heart beat faster.

"For the next hour you are."

"See you then." He nodded and then sauntered out.

Instead of immediately following him out to enjoy her own lunch, Tessa thought it was safer idea to wait a bit. And catch her breath.

To calm her nerves, she took a brisk walk before settling on lunch at the Aquagrill off 6th Avenue. To add to her luck, the sky darkened with rain clouds. After stepping into the line behind others waiting for a table, the sky opened to a torrent of rain. Great. She didn't have an umbrella, either. She could hide out here, but an afternoon of doing business from her cell phone didn't seem appealing.

Fifteen long minutes later, she was seated and waiting for her warm chicken salad lunch. As she checked her iPhone the shadow of a man crossed over her. She glanced up to see him peering down at her with black eyes. In stark contrast to his white-blond hair, his raven-colored irises bore into her soul.

Her grip on her phone tightened.

"Is this seat free?" He sat without waiting for a reply. Her waiter waltzed past without asking her new guest about a drink or menu. Blankets of powerful magic swirled around his head like hazy smoke, masking him from the world within this plane of existence. Not good. He stared at her with a sneer.

He probably *didn't* want her matchmaking services either.

"Tessa Dandridge. I'd hoped we'd meet someday under different circumstances."

"Do I know you?" She pushed confidence into her voice.

He stared at her for a bit. "I've seen you before, but we've yet to cross paths. I'm Dagger."

What kind of name was Dagger? She sure as hell didn't have the guts to ask him where he got it from. She sealed her mouth shut to prevent a quip from emerging.

The waiter appeared with her meal. She just couldn't touch it with Dagger sitting there. Dark magic rippled between the fingers of his right hand as he tapped the table. With each thump, black spots darkened on contact.

"You've been assisting someone who makes trouble for men like me."

Rob.

"I believe you're a respectable witch and I thought I'd warn you." He cracked his knuckles as he offered his hawkish profile. "That piano you took didn't belong to you. And you know you're over your head playing repo witch." He leaned forward, revealing straight white teeth like a shark. "The fun and games end now."

He pulled a cigarette from his pocket. With the flick of an antique brass lighter, he lit the end. Not a single patron noticed her uninvited lunch date was puffing away. The tainted energy leaking from his fingertips resembled one of the hissing wraiths from his home. The white linen under his hand turned dark gray as the shadows drifted in her direction.

As a child, she remembered her Uncle Orland discussing such men in hushed whispers with the other adults. Instead of playing with white magic for good, these men lurked in the shadows using their power to wring money from pockets of regular people. One of the greatest fears for warlocks, wizards, and witches was that one of these cretins would cast a great spell to undo the veil of secrecy that everyone had managed to maintain for centuries. In her quest for her scroll she'd leapt into a boiling pot.

Tessa squirmed in her seat before briefly meeting his eyes. "In all honesty, the only reason I dropped by was to snag a free ticket to Limbo. I kinda lost something valuable."

Before replying, he took a deep drag and exhaled. "Be that as it may, you're still meddling in affairs that aren't your own. When Mr. Shin took my imbued mask, I accepted the loss, but the piano wasn't an item I was prepared to give back." He laughed softly, and then twisted the cigarette butt into the blackened table cloth.

The stench of burnt cotton didn't hide the enticing scent of her lunch. Hunger bit into her growling stomach, but she didn't move an inch. What kind of fool would budge under such circumstances?

"Heed my warning, tell your friend to watch his back. If he'd kept his nose clean, he wouldn't have to deal with the likes of me." He grinned as his eyes darkened. "You're an attractive woman. Would be a pity for you to fall in line with the wrong kind of warlock."

His gaze never lefts hers as he stood. He strolled out of the restaurant into a down pour. Rain soaked the streets, but not a single drop touched him as he walked past the window. With each step he took, dread tightened her stomach until she released the breath she held.

Rob was so dead meat.

Chapter 9

Dating Tip #7: I've met a warlock or two who have fallen for ghosts. Let's be realistic here. If she materializes in and out of reality, then don't expect kids and a white picket fence in your future. Try dating someone with a pulse.

Being the ever attentive employee, Rob didn't show up after the lunch break. He'd left a short message that he wouldn't charge Tessa since he got paged for a quick job. How kind of him to disappear after her encounter with Dagger.

By the next morning, her fingers trembled as she dialed Clive's phone number. An answering machine message echoed through the phone with the voice of a lady who smoked way too many Newport Cools. With a nervous voice, she left a message to have Rob call her regarding someone of importance named Dagger.

She was expected at work but she spent her Tuesday morning at home hiding out in front of her Mac. Yep, she was spooked.

After fixing a quick breakfast, she checked her phone to see a message waiting from Clive. *"If you're looking for Rob, here's his address in Park Slope…"*

During the cab ride to his house in Brooklyn, she wanted to turn back a few times. Why didn't she call him, instead, to warn him? And second, why did she take the time to care about her appearance?

Deep inside, she wanted not to care. Why bother with a man like him? Yet she hungered for something, and it became alarmingly apparent with the skip in her step as she left her apartment that the something she hungered for was Rob.

Tessa's cab reached Park Slope and pulled up in front of a row of brownstones. The street was relatively quiet with a few kids playing tag down the street. As she stared at the homes she wondered, *Would he be alone?* Would he answer the door shirtless? In less than that, perhaps? As to how someone like her who interacted with guys all the time could feel this way seemed ludicrous, so she shoved her nervousness aside and used the knocker on the door. She didn't have long to wait.

Eventually, she heard a soft feminine voice say, "Just a minute."

Oh, God. Did he have a girlfriend? Tessa's heart sped up and her hands suddenly felt clammy. The pleasant breeze should've helped her keep her cool, but a line of sweat formed at the nape of her neck.

The door cracked open and Tessa had to look down to see an elderly white woman who held open the door. The lady peered at her from behind a pair of enormous light-purple glasses.

"Can I help you?" the woman asked.

Initially, her mouth moved, but nothing came out. "I need to leave a message for Rob."

Kind eyes squinted at her and the older witch smiled. "You must be Tessa. Come on in, you'll have to wait for a bit. I put Minho to work in my garden."

"Minho?" she asked.

"Oh, you didn't know his birth name?" She chuckled. "My sister, his step-mom, preferred to call him Robert, but he'd been born Minho Shin."

Tessa smiled at the thought. She'd learned one of his secrets.

"Come inside, I'm making stew."

As they weaved through the cozy home, the woman introduced herself as Rob's aunt, Matilda. In the sitting room they passed his snoring uncle, Arthur. A newspaper shifted up and down under his slumbering form. She wiped her damp palms on her sides and couldn't resist grinning. So his family had heard of her before.

The place had those subtle touches to make visitors feel at home. Handmade quilts over the sofa, family pictures all over the walls. She took a moment to peer at a picture of Rob with his parents. They looked so proud of him in his uniform. Right beside that photo was another faded black-and-white one of an Asian woman holding a slumbering baby. Was that Rob's birth mother? The woman smiled at the camera, her vibrant black hair pushed over her shoulder and head tilted to reveal beautiful cheekbones. The facial features were all too familiar. *So that's where Rob got his good looks*, she thought with a sigh.

Compared to her grandmother's upper-middle-class home, Matilda's house looked like someone truly lived here and didn't mind a tiny mess here or there. She especially loved the aspects that only a water witch could enjoy: Matilda grew her own herbs and placed plants around the house that Tessa felt an affinity toward. As they passed the living room, Tessa spied several vases with gardenias and fuchsias. The vibrant flowers both craved water and pulled at her to brush her fingertips against them.

As they entered the kitchen, the sounds of tea water boiling and a pot cooking dinner greeted her. Matilda lifted the lid and stirred the food. The rich scent of herbs, vegetables, and stew meat drew Tessa in.

A breeze from an open window to the backyard shifted Matilda's long gray skirt.

"Minho's outside. He should be done any time now. Feel free to check on him. He tends to get lost out there sometimes." Then the older water witch began to hum a soft tune as she sprinkled more spices into the bubbling pot.

Tessa's steps were tentative, but eventually she reached the back door and quietly opened it. The backyard was tiny but landscaped with care. Now she knew where all the flowers came from. Rob used a hoe to prepare a new row in the middle of the yard next to rows of other budding vegetables.

Dirt covered his jeans and his sweaty shirt had been tossed into a pile of tools nearby. He grunted as he continued to dig. Sweat poured down his back as she watched his shoulder muscles flex. She wet her lips and her thumbs anxiously rubbed their respective index fingers. He bent over and yanked out a weed. Tessa gulped as his buttocks clenched in his jeans. Damn it all to hell, did she just imagine herself butt-naked bent over in front of him pulling out weeds? She covered her face as a red flush crept into her cheeks.

She turned to see his aunt busy preparing a salad. The older woman continued humming under her breath, unaware of Tessa's burning desire to practice sexual gardening with Rob.

To distract herself, Tessa sat down in the breakfast nook, murmuring something to his aunt about waiting for Rob at the table.

He entered the kitchen a few minutes later. Matilda turned. "Wash up, we have a guest for lunch."

Tessa stood as Rob peered in her direction. In seconds, his eyes caressed her form. Sweat ran down the hard muscles of his abs and she stifled the urge follow the trail with her eyes.

"I don't need to stay, I have a quick message, that's all," she mumbled.

Rob took a step in her direction.

"Nonsense!" Matilda scolded. "And Minho,

get your dirty shoes off my floor and get cleaned up for lunch."

He towered over his five-foot aunt, but lowered his head when she spoke to him and grinned like mischievous teenager. Before heading out of the kitchen, he obediently took off his work boots. His feet thundered up the stairs as his aunt turned to Tessa with a smile. "Would you like to help set the table?"

A cheesy grin hit. All she'd wanted to do was deliver a quick message and now she'd been put to work. But the payoff of seeing Rob in the garden and a free lunch was the best payday she'd had all week.

Twenty minutes later, everyone was seated at a table covered with a light-gray linen cloth and gleaming white plates. His aunt and uncle sat opposite each other while Rob and Tessa did the same. The rectangular table comfortably seated four people in the soft-white dining room. Matilda passed around a bowl of salad, while Arthur selected the largest piece of baguette bread from another container.

"How's your foot, Tessa?" Matilda inquired before eating a bite of salad.

"It's better." *How much do they know about me?* "Thank you for asking."

"Arthur used to find those things all the time back in the day. Didn't you, hon?"

Rob's uncle nodded vigorously as he buttered his bread. "Nasty fuckers."

Matilda's mouth dropped open. "Arthur! We have a guest."

Arthur huffed and stuffed his mouth with

bread as Rob chuckled.

Arthur shrugged. "Back in the day, wraiths were just as evil as they are now. Unfortunately, in this day and age, we have a problem with dipshits using them for protection."

Tessa nodded as if she knew the real deal regarding her attackers.

"Robert, your military training wouldn't have prepared you for the likes of a rogue werewolf. When I was on the front lines in Korea, we found dozens of those crazy bastards hiding in holes."

Rob nodded with a hidden smile. Apparently his Uncle Arthur loved to dish out war stories like Uncle Orland. Tessa's poor father often had to sit for hours and listen to Uncle Orland talk about how he'd worked as a sniper on the front lines in World War II. Back in those days, he'd told her only the warlocks with *real* balls went to war for something other than a cash payoff.

While Arthur continued his diatribe about fishing out the pesky werewolves, something developed under the table. A leg brushed against hers, and she glanced up to see a pair of dark brown eyes staring at her. She moved back. Her stomach flipped when he moved again to rest his leg against hers. The heat from it burned against her bare calf.

She should be eating and not lingering in the fantasy of his hands slipping down her sides in the confines of a broom closet. How come none of her daydreams involved a regular bedroom? She tried to pay attention to the bowl of thick, meaty soup in front of her.

"Did you have something to tell me?" Rob asked before she could eat her first bite.

"A warlock named Dagger came to me yesterday. He told me to tell you to butt out of his business."

Rob's knuckles turned white as his fingers tightened on his fork. "He approached you?"

Tessa sipped her soup, savoring the delicious blend of herbs, trying to distract herself from Rob's hard stare. "Yes, during my lunch hour yesterday. Do you know this guy personally?"

"All I need to know is that he can't pay his bills on time. I returned property that didn't belong to him."

Matilda hushed her nephew.

Tessa scratched her cheek and took another generous bite of soup. In the middle of her third bite, she coughed as a strange urge to scratch her face deepened.

"I'll have to tell Clive to be on the lookout. Dagger isn't a man to cross—" Rob leaned closer to peer at her from across the table. His mouth dropped as his forehead scrunched in horror. "Tessa, you ok?"

Matilda glanced at her and gasped. "Oh no."

The itching turned into a burning which spread from her face to her fingers. Tessa glanced down to see angry hives erupting on her hands and arms.

Oh fuckity-fuck!

Everyone's eyes drifted to her bowl of soup.

"Do you have any allergies?" Rob asked, coming around the table.

"No, not really." Her tongue thickened in her mouth. "Only some rare herb called lovage. But how many people use that?"

Arthur frowned. "For some reason, my wife does. Matilda, go get my Benadryl." The elderly man took charge of the situation as Rob examined her. "Is her breathing labored?"

"I itch like hell," Tessa managed, "but I can breathe fine." The need to claw at her neck was unsettling. She rubbed the hives on her arms instead.

"Stop scratching yourself." Rob grabbed her water. "Drink this for a bit."

Matilda arrived with medication and offered a dose.

It was rather unnerving to sit there with three people staring at her wondering if at any minute she'd fall to the floor twitching and jerking in agony. Thankfully, her last allergic reaction had been over a decade ago. The reaction had been much worse with a trip to the hospital and a permanent ban from the leafy herb. Thank goodness she could still eat pineapples and tomatoes.

"Could you guys back off a bit?" The slur from her enlarged tongue was gone.

Matilda picked up plates from the table. "She'll be fine."

The men didn't back off. Matilda groaned and pushed them out of the way. "Tessa, come help me with the dishes."

"She's a guest. I think you and I can handle it," Rob suggested.

"Nope. We got some talkin' to do. You two go club yourselves over the head in the living room while watching TV."

With gentle fingers, he pushed her hair behind her ear.

"Shoo, Minho." Matilda waved her hands at him. Rob frowned but left her side as Arthur shuffled out of the room.

Tessa picked up the soiled plates and entered the kitchen to help Rob's aunt.

After ten minutes, she was still covered in lumpy hives, but she settled into an easy rhythm drying plates. Matilda's light conversation offered a diversion as the older woman passed her another dish. "We'd be destitute if Minho hadn't come home to help pay our mortgage and bills." She frowned. "Some hotshot investor type bought out our local bank. The rates went up and we didn't have a dime to spare."

Tessa nodded while rubbing a lumpy spot on her elbow.

"Arthur needs heart medication and, well, I have a laundry list of drugs that don't come cheap."

"You don't have any family in town?"

"Minho's dad used live here, but he passed away a few years ago. His birth-mother, my younger sister's best friend, passed away not long after he was born. A few years later his dad took my sister as his wife—but she too was called to the heavens. He doesn't have any parents so I try so hard to take good care of him."

The familiar ache of loss cut into Tessa. The pain of her grandmother's death still ran deep. Visits from her ghost weren't the same as the feeling Tessa had as a kid. The Kilburn matriarch might've been stiff at times, but she gave the best hugs when the people who irked her weren't around.

Tessa might've lost her grandma, but she'd never felt the loss of a parent before. Even though her dad wasn't the greatest guy, at least she still had him.

Another question came to mind. "If he's enlisted, how did he manage to come home? If you don't mind?" Tessa quickly added, "I don't mean to pry."

Matilda smiled. "Minho's been in the military since graduating from high school. Before coming back, we hadn't seen him for ten years. He showed up not too long ago saying he'd left the Navy." Her fingers played with the washcloth and she stifled a sob. "We never thought anyone would help us."

Tessa placed her hand on Matilda's back, sympathizing with the woman's money problems. Tessa was afloat now, but how long would that last?

Matilda sighed, offering a brave smile for Tessa's benefit. "Enough about me. Tell me more about yourself. I don't often have another water witch in my kitchen."

Tessa began by briefly describing her move

to NYC to open her matchmaking business. She then continued, chatting fondly of the women of her family—her aunts, mother and the antics of her matchmaker grandmother. Finally, she vented about owning a new business. How she rode the rough waves of financial problems. From slow-paying werewolves to picky, cranky warlocks, Tessa hated to admit that money problems revolved around anyone. "The hardest thing is the possibility of losing it all. Not only would I fail my grandmother, my primary investor, but I'd likely have to turn tail and return home to a dead-end job." After the words left her lips, she rubbed the last dish again for the umpteenth time. Matilda grabbed Tessa's hands and took the dish away.

"Perhaps fair winds may blow in your direction as well. The storm must end eventually."

Matilda's statement offered her temporary comfort, but Tessa couldn't help the apprehension that swiftly smothered it.

After they finished cleaning up, Rob walked with her outside and offered to take her home. "I wouldn't want you captured by the circus for the new elephant man exhibit." He poked at one of her bumps with a smile.

Oh damn, did she look that crazy? Time to retreat to the protected confines of a cab. "No need, the Privileged Princess Patrol can find her own way home."

She dialed for a cab and tried not to scratch the itchy blobs on her face. During the whole time, she avoided looking at his face. Why have him see her at her worst? She didn't need a mirror to know she resembled a pepperoni pizza.

When the cab arrived, Rob held the door open a second longer. Then he blocked her path—even when she tried to pass him. Less than a foot separated them.

Sooner or later a conversation would have to take place—she hoped. Where was this going? What was he doing to her?

"Are you sure you don't need help home?" he asked. "Dagger isn't a man to cross."

She nodded, reluctantly tearing her gaze away from his arresting brown eyes. "I'll be careful."

Chapter 10

Dating Tip #15: Taking a fairy out on a date requires planning, persistence, and a lucrative payday. Never take her on a cheap outing. If she's someone's fairy godmother then she's granting big-time wishes everyday and your cheap dinner at the local greasy spoon won't cut it.

Rob told himself he shouldn't have watched her cab pull away, but he did. Even as the car went around the corner, that same voice didn't stop him from walking back into the house, grabbing his satchel, and marching right back out.

Don't get attached. Don't start something you gotta let go.

Listening to something like that seemed logical, but the feeling remained and now that hold pulled him toward the nearest jump point. He glanced at his watch. With afternoon traffic it should take her a while to get home. He'd beat her to her house again no problem.

This back-and-forth game they played had

become quite an amusing distraction.

She was so sexy when she was flustered or angry. He couldn't help but grin. Then he laughed, remembering what had just gone down over lunch. Tessa's face had swelled before his family's very eyes, but she'd stayed calm when everyone else had panicked.

He'd panicked, too. Why have her over to eat and then kill her with the chow?

He'd never had a woman over to this house before. Not that he hadn't dated or had a woman hang out at his old apartment back in Queens, but his aunt and uncle's place in Brooklyn was off limits to brief flings. They pretty much expected him to bring home a good Korean girl like his dad had always wanted.

For a moment he was caught off guard when a thought came to mind: was she just a distraction from what he needed to do with the time he had left? The money she offered was nice and all, but was he wasting his time playing watch dog with her when he could be out making some good money? Enough to help his aunt and uncle?

A chortle rumbled from the satchel on his hip. His behavior wasn't missed by Harabeuji either. "Where are we going in such a hurry, *Doryeonim*?"

Rob stopped, his shoes scuffing against the sidewalk. It'd be so easy to brush her off. He was certain he could forget about her, but she'd warned him about that piece-of-shit warlock Dagger. The least he could do was keep her safe since she didn't deserve to be a target. With a decision made he moved again.

He'd keep her safe then focus on what was most important: wrapping things up with his relatives and getting back to where he belonged.

Tessa was supposed to have gotten a reprieve that afternoon. Or at least an opportunity to hide until all the bumps had faded.

Rob had different plans, though. He waited at her doorstep with a cheesy grin on his face. "I'm scared to think of what other means you'd use to get into Limbo, so I showed up."

Gee, thanks?

They spent the afternoon at her place until the daylight faded into the night. As they left her place, she'd asked him a few times what they needed to do, but he was as helpful as a tome with vanishing ink. She'd have better luck figuring things out on her own. Once they reached their destination, she really thought she'd seen it all.

Tessa stared at a factory across the street and scratched her forehead. "You're kidding me, right? We're breaking into a factory?"

Rob frowned and pulled an unusual hat from his satchel. She didn't have much time to check out the black, pointy hat. By the time he placed it on his head, it slowly transformed into a Mets baseball cap. "I hate when you say that."

"What did you put on?"

"A Korean troll's hat called a *gamtu*. C'mon."

She'd never heard of such a thing. Hopefully it kept them out of trouble.

After tonight, she could say to her friends she'd illegally entered homes, a meat-packing plant, and now a cheese-packaging facility. If Rob told her they needed to repo a magic staff from a peg-legged witch in a strip club, she would've believed him at this point.

The factory hummed from the machines constantly moving packages down conveyor belts. Large machinery chirped as cheese products flipped into plastic and fell into boxes. A light skeleton crew moved about as they slinked around in the shadows. She followed Rob's lead, darting between spaces and hiding behind boxes as they entered the main manufacturing floor.

"Our buddy, Dagger, has been a busy boy," he whispered in her ear. "He's trying to push around property instead of holding onto it. So we need to repossess an amulet from Jasper. He keeps our target in the office space safe. There is a jump point directly to the president's office from his home, but it's well-guarded."

"I think you're telling me I should be grateful we're not using the jump point to leap directly into the action."

He cocked a small grin. "About time you caught on."

Rob crept along the main manufacturing floor toward the stairwell to the second-floor office space.

She grabbed his arm. "Are there any security cameras around here?"

"Thanks to my hat we should be good. If you stay close enough to me, you'll be cloaked. I'd advise you not to head to the work line to test out the quality of the cheese."

She pursed her lips and followed him up the staircase. After the staircase door shut behind them, the loud noises of the main floor quieted. As they ascended the stairs to the second level, she heard a door creak open above. Rob froze, his index finger moving to his mouth. Footsteps plodded down the steps. She held her breath, hoping a pissed off warlock hadn't detected their presence. As the echoes of the footsteps approached, she couldn't sense any magic. Nonetheless, he inched closer to her, covering her body with his. She tilted her head to glance past his shoulder to see a security guard walk past. He fumbled with his iPod as he descended the stairs and left.

Rob poked her side. "Keep moving."

They walked down the marginally lit hallway to the main office floor. The faint glow of computer monitors from a small cluster of cubicles provided light as they weaved through the maze.

On the way to the office they walked through a narrow space used for storage-- someone skinny had stacked boxes of paper next to an ancient copy machine. As Tessa edged past the copy machine, a loud bleep startled her. She covered her mouth and turned to frantically search for a button to power down the device. Her heartbeat increased ten-fold as she scanned the rows of options. Power button? Power button? Why the hell couldn't copy machine designers put a bright "Turn This Bastard Off" button right where people expect it to be?

Rob cursed as the overhead lights flicked on. "What are you doing?" He grabbed her by the elbow and ducked low. After they scrambled through the two or three rows, they managed to find a storage closet along the wall. The lock opened with a soft click. Rob shoved her inside and closed the door behind him. Space in the closet was at a premium. The stacks of boxes extended into this room as well. Tessa stood on a single box against the wall so Rob could come inside.

"How long do we stay in here?" she whispered.

"Until the coast is clear."

"Why not use an invisibility spell? Or fight the guy?"

Rob rolled his eyes. "The hat has a time limit for spellcasters. Also, I can't cast too many spells here without drawing Jasper to his factory."

Faintly, the sounds of footsteps walking into the room crept under the gap in the door. The persistent bleeping of the copy machine died not long after.

Tessa froze in the stuffy space of the closet. She glanced down at the faint line of light from underneath the door. They watched as a shadow crossed the door twice. Her perch on the box tittered. Before she fell forward, Rob's hand locked on her hip to steady her. His other hand rested on the doorknob.

Time ticked on. Far too slowly.

Eventually the light lingered and the faint sounds of the guards arguing over sports filtered into the closet.

"I can't hold myself up for much longer. The box is collapsing." Tessa's legs buckled as her perch crumpled inward. One faint crunch echoed in the closet.

"I won't let you fall."

In the tight confines of the closet, Rob squatted against the opposite wall and reached for her to sit in his lap.

"Isn't this uncomfortable for you?" she asked.

He grunted. Apparently, his repo man skill set included hours squatting in closets hiding from the enemy.

"Am I too heavy?"

"Your weight isn't the issue right now."

She gazed at the door, ignoring the heat spreading from her body toward his. Her breath quickened as she snuggled deeper into his lap, shifting to find a comfortable position against his chest. How the hell did they always end up in a closet? She sensed a pattern forming as his lips brushed her ear. She leaned forward, apologizing softly.

A heavy silence followed. All she could hear was her heavy breathing. Rob's head drifted closer again. No matter how much she tried to remain still, her body trembled.

Rock-hard thighs remained steady, offering a solid perch. How did this man hold them up for so long?

His mouth lingered near her earlobe. "I wouldn't take you for a tease, Tee. You've been sending me all sorts of signals." His words sent white-hot shocks down the nape of her neck. No one had called her Tee before.

"No, I haven't." She licked her lips, intending to beg for him to leave her alone before her body betrayed her. He smelled so damn good. Her head turned away from the faint light under the door toward his.

She should've faced forward and waited like a good girl. Instead, she angled herself to give him direct access.

No hesitation. No words. Just lips brushing briefly together. She quickly shifted her gaze to the light shining under the door. That small move was foolish on her part. She tried to tell herself it wasn't a kiss, even as he closed in on her neck. A delicious shiver, like fingertips tracing a path, flowed up her back as he nuzzled her neck. A few nuzzles turned into delightful kisses, then a suck here and there. Weren't they here for something? She pushed against his chest and tried to stand. She was flush against the door, but at least she escaped Rob's magic mouth.

"I think the guard is gone." Why did she have to sound so turned on?

As Rob stood behind her, his hands slid up the outside of her thighs to her waist. She closed her eyes and bit the inside of her cheek. Tessa knew if she hadn't stood they'd be making out like two bunny rabbits in heat.

Rob leaned into her back and chuckled. "This isn't over. I'm not done with you yet."

She needed a diversion to cool her nerves. "Could you teach me, once and for all, how to properly do an unlock spell?" Her voice was less unnerved, more confident.

Rob didn't speak. Did he plan to touch her again? Was she strong enough to say no? His hands fell. "We can't cast too many spells right now, but I'll show you what I can."

With proper instruction, and patience, Tessa learned how to cast an unlock spell like the best of them.

Naturally, Rob had words of encouragement. "If I was unconscious and you were our only hope, I'd probably tell you to give up."

She stuck her tongue out at him for good measure.

Once they left the closet, Tessa followed Rob as they retraced their steps to the back of the office.

Soon enough, they reached the presidential office suite. The stronger magical lock blocked their path for a few minutes, but with a brief surge of powerful magic, Rob opened the door. Beyond the entrance, there was a small waiting room with two secretarial desks. Behind the farthest desk, another door loomed. On the opposite wall, an oil painting of Jasper hung on the wall. A rather creepy one. The warlock had a receding gray hairline and beady black eyes. Tessa wouldn't want to work in the office with his stern face eyeing her every time she passed by.

The lock on the main office door didn't put up a fight, and they entered the inner sanctum of Jasper's presidential suite. Rob made a beeline for the long mahogany desk as she crept around the office, eventually walking toward some gray drapes covering the windows. She trained her flashlight on Rob, but the curtains to her left drew her eyes. A faint tingle of magic tickled her nostrils.

As Rob fumbled with the safe underneath the desk, Tessa gave into her curiosity and touched the drapes. Jasper's magic dampened something large behind them. Curious fingers reached for the curtain, wondering what mysteries lay underneath the heavy cloth.

As expected, the bright lights from the outside of the facility shined with the night sky beyond. She closed her eyes and pried deeper into the folds of the magic. The spell's complexity had layers of masking magic to prevent prying eyes and ears from discovering the secret behind the curtain. Tessa unlocked the first layer and exposed the sound of rustling chains. A second layer pushed her from the window to a secret room hidden in the folds of the window glamour.

A room double the size of the presidential suite existed here. In the center of the room, a man sat in a gilded cage. The chains on him rustled as he stood to stare at her.

She took a hesitant step forward, before striding into the room across a white bear-skin rug. The muscles on his bare chest rippled as Tessa passed black leather couches. His strawberry-blond hair brushed against the top of the cage. Through the fuzzy noise of the magic in the room, she watched the barely contained energy bouncing around his body. The energy only a shape-shifter would have.

A hand touched her back. "What are you doing?"

Rob opened the curtain wider and took in the expensive baubles around the room. "I may have to report a few more items to Clive." He whistled appreciatively.

Tessa shook her head with disappointment. Rob ignored the poor man in the cage and started to dump stuff into an open Limbo gateway. Was he seriously whistling the tune from *Snow White and the Seven Dwarfs*, "Hi Ho, It's Off to Work We Go"?

She approached the cage. "Are you hurt?"

No reply.

"You don't have to be afraid. I want to let you out."

She reached for the cage.

The man inside jerked forward. "Don't touch it!" he snapped.

In seconds, Rob was at her side backing her away.

"I meant her no harm." The man continued to speak as Rob pushed her behind him. "The bars are cursed with a fire spell."

"I'm a water witch. I can disable it." Tessa

inched her way past Rob. He caught her arm.

"Haven't you learned anything from
Dagger? Don't get in the middle. I can protect
you from these people if I repo'ed the goods,
but taking a warlock's shape-shifter is another
thing."

She didn't know what warlocks used
shape-shifters for specifically, but locked
servitude for a sentient being was bullshit in
her opinion.

"I can't leave here with a man trapped in a
cage, Rob."

Rob shook his head. "A spell on his head
will prevent me touching the cage or him. He's
been marked to prevent other warlocks from
taking him away. You also need to make a
choice. Either free him or use your five minutes
in Limbo for your scroll."

She gazed at the open portal with longing.
After everything she went through to get to this
room, another opportunity was ticking away.
She took a step toward the opening, then
stopped. What if her scroll wasn't there?

"The clock is ticking, Tessa." He gazed at
her as if he knew what she planned to do. "I
can only mask us from the surveillance in this
room for so long."

Would she sleep well tonight knowing she
picked her scroll over another's life?

She approached the cage and prepared a
counterspell. Heat stroked her limbs. She edged
toward the bars with caution. Sweat formed on
her brow as she kissed her fingertips with
magic and touched the lock. With a loud click,

the door opened.

The shape-shifter waited, assessing her with sharp eyes.

"I mean you no harm." Tessa backed away. "You're free to go where you want." She returned to Rob's side.

"Ok, Mother Teresa, let's go." His voice was terse, but a small smile showed his approval.

After Rob left his repo calling card, they retraced their steps through the facility. She assumed the shape-shifter went his own way until flashes of his blond hair appeared around corners a few steps behind them; somehow he managed to hide, even as tall as he was, behind the crates.

They finally reached the streets outside of the factory, and Rob gave a rare grin. "Other than screwing up two or three times, you didn't do too bad back there."

Hints of a sunrise bled into the horizon as they strolled. "I'm not trying for my Repo Girl merit badge, but I did miss out on two opportunities to get my scroll in there."

"There'll be other times coming up. Plenty of deadbeat supernaturals who don't pay."

"I've always wondered: With your skill set, why are you a repo man?"

He grinned. "When I arrived back in the city, I searched for a few jobs. I didn't have time to go through rounds of interviews and bullshit recruiters out to make a quick buck."

"When I was in college, I dreaded interviews. I could talk to anybody on the street about anything, but when it comes to sitting in a chair with people staring at you like you're coming in to take their job I was more than happy to start my own business in a city far away from the prying eyes of my family."

"It can't be that bad if you've got money."

She scratched her nose, needing the distraction. "Money isn't everything. And well, my parents have money, not me. My grandparents wanted their grandchildren to make their own way."

"Sounds like great advice."

"It does, but well, my mom is a housewife. The only thing she's building up is a tab at the local shopping mall."

"I'd expect a beautiful woman like you to be some stockbroker's wife. Sitting pretty in an Upper West Side apartment eating bon bons."

She laughed. "Sounds like my mom. She married the first rich warlock my grandmother found for her."

"Your grandmother's a matchmaker?"

"Yeah, I'm trying to follow in her footsteps, hard as they may be to fill."

"My dad served in the military. There's nothing wrong with doing the family profession."

"Ever since Grandma passed away, she's pushed me toward her business. I guess I thought things would be so easy…"

She shuffled a bit, but he grasped her wrist.

His voice lowered. "So, are you heading home? Or would you like some breakfast at my place?"

She smiled. She'd hoped he'd forgotten their little episode in the storage closet. Apparently, his short-term memory was intact. Slowly, he stroked the skin on the pulse point of her wrist.

Tessa swallowed and focused on the road ahead to keep herself from asking if she could eat her breakfast from the comfort of his lap.

"I have to work this—" A truck beep behind them.

"Hey dumb ass, get outta the fuckin' road!" A stern man in a delivery vehicle veered around a dazed strawberry-blond shape-shifter twenty feet behind them.

She frowned. "He followed us this whole way?"

They'd used two jump points and trekked about two miles to reach the south docks in Manhattan.

"Pretty much. I assumed he's from the city."

Tessa stopped to allow their trailing ghost to catch up.

The shape-shifter eyed her but approached. In a thin t-shirt and tattered jeans, he blended into the crowd of workers heading toward the factories and docks.

"Do you need some money to get home?" Tessa searched her pockets, but she only had about twenty bucks. It wasn't much, but at least the poor man could have a hot meal.

"I have some friends somewhere in the city. I'll wander around Midtown until I find them."

"Wander around? I can't let you do that."

After imprisonment for who knows how long, Tessa didn't want to leave him roaming the streets. She sacrificed her time in Limbo for him, the least she could do was offer him some kind of temp work. Danielle and Ursula would lose their natural minds over another hot temporary employee.

Rob frowned and pulled her to the side. "You don't know this guy. He's free to make his own choices."

"I know that. I'm only thinking about giving him a temp job until he finds his friends."

"How much do you know about shape-shifters?"

"Enough to know they're afraid of us." She returned his hard stare. "Rob, I'm a pretty good judge of character. Not every man is a rapist or nut job sorcerer. I think he's a nice guy."

From behind Rob, she heard the man grunt, "I'm not a man."

Rob tilted his head. "Excuse me?"

"I'm a *woman*."

Chapter 11

Dating Tip #4: Most of my clients are men, but witches are guilty parties as well. It's great to have a career and build a name for yourself as the Wicked Witch of the West, but remember that men are looking for love as well.

Tessa's mouth dropped open as Rob chuckled with amusement. She reddened, thinking of how less than an hour before she had been admiring the shape-shifter's fine physique.

"As much as I appreciate your offer, I just wanted to thank you personally for helping me." The shifter's hard face softened as her height decreased. A second later, a brunette in oversized clothes stood next to Tessa.

"If you're in the same position to help someone else someday, I hope you help them, too." The temptation to ask the woman's name was there, but now that the shape-shifter had her freedom, Tessa didn't want to know. The choice to live her life as she saw fit was now in her hands.

Tessa dug into her pocket. "I don't have much—"

Rob pushed her hand away and fished a few bills out of the satchel. "Stay off the streets for a while. Don't go uptown. Matter of fact, you're better off leaving New York entirely."

The shape-shifter reluctantly took the money and nodded.

From that point, they parted with a round of quick goodbyes. As Tessa watched the woman walk away, she grinned with satisfaction. *This feeling is much better than matching a high-strung warlock with a witch, Grandma.*

She turned to see Rob staring at her. "What?"

He merely shook his head with a small smile. "Let's get you home."

The trip was quiet—although the kiss lingered on her mind with each step. When he delivered her safely to her door, she took her time messing with her key-ring, wondering if he'd kiss her again, but when she turned around to say a few words, she found him long gone.

He had too many annoying habits.

She rolled her eyes and went inside. She'd deal with him again soon enough.

After a nice power nap, Tessa ambled into the bathroom. As she passed the wall mirror, she caught the first faint circle of red on her neck. Oh, damn! She faced the mirror with wide eyes. Then she craned her chin up to view the carnage. Hickies sprinkled over her neck screamed out, "You sure got it on last night!" One in particular was bright red with a light-purple spot in the middle.

Once the shock wore off, Tessa dressed for work. Her makeup though, took longer than expected. Twenty minutes later, her neck's giraffe-like appearance was covered in enough foundation to put Mary Kay out of business.

A few hours later, Tessa was in the middle of assessing a client's file when Ursula sent a call her way. "Phone call from the accountant."

Her eyebrows lowered. Why would Aunt Daisy call her? Her aunt usually sent an email if there was something wrong.

"Aunt Daisy, how nice of you to call."

"Ursula left a message regarding the mishap with the car payments. Sorry about that." Aunt Daisy added stiffly, "You should pay more attention to your account."

"I thought that's what I hired your firm to do."

"Tessa, I contacted you as a courtesy since you're my niece. We balance your books and pay your debts, but you're responsible for guaranteeing that there are enough funds for withdrawals."

Tessa's fingers tightened on the pencil she held. A pencil that would snap any minute now. She stood and started pacing the five feet of her office.

"Help me understand this here. Is there some kind of policy that prevents you from acting like a family member who cares for the welfare of my business?" After she spoke, she wanted to take back her words. But her anger couldn't be contained.

Aunt Daisy snickered into the phone. "Just 'cause my mother favored you over everyone else doesn't mean I give you any breaks. You should be grateful I called."

Grateful? She's kidding, right?

"Don't think most of us didn't know about the extra gifts."

Not again. "Both you and Aunt Lenore can't let it go. Grandma's gone and I can't change her will. She wouldn't want you to be unhappy like this. She'd want you to find your own happiness and let bitterness go."

Her aunt huffed. "Let bitterness go? What about the car for your high school graduation or the extra money to ensure you'd afford the scroll, yet have enough money to start your business? Didn't think we knew about that, did you?"

Tessa's teeth ground together. "I never asked for any of those things." Aunt Daisy always went for the jugular when Grandma Kilburn wasn't present.

"I could go on and on. But we all know you'll waste it all. My mother thought you were so perfect. At the rate you're going, you'll be back in Chicago quite soon."

"Do you have anything else to tell me? Something related to doing your job correctly?"

"There will be plenty to talk about in the coming months." She could sense Aunt Daisy's smug smile through the phone. "By the way, you keep transferring funds from your savings. I suggest you generate more income from those clients of yours. If that doesn't work out, you could always find work as my assistant."

Time passed far too quickly for Rob. He'd been apart from her for four days, but he'd used his time wisely. He'd managed to pay enough money to stop the creditors from calling, but a couple thousand wasn't enough. He needed to keep working. He'd pulled a few all-nighters and still had strength in his hands.

One month wasn't enough time to get a job, work for a bit, then quit.

With a sigh, Rob sipped a cold coffee at a local bakery and scanned the want ads. No one really wanted temporary workers these days. Not for a few weeks anyway. He'd hauled around boxes in stuffy basements, swallowed his pride as he packaged blow-up dolls, and even worse, he'd dressed in a chicken outfit to drum up business for a store. He refused to use magic to make an honest dollar.

"Don't be a *gumbengi*," his dad used to say, blending Korean and English. He'd heard the word often during his old man's "pep talks." The term, which meant maggot, also roughly translated to someone who was a lazy loser with no job.

The best way to avoid the label was to work. And that meant doing repo gigs. That was the only job that paid very well and made him feel good about what he did. But those prospects didn't look so good tonight. Bad luck seemed to cling to him like a stick of gum smeared on a sidewalk. Scrapping it off would be a sticky mess he didn't want to handle.

Pedestrians continued to walk outside, enjoying the cool evening. They had places to go, plans to have fun. He didn't have such time and thanks to Clive, his trip with Tessa tonight wouldn't go as planned. No golden amulet meant his access to Limbo was toast. He guessed that would be like a repo man without a tow truck — a truck with inter-dimensional abilities anyway. Rob snorted and crumpled up the empty cup.

Time to face the matchmaker.

Rob met her in front of Clive's Repossessions.

"What crazy place are we going to this evening?" she asked. As usual, she looked casual, yet put together enough to have him wondering if he'd been keeping an eye on her versus the problem at hand.

"At this point, not to a job," he grumbled as he walked west.

She followed close behind him and grasped his arm. "Rob, what's wrong? No job tonight?"

"Not until I get another amulet. The cheap piece of shit Clive bought died a few hours ago."

She frowned. "Can you get another one?"

"That's where we're going. It's a rough place. If you want, you can go back home until I get another one."

"I'll be all right. How rough are we talking here?"

"I'm going to a wizard's bar in Queens."

She kept a straight face the whole time. He could almost imagine all the things that came to mind. Had she ever left Midtown to see the other boroughs?

"Let's go." She strolled ahead of him, keeping her face hidden, but he wondered if he caught a flicker of doubt in her eyes.

Instead of taking a cab or jump point to Queens, Rob took her to the subway station. As they entered the train, Tessa asked, "I'm surprised you haven't suggested a jump point. Aren't there any to take us to Queens?"

Rob directed her to a set of seats and plopped down beside her. "The wizards in Queens blocked off the warlock jump points around a hundred years ago."

"You have turf issues here too, I see."

"You could say that." Warlocks and wizards dealt with magic, but in different forms. Warlocks, like himself, had the ability to play with dark and light magic, while wizards were restricted to light magic. Not that this problem didn't stop wizards from using magically imbued shit to perform dark magic.

In some areas, warlocks and wizards didn't get along very well. He remembered his father telling him that during riots, like the one in L.A., warlocks and wizards often took advantage of the chaos to make war against each other. Dad had been visiting family there during the time. His old man had said, "I'd just

stand there and let 'em fight. Most of our kind
don't have a spit's worth of common sense, I
tell ya." Based on Dad's eloquent words, Rob
just saw the fighting as an excuse for men to act
like idiots and beat the shit out of each other.

"Do you have any wizards in your family?"
she asked. "I have a few extended relatives
sprinkled here and there. They don't attend
family functions all that often."

"I grew up in a house with both warlocks
and wizards." He sighed. "Over the years, I've
seen relatives go rabid over differences in ideals
and a bunch of other bullshit most folks would
deem trivial. Who cares about the path you
follow or what kind of wand you use?" She
nodded while he spoke. "I don't have time or
the patience to support one side over the other.
I'm trained as a warlock and that is all that
matters."

The ride on the F and A train took around
an hour. They were alone for most of time, with
a few people entering and leaving the trains.
For the first half, he didn't have much to say to
her. She glanced at him a few times, making
him wonder what thoughts swirled around that
pretty head of hers.

Harabeuji was thankfully silent the whole
time.

"Are your aunt and uncle okay?" she asked.

"Yeah, they're fine. My aunt still asks about
you."

A light blush rose in her cheeks as she
smiled. "Did you finish the garden for her?"

He chuckled, remembering the way she

looked him over after he entered the house. "Yeah, she's got rows of squash for days."

"Hopefully with less pots of lovage."

He laughed. "She still has a pot or two."

The noise from the train was the only sound between them. Rob gazed at her profile, taking in the curve of her neck to the soft angles in her face. Her glossy lips parted, reminding him of their heated encounter in the closet. A hunger hit to touch her again. A hunger that hadn't disappeared after four days. He didn't stop his hand when it reached for hers. He traced a circle on the soft skin of her wrist.

She swallowed visibly and avoided his eyes.

"I can see you recovered," he whispered.

"Yeah, a few days of drinking Benadryl is the best cure."

He'd never admit it to her, but he wanted to kiss her. A real kiss this time. For the past few days, he thought over and over again of a situation like this where they'd be together again. And none of them involved a closet.

The tension in his body increased. He itched, no more precisely, he yearned to touch her. The train jolted to a stop.

"Are we there?" she asked.

"Yeah." His chance would come again soon enough.

He wouldn't hold back next time.

Chapter 12

Dating Tip #19: Dating websites on the Internet offer the opportunity to seek out people you wouldn't have likely met in person. But stay true to yourself and don't post a picture of the current celebrity du jour, even if HR declined to post your photo for Employee of the Month.

The ride with Rob had turned out nicer than she'd expected. The moment they left the subway station, such niceties ended. The neighborhood, with its revitalized homes and businesses, appeared small-town cozy and such, but supernaturals prowled the streets offering services she didn't want, even if she were sloppy drunk. After walking for a few blocks, she spotted a succubus among a group of prostitutes across the street. One of the streetwalkers approached Rob asking if he wanted her to join "their little party." Tessa kept her mouth clamped shut as Rob shook his head. "No, thanks."

They were propositioned four more times to

do things she'd rather not remember. Most of them whistled cat calls to Rob, including a man dressed as a woman—with a better fashion sense than most women in Manhattan—who wanted to count the tattoos Rob had on his body. Her escort declined the show-and-tell opportunity.

Eventually, once past the prostitutes and drug pushers, they reached a street where the lights of The Bubbling Cauldron could be seen. The faint sounds of music drifted across the street. An old Chevy without front wheels had the words, "Piece-O-Shit Car" on a bumper sticker. Tessa assumed she wouldn't find the honorable elements of society inside.

"About time we got here," she said.

He laughed. "I should take you here more often."

"The next time your amulet breaks, I think I might sit things out."

"Oh, we've only had half the fun. Are you sure you don't want to turn back home?" He swung open the door to the bar.

"And go back to be propositioned to a party in an alley? I think I'll pass."

The roar of rock music hit her ears. The door definitely did its job of noise control.

Inside, the bar appeared much larger. Magical folk sat in rows of tables with the bar located along the wall to her right. Two patrons snored beside their drinks as others partied around them. A few gazed in their direction with various states of emotion: lust, anger, and indifference.

Tessa's attire, or the fact she had *too* many clothes, made her stand out like tooth fairy at a dental conference. A few biker nymphs at a table pointed in her direction and cackled.

Rob headed toward the back, searching the faces for someone.

"Who are we looking for?" she bellowed over the music.

"I'll know him when I see him."

Rob searched for a few more minutes before he pulled her to the bar. A humongous cyclops bartender served him a beer. How did he maneuver behind the counter anyway? Somehow, he managed to serve another patron a double shot of Jack Daniels. "Hey Rob, what does the lady want?"

"She'll have—"

She squeezed between Rob and a wizard who laughed it up with his friend. "I'll have a *light* Corona with lime please."

The one-eyed giant made a disgusted face. "To each his own." He gave her the drink and Rob tossed a few bills on the counter.

"Your friend isn't here?" Tessa tried to take it all in. College bars didn't come close to the rowdiness here. The place was swarming with supernaturals.

"He'll arrive soon enough. Harry can't go an hour or two without being slightly inebriated."

As Tessa took a sip of her beer, a large hand clamped down on her bottom. "Well, aren't you a sweet treat?"

She whipped around. "Hey!"

In an instant, Rob stood. He grabbed the wizard's wrist and twisted it behind his back.

The air cracked with magic around them. A strange buzz tugged her ears. The offending wizard's meaty face contorted into a snarl. The stench from the greasy gel in his hair intensified.

"Rob!" the bartender barked. "Take it outside, or else I will."

Rob released the man. The wizard slinked to the front of bar cursing.

"You all right?" Rob asked her.

She nodded, wiping away an invisible film of disgust from her rear-end. After taking a few more sips of her drink she wondered what else was waiting to greet them. "What does Harry look like?"

Rob tilted his head toward hers. "I'd say he's the chunky guy behind those five pissed off wizards."

She turned around to see the head of an overweight man dressed in biker gear. It was rather difficult to make out his features with five glowering dudes snarling in front of him. The one who grabbed her stepped forward and pointed at Rob.

Uh-oh.

They moved through the crowd as a rendition of the "The Devil Went Down to Georgia" thundered from a jukebox.

As they approached, she turned to Rob. "Is it time to go yet?"

"Nope." He finished his beer and put the strap of his satchel over his shoulder. "But I suggest you stay out of trouble and find a seat somewhere else." *Stay out of trouble?* Shouldn't Rob follow his own advice?

Tessa picked up her drink and searched for a free table. The bar was packed. She decided to pick a spot close by, behind the table of biker nymphs. They didn't care anymore about harassing her. They had front-row seats to a fight.

Five greasy wizards stepped up to Rob. Two matched his height, while the others peered up.

"Our friend here says you need to be reminded of your place, Warlock," one of the taller ones grunted.

Rob's right eyebrow rose. "Why don't you come teach me?"

The other taller one with a military buzz cut jabbed Rob's chest with his index finger. "Let's see how tough he is with all of us standing here."

"Rob. Don't. Do. This," the bartender warned.

"Shut up, Stan! He don't belong here," one of the shorter ones with a missing eye said.

Rob glanced at the finger on his chest. "Move it before I break it."

Tessa sighed. They should've left. Did he thrive on danger like this? She knew he was ex-Navy, but damn, did he need to stand up to everyone?

The biker nymphs in front of her giggled as some of the patrons backed away.

The wizard with his index finger pointed at

Rob waved his hand again. Suddenly, Rob snapped. Grasping the finger, he jerked it wildly to the side. The wizard's face contorted in pain as Rob's firm grip drove him to his knees.

His friends surged forward. Rob barked, "Take another step and I break his hand."

Behind him, Stan gritted his teeth. "Take it outside, Rob. Bart, call off your friends or I'll step in to end this."

Rob released the wizard's finger. With a sneer, Bart motioned with his head toward the door.

Rob grinned wolfishly. "You first."

Tessa took a step forward. "Rob, why don't we find a table? Let's talk to Harry and—"

"Oh, shut up!" One of the biker nymphs tossed peanuts in her direction. Another with a nose piercing joined the assault, forcing Tessa to follow the men as they left the bar.

She reached the door, only to find herself flung backwards as the military-hair cut wizard flew through the glass pane in the door. His momentum threw them into a table of wizards playing cards. Their goblets of brandy soaked her shirt as the blubbering wizard rolled off her. The hard imprint of poker chips pressed into her back. Grimacing, she removed a spicy chicken tender from her shoulder.

"Sorry… I'm so sorry," she mumbled to the old men as they continued to play. One of them tossed a card on her head as another raised a bet.

Cackles of laughter from the biker nymphs

and a few other patrons floated through the room over the screeches of the fiddle music. The fallen wizard wiped a line of blood from his mouth as he stood. Then he opened the broken door and bounded outside.

She followed him to find Rob tossing around wizards like hopscotch marbles. One would attempt to throw a punch, which Rob would block then respond to a swift jab of his own.

Like fools bent on being punished, the wizards continued their pattern until one of the men grabbed Rob from behind. Before Rob could twist out to throw the attacker, another swept in and punched him in the ribs. She expected Rob to glance off the blow, but his face contorted in agony. The shorter wizard used the opportunity to hit Rob across the jaw.

Rob shook off the blow, sidestepping out of the hold. "Is that all you got!"

This had to end. *What to do? What to do?* The closest thing was a stack of newspapers. Read them to death? Need something better. As her eyes darted over the street, Rob snarled as he threw one of the wizards into a car door. The man rolled into a puddle of rainwater flowing into the sewer.

With an idea in mind, she sucked in a deep breath and gathered the energy necessary to summon the water to her will. With a flick of her fingers, the water rose, then drenched the men in the street.

They turned to her, dumbfounded.

"Works on dogs. I can see it works on

wizards as well," she sneered.

"What the hell did you dump on me?" a taller one moaned.

"It smells like shit," another said.

NYC streets weren't the cleanest in some places. A jump into the East River might've been a cleaner option than being doused in puddles heading for the sewer.

Rob flashed a dark look at the men, then clenched his side and limped toward the bar. He ignored her wide eyes and stepped through the new opening in the front door. His wet shirt clung to his torso.

"Tessa, get your butt in here," he yelled from inside the bar.

She backed away from the wizards as Bart tried to help one of his fallen comrades.

Once she returned, she found Rob sitting next to Harry at the bar. The table of card-playing wizards continued, their table now reassembled through magic, as if she'd never interrupted their game.

Stan tossed Rob a tattered towel from behind the counter.

"You always make an entrance, Shin." Harry completed his shot with a single gulp. He scratched his straggled mane of dirty-blond hair before belching.

"If you would've made it during the appointed time, I would've stayed out of trouble," Rob grumbled.

He no longer held his side, but leaned inward with a scowl. "How much is it this time? And don't think I haven't checked the market prices."

"The usual price. I could've added a fee for transport, but I can see—" He plucked a small piece of plastic from Rob's shoulder. "—that you've had enough drama this evening."

Rob reached into his jeans and pulled out a single ruby the size of a fingernail.

Harry snatched the gem from Rob's hand and examined it with glee. He bit into the stone then stuffed it into his pocket.

"Feels legit." He turned to Stan, tossing a few bills on the counter. "Another double Jack Daniels."

He dug into his biker jacket, pulling out a crumpled paper bag. He tossed it to Rob.

"This one should last a lot longer. The magic is setup for one trial opening. After that, Clive will have to register its use with the Supernatural Municipal System."

Rob nodded.

Harry chuckled. "You could've waited for Clive to buy another one of those."

"Last time this happened, Clive told me he waited three years for a replacement. I don't have that kind of time."

A double shot of Jack Daniels was placed in front of Harry, only to be snatched by Rob. After slamming the drink in one gulp, he hissed while clenching his side.

Was he hurt worse than she'd thought? "Rob, are you hurt?"

"Old injury. Nothing that a quick handshake with my friend Jack Daniels won't cure."

Most men like Rob didn't walk around with rib-based injuries. His aunt had said he'd worked long hours. Maybe he'd pushed himself too far?

She touched his shoulder. "How about we head on out since we have what we came for?"

Rob nodded slowly.

Harry rolled his eyes. "You already took my drink. If you ask nicely, I'll bandage you enough to get home without pain."

"How much will it cost me?"

"You're already a valued customer. Consider it on the house."

Rob took a step forward. Then paused. "No tricks, wizard. The last spell you cast wasn't funny."

"You can't take a joke." Harry turned to her with a wink. "I gave him a magical dose of Viagra. To help out. Apparently, he doesn't have a sense of humor."

"I would have to agree on that one," she chimed in.

Rob frowned at her. "I had a hard-on for twenty-four hours. That kind of shit isn't funny."

While stifling the urge to laugh, Harry rubbed his hands together, drawing magic into his fingers. Light danced from hand to hand.

Rob offered a small smile. "Thanks."

"No tricks, I promise," Harry said. "If you feel anything funny, you can taint all my wands."

Rob flashed a grin that made Tessa's insides melt. "Is that even possible?" he asked.

"With the right tools, all of them rare, warlocks can jack up any weapon." Harry lightly pressed his palms against Rob's side. "Just give em' cursed shit from each of the elements—fire, earth, wind, and water—and they'll grow an ego big enough to think they can mess with the wizards." The wizard backed away, apparently done with his work.

"The right tools…" Rob appeared thoughtful then made a move toward the door. "Thanks again for the quickie."

"I treated you right, didn't I? Last thing I think your lady friend needs is an injured boyfriend trying to tuck her in."

"H-he's not my boyfriend," she stammered.

Rob leaned in to his friend, whispered something into his ear, and then patted him on the shoulder. Harry laughed with an evil glint in his eye. What secrets was Rob keeping?

"Nice doing business with you, Shin," Harry said.

Silent as always, Rob pulled her out of the bar.

A little over an hour later, they arrived back at her apartment. Ever since they'd left the subway entrance, their walking had slowed down. Almost to a casual stroll. She hoped he wasn't in pain.

"You should get some rest. Are you sure we shouldn't go to the hospital or something?" she asked.

"I'm not one hundred percent right now, but I'm fine." He was staring at her again. His body was hard to read, but his eyes said something else. The message made her stomach flip.

"Maybe we can go out tomorrow then." She tried to avoid his eyes and ended up glancing at his full lips. Not the best place. She daydreamed often as to whether they were as delicious as they appeared. "Oh, thanks again for watching out for me."

"Not a problem. Although I'm surprised you made it out of there in one piece."

"I'm not doing too bad."

"Was that before or after you ended up covered in brandy?"

To distract herself from the heat rising in her face, she handed him his satchel. Then she pulled up her shirt to her nose and frowned. Her clothes smelled like a smoky bar that had been doused in hard liquor. Also, a bright orange smudge of Tabasco sauce caked her shoulder. She had hot stuff written all over her.

"So we can try again in a few days?" Persistence was how this game had to be won.

"Sure." He hugged his side again. Harry's healing spell must've not been as strong as his Viagra spell.

"See you around." She backed toward the apartment. He didn't step forward. She faced the doors, battling the need to reach for him. With eyes closed, she made a split-second decision. If he was there when she turned around, then she'd make her move. She'd walk right up to him and say *something*. After she pivoted, she found him mere inches away. Her lips parted as his nose brushed against hers.

Her heart began to race. Did he know she'd make her move?

His free right hand drifted up her arm, finally resting on her shoulder. With a gentle tug, he drew her forward into a brief kiss. Was that it? Breathless from a single peck, she was about to burst at the seams. His mouth was so deliciously close. She wasn't sure how much time passed as they stood there, eyes closed in a stand-off.

His tongue darted out to slide between her lips. She sucked in a breath. If this man didn't stop teasing and kiss her, she'd hurt him!

As if under a spell, her eyes opened to see Rob returning her hungry gaze. For a split second, her mind delved into a fantasy of events: their fevered ascent up the stairs, their discarded clothes in the living room, and finally him pounding into her body as she braced against the doorjamb of her bedroom.

Tessa's eager hands reached for his shirt to reunite their mouths. The sounds of the city disappeared as they made-out under the streetlight. His hand slid down her back to rest against her bottom. As his fingers gripped her heated flesh, he kissed her with a possessiveness that left her breathless.

Suddenly, he clenched his side. He spoke against her mouth. "If I wasn't… injured…"

Something buzzed in her pocket. She ignored it, but her phone kept vibrating. Whoever it was, they were quite persistent.

Once their heavy breathing settled, she glanced down and retrieved her phone.

Her fingertips went numb as she stared at the screen. The text message had been sent multiple times, each line more ominous than the next: *Don't forget about the loan you made with us. We will come for you.*

Chapter 13

Dating Tip #15: I had a client of mine brag that his "connections" with Cupid was the key to his success. A single wizard living at home with his mother doesn't have Cupid on speed dial. Women, avoid men who are all mouth and no action.

"Is everything okay?" Rob asked Tessa.

"I wish. Everything would be okay if I found a spell to send me to the moon. I'd be problem-free living in one of those humungous craters."

Rob's face reflected confusion.

"Don't worry about it. Let's just say I'd like a long vacation in a far, far away location."

Rob leaned in to kiss her forehead and bid her goodbye. The touch left her heady as he added space between them. She watched him walk away before she ambled up to her apartment. The lights of her apartment were dim when she returned. Perfect for her somber mood. With nothing to purge the empty feeling that clawed at her, she plopped down on her bed. Eventually, she drifted to sleep.

A few days later, things weren't getting any better. The calendar on Tessa's iPhone stared back at her with red dots on critical dates. The crimson specks were stark against the white background. Other than reminding her of impending doom, the electronic device also admonished the fact that she hadn't seen Rob for a while. After that crazy night at the bar, he'd disappeared.

Her mind kept flashing to him protecting his side. The fight must've hurt him pretty bad. She kept the card holding his phone number, itching to check on him. But was she satisfying her need to see him again or simply seeing if she could use him to find her scroll?

The evening shows on her TV didn't distract her from her wandering thoughts. Her gaze darted to the phone across the room as if it would ring any minute now with the loan sharks would be on the other line.

Time to go for a quick walk for some ice cream. She'd buy something fattening for good measure.

The trip for ice cream didn't cheer her up like it was supposed to. Perhaps she should've gotten three scoops of gooey double brownie fudge instead of two. She expected to come home to an empty apartment, but she found Rob relaxing with his feet propped up on her coffee table.

She couldn't hide her smile. "How did you get in?"

"An unlock spell. I could've waited outside,

but breaking in and making myself at home with your ghost cats seemed much more appealing."

Tessa placed her keys on the tiny stand near the door. "What are you doing here?" She plopped down on the couch while he watched a baseball game on TV. A single cushion seat separated them.

"My aunt cooked some homemade New England clam chowder for you. I put it in the fridge." He gave a soft laugh. "Something about it bringing luck to water witches."

Tessa sighed. She could use some luck about now. Was he here to see her or was it something else? "A job tonight?"

"Yeah. There's something that needs to be done tonight." The velvet smoothness of his voice brought delicious chills down her back. He continued to face the TV, his hands kneading the soft purple pillow from the couch. She squirmed in the seat as his hand grasped the pillow. She shook her head. Pillows weren't erotic objects.

"How are you feeling?" she croaked.

A small smile. "Much better."

"What happened? Did you break a rib perhaps?"

"An old injury I can't shake." His words faded away.

She reached out and touched his satchel on the coffee table. Her fingertips rode the ridges along the soft leather. "This is beautiful."

"It was my dad's." He picked up the bag and offered it to her. "He told me the leather used to construct this came from an elder warlock in the family."

Tessa lifted the flap and marveled at the foreign symbols burned into the material along the lighter inside. "What language is this? Is this all Chinese?"

"Most of the top row is Korean." His warm hand brushed against hers to point out the difference. "My dad said most of those are spells to more-or-less give me access to his old stuff. All wizard coats use the same means to create compartments for holding weapons and tools of the trade in their pockets."

"So most of your wands and such are from overseas?"

"Yeah, they've been in the Shin family for a long time. My dad never took the time to tell me what everything does, but through trial and error I've figured out a few things."

A faint whisper emerged from the bag. She almost dropped it. "What was that?" A chuckle came next.

"You're not very good at keeping secrets, Harabeuji," Rob whispered.

Tessa quirked a brow and pursed her lips. "So the voice is Ha-rah-bow-jee? Is the bag enchanted?"

"Someone, I don't know who, trapped Harabeuji's spirit in the leather. Through circumstances my ancestors never revealed, Harabeuji has come to serve the Shin family. I don't know his real name, so I call him grandfather in Korean."

A hard-to-hear response, in a language

other than English, flowed from the folds.

"What's he saying?" she asked.

Rob sighed. "All right. All right, I'll tell her. Harabeuji says you have good taste in purses, but the Coach knockoff has gotta go and..."

She couldn't stifle the chuckle from the back of her throat. "You're kidding me, right? That was a present from a friend. I just can't throw it away!"

"I wish I was kidding." Rob switched his gaze to the bag and spouted something in what had to be Korean. She couldn't tell.

"What did you say to him?" she asked.

"My bag spirit is feeling chatty today. He also said you remind him of a fire witch named Sooin. She…was capable of so much, but never showed how powerful she was until it was far too late." He chuckled. "She had such a quick wit and timeless beauty he couldn't forget."

Heat tickled her cheeks as she sounded out the name. *Sooin*. "Very pretty."

"All right, Harabeuji." He threw a glare at the satchel. "I don't know why you're doing this, but you owe me." He spread his palm across the front pocket, his eyelids fluttering. After coughing deeply in his chest, Rob's voice deepened, cracking with old age.

"My sweet Sooin lived in a different time," Harabeuji began. "A turbulent time when those animals, who you would call the Mongols, swept in from the north to take over Goryeo. Slowly they crept south, closing in on the city of Gaesang where I lived. During the invasion, I was hired as a magician to protect an affluent

scholar's family while Sooin acted as a
protector for their children. An elder wizard
named Nokwon provided support as a healer.
We didn't always get along, but we got the job
done." He paused as in thought. "I don't
remember much about the night the compound
was attacked. It's all a blur in my mind. One
moment the guards called us to action and in
the next the night sky lit up as if on fire. The
men scrambled like frightened children at the
unnatural light, leaving me alone to face what
couldn't be Mongol troops."

"Wow," she whispered.

"I have fended off countless humans. Most
of them ruthless and armed, but in my opinion,
the deadliest foe for any warlock is another
warlock with equal skill. Men who are driven
are far more dangerous than you'd imagine.

"That had to be what happened when the
compound's west wall exploded and an unseen
force drove me into the main house. Our
attackers closed in from all sides, leaving me,
Nokwon, and Sooin to defend the family. Not
long after I got inside, my memories become
hazy." Rob's jaw tightened. "The last thing I
remember was hearing the children screaming
from down a long hallway. I felt a blow to the
back of my head. As I collapsed, Sooin called
out my name and all I could think about was
how I couldn't reach her.

"I wished I would've…" Rob's hand slid
away and his eyes opened.

"Would've what?" The once quivering
satchel had become still in her lap.

"He's quiet now." Rob's voice returned the normal and now he appeared thoughtful. "He's never told me about Sooin before. And I've heard countless tales. On repeat."

"So what does that mean?" She had to ask, quite caught up in the tale.

Rob snorted. "That he needs to keep quiet before he gets into trouble. I usually don't reveal Harabeuji to others, but he's apparently taken a liking to you and trusts you."

She ran her fingers over the lettering again. "You could've stayed quiet about him. Yet you mentioned his name to me."

Rob shrugged, but she caught the smile in his eyes.

She laid the satchel back on the coffee table and a silence fell over them. The images on the TV didn't hold her attention. She'd learned so much tonight about Rob and his bag spirit. What other secrets did he keep? A sigh escaped her lips as his bicep clenched under his shirt.

"What are you watching?" she finally managed to ask him.

He flipped through the channels. "Nothing much. Highlights of the Mets on the local ten o'clock news."

"You were gone for a while there," she blurted, unsure of what to say. "I didn't know if I'd have another chance to enter Limbo."

He huffed. "From the way you sound, I'm not sure if I should feel used."

"I didn't mean it like that." She looked away. "I-I didn't know if you were hurt in a hospital somewhere." Or if he had run off to never return.

"We have to wait until the place opens. We can head there soon enough." He was silent after that.

The news droned on in the background as her mind lingered on the things that bothered her: her business and the scroll. She didn't want to admit Rob had somehow jumped into the pile. The TV's sounds faded for a moment as her head bobbed.

"The first time I went on a job was the hardest," he whispered, drifting a bit closer to her. "I needed to make some fast cash. And Clive didn't want to spend his valuable time going through a résumé I didn't want to write."

She lessened the space between them even more.

He chuckled softly. "Would you believe my first job was to repossess a mask from Dagger?"

Her lunch with the disturbed warlock came to mind. The scent of his cigarette and his black eyes made her shiver.

"He said you two had a history."

"Yeah. I picked an interesting night for the break-in. A long weekend. Most warlocks like Dagger are busy trying to scope out a magic-magnet for the evening, so I took advantage."

"I can't believe there are women out there who'd want to jump from a broomstick to the bedroom with that psycho."

"Evidently, within the many boroughs of NYC, there's a small group of witches who get off on that." He continued to speak. "So there I was, thinking this would be an easy, in-and-out of this guy's penthouse apartment. I broke in easy enough. Managed to search a few rooms. For some jobs, Clive doesn't have exact coordinates for retrieval. I was in the process of searching his bedroom when I heard activity in the front room. After checking the windows, or for a hiding place in an adjoining room, I settled for a heavy mask spell in the bedroom closet."

She yawned, but couldn't stifle the giggle. "He didn't do what I think he did? Please tell me he didn't with you in there?"

Rob chuckled. "He did that... And more."

She ignored Rob's subtle move to snake his arm around her shoulder. The warmth from his body was pleasant.

"At first I thought, he'll find me. If he's at the top of his game, then I should expect him to fight, but he didn't."

A commercial flashed across the screen with an advertisement for a cruise line. Rob stared at the sea with longing.

She slapped his shoulder playfully. "I want to know what happened."

"I sat in the closet for two hours masking myself while Dagger got spanked by some woman he called Hilda."

She covered her mouth with her hands. "*He* got spanked?"

"Oh yeah. 'Dagger, you've been a naughty boy.' Every man's got secrets." Rob shrugged. "Some of them involve paddles."

"Wow, when I met him he came off as dangerous. Little did I know he could purr like familiar on demand."

He turned to her, his eyes serious. "Dagger is dangerous, Tee. Just because I caught him in a compromising situation doesn't mean he couldn't take us both out. He has an arsenal of demons. Shit even I don't mess with in my line of work."

From confident witch to lowly spell caster tugged down a peg or two, she crossed her arms.

Using his left hand, he slid his fingertips along her arm. She sighed softly. "Dagger kind of reminds me of my first client also."

"I wouldn't see a man like Dagger using a matchmaker service."

"There are men out there who think they're ready for love." She turned to talk directly, but caught him staring at her profile. She avoided his gaze and focused on the TV. "But they're more suited for a mental hospital. My first client was the worst imaginable. I expected some glamorous CEO to walk through my door. Instead, I got a pompous jerk who complained every step of the way.

"You see, I was new at owning a business, at matching people for love professionally. All I had were hours of advice from my grandma."

Rob nodded, his head leaning closer to hers. She tried so hard to keep talking.

"My client had gone through practically every matchmaker in the NYC area. No one wanted to work with him. And after a few days I understood why."

"I thought you had it easy. All you have to

do is place some guy in a room full of women. Wait for the dames to jump him." He gave a brief chuckle that died as he nibbled at her neckline. Tessa's toes curled. His warm lips brushed against a sensitive spot under her earlobe.

"It's never that simple when it comes to men and women. We all want different things, but if someone isn't ready for a relationship, then they may unknowingly do everything to mess up their chances."

"Like not giving in to what they need?" He kissed her nose, only return to her neck.

She leaned back, hoping she wouldn't push him away. "You left a bunch of hickies on my neck last time," she teased.

A single finger brushed against the side of her right breast. "I could add more if you like," he whispered as his tongue darted out along her neck, searing a path to his next target.

"Tessa, are you there?" The paper-thin voice of Grandma Kilburn wafted from the kitchen.

She scrambled away from Rob. Thank goodness her grandmother's ghost materialized and dematerialized from the same spot each time. Tessa might've been a grown woman, but who wanted their grandma catching someone feeling them up?

Grandma loved popping up like this. Her last impromptu visit was during a date night nearly a year ago. Tessa had managed to get the guy to go to second base after a romantic candlelight dinner, and Grandma decided she'd visit New York and teach her granddaughter the finer details of managing clients.

Grandma stopped when her opaque form reached the doorway to the living room. "I see my granddaughter has a guest. Is this a bad time?" Her grandmother didn't wait for an answer, simply sitting down between them. A chill passed through Tessa's body as Grandma Kilburn hovered close.

Rob stood quickly like a nervous gentleman. "Ma'am."

Grandma glanced at Rob before speaking again. "It's been many months since I've checked on you. I feel awful about that since I used to visit often."

Tessa sighed. Advanced notice would've been nice.

"I'm sure your business is doing well and growing. Your mother is constantly bragging about your exploits."

Did her grandmother know about her problems? "Y-you know how she is."

Rob sat down in the chair next to the couch.

"Yes, I know," her grandma said. "Quite unfortunate that she never had your aspirations. I always assumed it would have been her to take over my business. But apparently, she found true happiness with her local shopping center after meeting your father."

Grandma had often told her about how she'd placed them together. Tessa's mother didn't want to be a matchmaker, so Grandma had moved on to the next candidate.

The deceased Kilburn matriarch focused on Rob with a small smile. "I've never seen you before. By what name does a handsome man like yourself go by?"

"Robert Shin, Ma'am."

"He'll make a fine client, Tessa."

Tessa's gaze darted to Rob's, imploring him to play along. "Thanks, Grandma. I'm pleased with the progress I've made in his regard."

"What an interesting satchel you have." The shadows of her hand hovered over the coffee table.

Tessa stood, grabbing the bag. Did her grandma see something she couldn't? "Didn't we need look into something important, Rob?" She avoided his eyes and kept her body language neutral. With sharp eyes, the elderly ghost glanced at them.

"You two go ahead," she beckoned.

Rob saved her with a curt, "Yeah. Let's go before you get into trouble."

Chapter 14

Dating Tip #20: Take your date to a romantic location to inspire romance. This doesn't include the local haunted house which may be creepier than you are.

A couple days ago, Tessa thought she wouldn't be surprised if Rob had to take something from a supernatural strip club. It seemed rather hilarious. She wasn't laughing tonight. Not only did he need to repo something from a pimp, but a leprechaun pimp at that.

As they stood outside the strip club, she rubbed her shoulders.

With a devilish grin, he said, "You can always pass on this one."

After several missed opportunities to reach her scroll, she couldn't pass up this chance. "Couldn't you open the portal as a favor?"

He crossed his arms.

"I won't tell anyone. It could be between you and me."

"Nope, proximity issues. Have to be within a certain distance of the repo'ed item."

Two warlocks left the club, allowing the booming beats of dance music to escape into the street.

Tessa frowned. After the episode with her grandmother, she hadn't come prepared for a night at the club. Jeans and a T-shirt wasn't her standard attire.

"Before we go inside, who's our target? I prefer to be aware of things from now on. No more crazy surprises like weirdo warlocks or pissed off wood nymphs."

He walked toward the door. "The client wants an ancient goblet, a tenth-century wooden mug imbued with warding magic."

The bouncer at the door eyed their attire with distaste. His eyes swept over her clothes as if she had wriggled into the gutter and came back hoping to enter.

Rob leaned forward and whispered into his ear. The man nodded and allowed them to enter.

"What did you tell him?"

He grinned. "That I was your boyfriend and you wanted to talk to the owner about a job."

"You're joking, right?"

"It got us in the door, didn't it?"

"Yes, but now he thinks I'll be swinging from one of those poles in a few days."

A sizeable crowd circled three stages with a bar in the back. The performers undulated and gyrated as a mixed crowd of humans and supernaturals cheered them on. She'd never

been to a strip club before. Not that Tessa had
never seen stripping acted out on TV, but that
wasn't the same as seeing a woman on stage
flinging her business out to customers hoping
for a tip. Groups of men and women danced
not far from the stage.

Tessa tried to avoid the feeling of being
underdressed, but as they weaved through the
crowd, she couldn't help folding her arms to
cover her clothes. Her nervous hands checked
her hair, smoothed over her shirt.

She hated casting spells related to clothing,
but the desire to put her best foot forward
drove her toward a corner. A powerful masking
spell would require concentration to maintain
and hold, but she had only a few options. With
a flick of her wrist, she created a black pencil
skirt. For good measure she clipped two inches
from the hemline and fit the garment more
snuggly on her hips. The drab shirt
transformed into a blood-red blouse. Her
breasts peeked up from the decreased neckline.

Rob finally noticed her departure. Her
choices must've been good. His eyes weren't
focused on her face. "Get a drink. I need to find
my target."

"Can't I follow you?"

"You'd slow me down. Sit tight, it won't
take long."

Tessa harrumphed. With the way the last
redhead performed on the stage, she wondered
how Rob planned to scope out his target with
that kind of distraction. By the time he
disappeared into the crowd, the dancer's

sparkling green ensemble lay in a heap on the floor. At the bar, Tessa settled into a seat. She expected her arrival to go unnoticed with the entertainment on the stage, but several pairs of eyes followed her as she passed them.

Thirty seconds later, she had declined two offers for drinks. Another asked her when she'd be heading to the stage. How about never?

She glanced around. What happened to Rob?

"Your eyes are hypnotic."

A Hispanic man with a thin black mustache leaned in behind her. "They remind me of a cat. Very seductive." His brown eyes drifted to her chest, before meeting her eyes. "You look nervous."

"I'm waiting for a friend."

Another patron left his seat beside her, freeing space for the well-dressed werewolf in a white suit and black shirt. Tufts of black hair, which for some reason resembled taco meat, poked out of his partially opened shirt. The lingering scent of his spicy aftershave intermingled with cigars. He smelled like a club.

"I've never seen you here before. I'm Claus."

"You wouldn't have seen me here." She didn't hunt for clients in a strip club.

Her cosmopolitan arrived as Claus leaned in closer over the loud music. His breath stunk of cigars.

"What line of work is that? Do you work at another club?"

Her sip went down hard. Did she look like a stripper? "I work in Manhattan as a matchmaker."

His eyebrows rose. About two out of three men took her occupation with surprise. It wasn't the same as announcing she was a stockbroker or an intern at a fashion magazine. The 'what do you do' question usually didn't follow with: *I take supernatural millionaires and find them wives.*

A blonde with streaks of pink in her hair jumped on the bar and marched down, gyrating to the beats of the club music. Unconcerted, Claus continued to chat as she stopped in front of them. Tessa turned away as Claus continued to speak. "We're in the same business, then."

"Oh, really?" Now, this ought to be good.

"You match people for life, while my enterprise is aimed for the moment."

Not bad. A little skewed, but one could think of it that way.

He spied the ten-dollar bill Tessa left on the counter and pushed it toward her. "Could I offer you another drink? I treat my guests well. Perhaps some Cristal in the V.I.P. section?"

His finger pointed briefly to an elevated section of the room. The affluent patrons sat clustered in tables with attractive women buzzing around them like eager insects. A bright glint of green caught her eye. The leprechaun pimp. On his table in front of him sat a wooden goblet.

Tessa smiled at the owner of the club. "A

quick drink would be nice."

As he led her to the V.I.P section, other werewolves moved to allow him to pass. The other partiers continued to dance and whistle at the dancers on the stage. She glanced around for Rob, but the mess of bodies made it difficult to make out a head of black hair.

Claus led her up a staircase to the exclusive set of tables. A few groupies remained by the stairs, hoping for an invitation up to the top.

"You can sit at my private table if you like?"

The leprechaun sat in the back with three women clamored around him chatting. Tessa spotted a celebrity or two among the tables. Claus' table was adjacent to the pimp's.

"That would be perfect," Tessa said.

Claus pulled back a chair so she could sit. A waitress appeared with the bottles and drinks. She'd never tasted Cristal, but after a sip, she decided the champagne tasted good.

"You most certainly don't behave like most of the women who frequent downstairs." He grinned as he took a seat. "You practically turned down every man who offered you a drink."

She returned a polite smile as her gaze trained on the rough grain of the goblet.

The leprechaun pimp barely reached the chest level of the women sitting around him. He masked himself well as a businessman with a green blazer and black shirt. Tufts of red hair peeked from under a black fedora. A nose ring completed his glamour. Underneath the disguise, the standard appearance applied:

rosy-cheeks, short height, and a sprinkle of freckles across his nose. But this wasn't a cheery creature protecting his stash of gold. This one protected his stable of girls who could be bought with an American Express, no Traveler's checks accepted, please.

From their table Tessa overheard a man speaking. "Seamus, you owe me four hours with Melinda."

"Four hours? I don't owe you shit, boy."

The girls cackled as the man's face reddened.

"Why am I negotiating with a bastard like you? I could just as easily beat the time out of you."

The eyes of the leprechaun darkened. "I'd love to see you try me, boy."

The women continued to smile. The poor human had no idea who he was trifling with.

A hand touched Tessa. She had almost forgotten about the strip club owner. "I never learned your name?"

With a smile to Claus she offered her middle name.

"How lovely. Perhaps I may need to use your services in the future."

"I don't know if you could afford me. I have an exclusive list of clients."

Men like Claus fell for this line each and every time. Question a boastful millionaire on his value and a laundry list was guaranteed. As Claus droned on about his personal holdings, the fight between the leprechaun pimp and the pissed off trick continued.

"How about I come across the table and kick your ass?" the man spat.

Seamus gulped his drink. A leggy blonde refilled the glass from one of the many bottles of premium vodka on the table.

The young man stepped forward. Claus sensed the confrontation and alerted his bouncer. A larger werewolf in a suit approached the table. "Is this gentleman bothering you, Seamus?"

The leprechaun laughed. "Bothered? Would help if I actually *saw* someone in front of me."

Red-faced, the young man jumped across the table, knocking over bottles. The wooden goblet rolled off the table and disappeared in the direction opposite where she sat a few feet away. Simultaneously, Seamus cursed as drinks spilled over on him and his girls.

"You're gonna wish you hadn't done that, lad," Seamus growled as he gave the young man a strong wallop across the head with a cane.

The bouncer grabbed the man as something hit Tessa's foot under the table. Claus directed the bouncer while she glanced at her high heel. Right next to her foot was the goblet. What the hell? She stared at it for a second before a strong compulsion urged her to pick it up. It tickled the back of her neck and confirmed her suspicions. *Rob?*

Tessa picked up the goblet and placed it behind her back in the seat. Transforming an imbued object required power and ability she didn't possess. With time she could mask it from prying eyes, but she had to act fast.

The stilted john turned over a few drinks as he was carried out of the V.I.P. area. Angry patrons cursed as their drinks were jostled from his kicking feet.

"If you'll excuse me, I need to do damage control," Claus told her. "Please continue to enjoy the drinks on me."

By the time Claus left, she'd prepared a masking spell for the goblet behind her. From behind her back, Tessa retrieved a camel-brown clutch purse — an ideal disguise. She made her way toward the stairs.

The leprechaun stepped into her path.

"What a pretty witch you are."

Her heart skipped a beat as the liquor-stained leprechaun leaned forward. Did her mask spell work?

"Seamus, I can't find it," one of his women called out. She was bent under the table.

His eyes never left hers. "Keep looking," he barked.

"I haven't seen you around here before," the leprechaun said. "You're new here."

Her mouth opened, but nothing came out. Thousands of excuses crossed her mind: bathroom, girlfriends heading back home, or boyfriend ready to go. Instead, Tessa mumbled, "I don't frequent here often."

"Quite a shame I missed you. Would you like to come sit at my table?"

The faint sliver of Seamus' compulsion spell glossed over her. One foot scraped forward before a counterspell in another location pushed her back.

His smile faded as he peered toward the crowd below. Did he sense the intervention?

With a push of confidence, Tessa sprang into action. "Thank you for your kind offer, but I have to..." Oh, shit, she'd had fifty million excuses ready to go. Her empty brain refused to work as she stepped backwards.

"I'd love to discuss business with you." He offered a cocky grin. "A fine lady like yourself could make some nice money."

His last statement kicked her in the gut. She'd just been propositioned by a pimp...

"I already have a job, thank you, but no thank you." She skirted around him and bolted for the stairs. When she reached the bottom, she made a beeline for the door. A hand grasped her elbow in the middle of the crowd. She whipped her head around, expecting to see one of Seamus' girls with an angry snarl. It was Rob.

"I bet it was that witch," someone in the V.I.P. section yelled.

"Go down there and check her," Seamus screamed.

"Time to go." Rob pulled her toward the entrance.

Once outside, they darted across the street toward the closest side street. Rob kept checking for cabs or subway entrances as their brisk walk turned into a light run. High heels weren't meant for running.

After she stumbled a second time he growled, "Lose the heels."

After she removed the mask on the shoes, they sped a few blocks until they arrived at a quiet park. He allowed her to catch her breath as he watched the direction they came from.

"Not bad," he said.

"Where were you?"

"Apparently putting myself out of a job at the rate you're going."

"I think your job security is safe this time." She plopped down on a park bench and tossed the masked goblet to him. "You can have it."

He eyed the purse and chuckled. "This doesn't match my shoes."

She flicked her wrist to free the magic of the mask.

"We need to keep moving. I can't open a gate in the open like this."

Ten minutes later, Rob opened a gateway in a Japanese pachinko establishment a few blocks away. The *hengeyokai* owner accepted a few dollars from Rob for some time alone in the private dining room. They could hear the chirping noises from the gaming machines as the Japanese shape-shifter, with the body of a man and the head of a rat, left them a service of tea.

After tossing in the goblet, he waved for Tessa to enter. She jumped into the junk pile, hoping this would be the last time she'd have to go through this madness.

As she stared across the piles and piles of magical items, she didn't see her Honda anywhere. She wanted to move to look around, but she could barely make progress forward in her skirt. She hiked up the garment, but this did little good to boost her morale. For miles and miles there were capes, wands, and broomsticks. A stray vehicle here and there didn't resemble anything from this decade. Were all her efforts with Rob in vain? Her shoulders slumped.

"You have four minutes. Move it, woman!"

She took a lumbered step forward and scowled when something caught her skirt—the bristly end of a weathered, light-brown wand. A water witch wand. Could she? It wasn't like there was anyone patrolling around to stop her from using the returned merchandise.

"Three minutes, Tessa."

She freed her skirt and picked up the wand from under a pile of torn hardback books. The stick shook for a moment under her hands before settling into a comfortable buzz. She knew somewhat how to wield a wand. Like every curious young witch, she'd crept into her mother's bedroom and tried on her clothes. After the clothes came the makeup, then the magical goodies stored away under the bed.

Wands could detect experienced users bent on world domination compared to young girls with fantasies of teenage boys. The twig twitched, tugging her to the right. It pulled Tessa along for a few feet before Rob yelled about the ticking clock.

With a frustrated sigh, she returned to the opening. Another chance gone. She gazed at the beautiful wand in her hands. It didn't belong to her, but how she wished she could use it again.

Tessa couldn't afford such a powerful tool. Not until her business turned around. She left it on top of a pile of shiny men's shoes and scrambled to the entrance.

The portal closed behind her not long after. Rob waited on one of the seats he shoved out of the way for the portal.

"My chances don't look too good right now."

"You give up too easily. Perhaps you need to change your approach."

"Well, I can call my father and see what his associates could do. But asking my family for help would be opening a can of worms I want to leave closed at all costs." She plopped down on the chair beside him.

"Who are you trying to contact?"

"Archibald Cramer."

"Sounds vaguely familiar, but I don't know him personally."

"Most wouldn't. He's too busy pissing on everyone's parade from the fifth dimension." She leaned forward so she could think. There had to be another way for her to directly reach the car. If she'd managed to wrangle a goblet from a leprechaun pimp, the sky sure as hell shouldn't be the limit.

"What's that on your back?" he asked.

"What?" She tried to reach behind her back. Her fingers brushed against something rough and pointy.

Oh no.

"There's a wand on your back," he said. "Can you take it off?"

Rob pulled and yanked, but the wand refused to budge. With little effort, she managed to grab the wand.

"It's a water witch wand. I used it to try to find the scroll."

He grinned and cocked an eyebrow.

"I did not steal this! Don't you dare think such a thing."

He chuckled.

He probably thought she waltzed out of there with it. "Can you open the portal again? I'm perfectly willing to toss it back inside."

Rob pulled the golden amulet from his pocket. He waved it in the air, but nothing happened. He forcefully shook the amulet again. "It's activated by a repo'ed item."

She checked the wand. There weren't any markings or names.

"Any way to find out who the owner is then? Maybe the wand isn't on any records. Either way, you can hold onto it until you open another gate." She offered him the wand. He tried to grab it, but the twig refused to release its hold on her hand.

"It's chosen a new owner."

"You can't be serious. Wands don't choose owners. My aunts used to buy them all the time. None of them did this."

"Those were cheap wands from outdoor flea markets. You wouldn't see me coming to repo those pieces of junk."

"Well, until I can find the owner, I'll store it somewhere." She held it in her hand, wondering where she could hide it until she returned home. Only crazy people with carts and folks heading to a costume party carried sticks like this.

With a verbal command, she willed it to collapse. Nothing happened.

"You're its owner. Command it to disappear."

She gave him a dirty look.

He positioned himself behind her. All up close and personal. "Like this." He grabbed her hand. Directed her movements as he recited an incantation for her to repeat. The wand twitched, and then blinked out of sight.

A soft laugh emerged from her lips. "How nice…"

His hands slipped down Tessa's sides and rested on her hips. Through the thin material of her skirt, she could feel the heat from his hands. His lips grazed her head as he inhaled deeply.

Fire coursed through her veins, leaving her heady with yearning. All this back and forth between them, she was ready to burst. One hand slid over her belly, while another gripped her hip. The evidence of his arousal pressed against her as his head descended to rain kisses along her neck.

"Come with me to my place," he whispered.

Could she head to his home, where his aunt and uncle potentially slept a room away? Not that she expected to have wild monkey sex from wall-to-wall, but the prospects dampened the mood. She stepped forward, taking a moment to catch her breath. He didn't speak a word as she gathered her thoughts.

Hadn't she told all her clients to follow the rules of courtship? To go on dates and meet the right man? No trysts. Establish a long-term relationship. But at this very moment, she looked at Rob and didn't give a damn.

Weren't certain rules meant to be broken?

They'd approached this point together, but right now she had an opportunity for an out, for an escape. The words didn't come out. Instead, she offered a trembling hand into his outstretched one.

Chapter 15

Dating Tip #11: Keep reevaluating your growing relationship for positive forward movement. Especially, if your date is gazing at your leg considering how tasty you would be if she took a bite.

The ride to Rob's place was a blur. They didn't make a sound as they bounded the stairs to his room. A single lamp illuminated a dim corner in the sitting room. Once they reached the darkness at the top of the stairs, he pulled Tessa along into a suite at the far end of the hallway.

With the door shut behind her, she expected him to fling her on his king-size bed. Instead, his eager hands cornered her at the door. Her back pressed into old wood, she leaned forward to capture his lips. He avoided her, grinding his hips against hers. She was ready to reciprocate, to offer everything.

"You've teased me all this time. No more games."

A soft moan escaped her mouth when he foiled her next attempt to kiss him.

He pushed her against the creaking door again.

"Rob, the noise!" she whispered.

"There are many things I'm capable of. If your screaming is a problem, then that's the least of our troubles." The thin veil of a masking spell descended along the walls. The buttons of her red blouse unsnapped. The discarded buttons echoed along the walls.

To prove his point, he pounced, nipping Tessa's neck as his hand snaked up from her waist to rub the nipples that poked out underneath. Another hand yanked her blouse open so his head could descend. As his mouth worked its way downward, she tried to hold back a whimper. Shirt gone. Bra discarded. She bit her lip, the shiver uncontrollable as he found his target. All she could do was grab his hair as he traced a circle around each nipple then sucked. His warm kisses between her breasts turned into future sites for hickies.

Invisible fingers unzipped her skirt. The masking spell she placed on the skirt wavered but held. Rob worked overtime tonight on spellcasting. Would he have enough energy to complete what he asked her to come here for? "Pretty big spell to hold for a span of time."

He ignored her and pulled down her skirt. She averted her eyes as he grabbed her panties and jerked them down for her to step out of them. Instead of standing, he shocked her senses with kisses along her thighs.

These weren't short and quick. Every kiss included a brief swirl of his tongue before his lips connected with her skin. Tessa sucked in a breath as his head hovered below, his lips resting only inches from her inner thighs. With a firm grip, he squeezed her buttocks. He came up for a brief moment to dart his tongue into her belly button.

Damn it, he was so good with that thing. Each touch fed the fire within her. Then he descended until he traced a path along her bikini line. Lower and lower. Her legs quivered, but he held her in place. Then he stopped.

Fully clothed, he led her to the bed, his warm hand intertwined with hers. He pushed her onto her back so he could undress. Her body burned with need as he pulled his shirt off and tossed his pants aside. Based on the way his eyes blazed and the tight line of his mouth, she knew he enjoyed watching her watching him. Especially when he discarded his briefs…

Now that is a wand I'd like to wield.

Her eyes lingered on his length before they admired his hardened stomach. The muscles clenched twice before he leaned forward. She spied the dark rings of tattoos along his long arms, the faint scars along his left shoulder.

Rob climbed onto the bed, sliding the hard muscles of his body along hers. Tessa ached for him to kiss her. To kiss her like that night during the bar fight. But when she leaned toward his lips, he shifted downward until he opened her legs. Would he really go there their first night? Would he really… Why yes, he would. She tried to squirm away as the manipulation of his tongue turned from a burning bonfire into an overflowing eruption. He nipped, sucked, manipulated flesh like a master. She bucked again. Hands clasped her bottom to hold her in place again. Panting turned to begging.

"Rob, please…"

Suddenly, her back arched. She climaxed. She released months of pent up frustration as she grasped for anything to hold onto: His hair, the bed sheets, and finally a pillow within reach.

As her breathing slowed, the sweat bathing her skin cooled. She'd never made such noises before. She hoped he really did mask the room, or else his aunt and uncle would've heard enough to convince themselves to never have dinner with her again.

After he brushed his lips against her inner thigh, he trailed kisses along her hipbones, pausing briefly to nuzzle her belly button. Almost as if there was no rush. He slowly positioned himself between her legs.

Dark eyes caressed her nakedness. "If you tell me no, I'll stop now." Ragged breaths fanned her face. She could feel his cock against her thigh, so tantalizingly close to the place where his head had been before. All of this teasing, all of this maddening manipulation of her limbs to bring her to this single point where she had to make a choice again. Hadn't she come here willingly? And climbed up the stairs to his room two steps at a time?

"Tessa, I'm not a man who pursues any woman," he growled.

She lifted her hips with urgency. He moved out of the way.

"Tell me yes…"

"I think I already said that more times than I can count." She grinned.

"I'm serious." He pressed the swollen tip against her center and then withdrew. *Oh, mercy!*

What did he want her to say? Was he telling her this wasn't a one-night stand? "Yes, Rob…" Tessa's words trailed into a long guttural moan as he pushed into her body. He punished her for her reluctance, pumping his hips as she held onto his back. The whole time, his eyes stayed locked with hers, watching her face as she tried to resist the ever-increasing pleasure.

"I need you…" he whispered.

Finally, he reunited their lips. Her hands moved to caress his face as the kiss deepened. All she could do was hold onto him. Savor his touch. Why did she wait so damn long? The grip on her hips tightened. The pleasure rose to agonizing levels. She thought the pain of his hands would surpass the sweet agony of release, but with an urgent whisper of her name his hard body turned to stone above her a few seconds afterwards.

After things settled between them, he rolled off, pulling her into the crook of his arm. A contentment Tessa hadn't felt for years washed over her, leaving her grinning from

ear-to-ear like a goofy college freshman. And all
it took was one night with a repo man.

The next morning, Rob woke up to arms
wrapped around him and a warm breath
against his shoulder. A beautiful woman
pressed against his back. As he stretched, he
couldn't help smiling. He turned over to draw
her closer to him. She was soft in all the right
places.

"Why can't I wake up like this every
morning?" she purred.

He kissed her lips again. They might be at it
for hours again with the way she knew how to
kiss. He drifted to her neck and licked her pulse
point. Her heart raced for him. From that spot
he drifted upwards. Against her cheek, he
inhaled, taking in her perfumed skin. Asking
her to stay the night hadn't been planned. If
he'd truly thought about it, he would've held
back, but as he nibbled on her sensitive earlobe,
he decided he'd made a good decision.

There was no turning back now.
Consequences be damned.

"You know, if you let people get to know
you, they might find out you're not such a
burly bear," she whispered between kisses.

She'd gotten chatty. He'd have to remedy
that. "My attitude keeps the crazies away."

"But what about acting nice—" She tried to
speak and only managed to gasp. "That tongue
of yours is the bane of my existence."

"I enjoy putting him to work." He turned her around so her back faced him. A much better position for what he had in mind. His hand left her waist to trail up to her breasts. Gently, he rubbed his fingertips over the nipples, grazing them again and again. Her gasps excited him, hardening him even faster. She was so soft, so warm. He couldn't help thrusting forward, attempting to position her legs for spooning.

Rob whispered an incantation for "protection." There was nothing more reliable than a spell-based condom that wouldn't break. His uncle reminded him at length before he'd entered the service that no magical *oops* were allowed.

She hissed as he slid into her wet warmth. He tried to go slow. Maybe even build a rhythm to give her the pleasure she'd given him last night.

"Rob!"

He squeezed his eyes shut in agony. She called his name again and again, tightened around him until he wondered if he'd finish quickly. Damn, she felt so good.

"You want it harder?" he whispered at her neck. He quickened his pace, unable to hold in the curse that slipped through his lips.

They soared higher and higher, cresting at some unknown peak again and again. He whispered words in Korean she wouldn't understand — that she was his flower, his perfect moon — but that didn't matter. The only important thing was that she was here with him. Overwhelmed with emotion, he stiffened with another climax as she reached her own release.

Slick with sweat, they lay quietly for some time before he withdrew. Instead of pulling her into his arms, he propped himself up on the pillows and glanced down at her.

She smiled back at him. A sweet expression he wanted to remember for the long days to come. Just her, lying like this with him.

Tessa reached for him, gripping his shoulders before grabbing his waist. Her hand kneaded his muscles—far too roughly. Pain shot through his side—an area that had been pain-free for the last couple of days.

He pulled back briefly. "Please don't do that. I need some recovery time."

"You've had a whole night." Her hand moved to caress his chest before pulling him into a hug.

The pain that came again was sharper than he'd expected. He'd wasted far too much energy last night. He cringed as she brushed against the muscles of his ribs.

"Sorry!" she blurted.

Her eyes formed slits. Cautiously, she touched his skin. "Rob, you should really get that checked out." Her fingers tentatively touched the area.

Before he could stop her, she discovered the hidden layer of magic. Rob recoiled and sat up, but it was too late.

She squinted, attempting to unfold the spell he placed on his midsection.

"Don't," he warned through clenched teeth.

He'd worked so hard to bind his midsection like a corset. All he could do was stare at the ceiling. Damn, what could he say now? What he had wasn't a minor sprain.

"Tessa, there's something I need to set right with you."

She looked horrified. "Are you marr—"

"No, I'm not married. Why would you think that?"

"In my business, when most men are hiding something, it's usually another woman."

He shook his head, not meeting her eyes. "It's not another woman." He paused. "Remember when I left you after the fight at the bar?"

She nodded.

With a whisper, he released the folds of magic around his middle and they dissipated. Layer after layer around his midsection. It was both freeing and quite painful.

"I went down to the Bethesda Naval Hospital for treatment for an injury I received during a rescue-and-recovery mission a few months ago back in South America."

"An active-duty mission—as in one for the Navy SEALs?" Her whole body clenched against him. "I thought you weren't in the military anymore."

Rob bit his lip, and he stared at the far wall. "I didn't want my aunt and uncle to think I'd have to suddenly up and leave. I just wanted to help them out while hiding my problems."

He said a final incantation. In moments, the veil over his injury cleared. He didn't need to look down to see what her wide eyes took in: a large scratch marred his skin under his chest muscle to curve toward his ribs. Bruises were a mottled yellow in places. Stark-white bandages were draped around his middle. A costly hour with a local wizard had only done so much.

"I've been doing repo jobs at night and reporting to the hospital for treatment once in a while. I'll be going back to Fort Briggs as soon as the doctors sign off."

Anger practically boiled off her skin. "You lied to me. To everyone."

His head dropped. "Tessa, I—"

"No. Don't try to explain." She scooted away from him.

He tried to reach for her, and he winced.

Damn it all to hell. This moment should've been funny. They should've laughed it off while he groaned in pain, but not everything worked out that way. He should've trusted her and told her he was active-duty and on medical leave.

And now the look of pain in her eyes was one he wanted to take away.

What a fool she was. Tessa had given into this fantasy for the moment, hoping Rob would offer her something different. But like some of her matchmaking clients, he withheld the truth until it suited him. "I knew you were rough around the edges, but I didn't suspect you to be a liar." She left the bed, searching for her clothes.

With clenched teeth, he stood and snatched her pants away. The mask on them had faded overnight. "I think you're overreacting. I haven't lied to you."

"Lied — withheld. It doesn't matter. All I know is that I can't deal with this right now." She pushed him out of the way. "Move!"

She knew this would happen. This revelation was punishment of some kind. She was already failing at her business. Why not screw up a relationship, too?

Not only had Rob lied to her, but, even worse, he'd lied to his *family*. His poor aunt had no idea her nephew was active-duty and soon would need to leave. As to when, she didn't know how the system worked. Probably not any time soon since he was in pretty bad shape. One thing she did know was that once Rob left, he wouldn't be around to support his aunt and uncle.

Her thoughts flashed to his aunt, a woman she'd gladly place above her own Aunt Daisy.

"I need you to let me explain myself."

"No need. I've heard enough." She grabbed her pants. He didn't fight her as she dressed.

"I'm trying to hold things off as long as I can. I'm supposed to be convalescing until the hospital clears me to return."

He grabbed her arm as she tried to pass. "I'm taking a big chance doing my job to help both you and my family."

"How kind of you," she said. "Telling the truth should've been a chance you had taken, too."

Tessa left and didn't bother looking back.

Chapter 16

Dating Tip #5: Grow from the positive and negative dating experiences. And ladies, be sure to remove that chastity belt. Nothing says, "I'm not playing the field," more than a medieval device used to barricade horny knights.

Why did the pain of betrayal always sear so deep—deep enough to make her wonder if she'd ever dig herself out?

Tessa had thought her dad knew how to do a number on her. Rob evidently worked just as hard. It was on early mornings like this one that she couldn't help but think about a corner similar to the one where she stood now. She wasn't waiting for a taxi or a bus at the time.

She was waiting for another man—the first one in her life. She'd been waiting for her father to come pick her up for her rite of passage, the once-in-a-lifetime event for witches who'd soon leave their homes to be educated in college. She had another year of high school left, but she'd been accepted to attend Northwestern

University. She was on the path her parents had set out for her.

A few hours earlier, her mom had said, "Are you sure you don't want me to take you? I know it's a father-daughter thing, but I could give you a ride."

"Dad will show up, Mom. He told me he's cleared his evening and he's wrapped up his case load."

Clark Dandridge was making a name for himself among the supernatural trial lawyers in the Midwest. She'd often heard her father's name during her grandmother's dinner parties. He was a man to be respected—especially since he fought for the disenfranchised.

Meet me outside of my office, sweetheart, his note said. *I'll be there at six o'clock sharp.*

It was seven-thirty, and her feet hurt from standing in her heels so long. The fall wind had picked up as well.

Cars passed by on the busy downtown street in Chicago. After all this time waiting, she sensed everyone's eyes on her. Who was this girl in the pretty red dress? Why did she look at each car with expectant eyes?

Each time a black car approached, her heartbeat sped up. Would it be him this time? Wouldn't she feel silly that she'd doubted him?

Like all the other times. He'd taught her to stand behind her words, to uphold the truth.

Tessa took a step toward the curb and tried to ignore a growing feeling of regret. He promised he'd come this time. It wouldn't be like the other times when her dad had told her he'd leave work early or take her out to eat and not show up.

A black car pulled up. It was one that she recognized, but the woman who opened the door and ushered her inside wasn't her father. It was her mom.

She didn't say a word as they rode to the dance.

Tessa cried the whole way.

The event was everything she'd expected it to be, minus the man who was supposed to be at her side.

The ceremony at the country club was simple yet profound. Fathers offered their daughters a gift, one that would prepare them for their journey in the magical world. Most got jewelry; others got rare wands and capes made from exotic materials.

· "I'll get you something tomorrow," her mom told her. "Something really nice." Her mom's kind words touched her, and Tessa tried to hide her disappointment. She was the only girl without a gift—rather embarrassing with all the money that flowed around her affluent friends.

The dance began, and one of the teachers took her hand to lead her to the dance floor. Dr. Parks wasn't the tallest guy, either—the top of his head was at the same level as her eyes, but he beamed at her the whole time. The math teacher's eyes shined as if to say to everyone, "She's my daughter tonight."

If only such things were true.

After the father-daughter dance ended, Tessa sipped her punch and gabbed with her friends.

The evening almost came to a close — then someone lightly touched her shoulder. She turned to see her aunt Daisy.

"What are you doing here?" When she noticed the distraught expression on her aunt's face, Tessa's smile vanished.

"Tessa…I'm so sorry." Daisy swallowed visibly. "We need to talk somewhere else." Her mother wasn't standing with the adults anymore. She was by the door leading out of the ballroom, holding both of their coats. Grief was etched in her features.

Something was very wrong.

As her mother led her out, Tessa kept repeating, "What's wrong, Mom? Is it Dad?"

Had he gotten in an accident? She should've waited a bit longer. Had he missed her and gotten hurt?

By the time they'd reached the hallway outside, her mom broke into tears. Her sobs stabbed into Tessa. "It's Grandma. She's gone. She died a half-hour ago."

The trip home didn't exist. The house where her family gathered to mourn didn't exist. All she had left was her family's love, but even at that moment in time, what she really needed was her dad. And he didn't bother to exist either.

Clark Dandridge didn't bother to show up until her grandmother's will was read.

The ticking clock left Tessa hungry for a repo mission. Ursula's hard work proved fruitful. After reading and arranging the paperwork for the agency, she managed to determine the contact information of four of the seven warlocks on the list. The intern could alter her voice and contact relatives or old golf buddies, fishing for information on the location or contact details on the missing client.

Tessa was reading the profiles for an upcoming dinner party this week for Clive when the phone beside her rang.

She heard the haggard voice of Rob's aunt.

"Thank God you answered. I've no one else to call."

"What's wrong?" Was Rob hurt? A thousand ideas popped into her head.

"Arthur isn't feeling very well. We were out for a walk in Central Park and he started having chest pains. I can't get a hold of Rob."

His aunt's worried voice sounded strange. The woman's fright broke her heart.

"It's not that bad, Matilda. Come sit down with me," her husband's voice barked.

She could see where Rob got some of his stubbornness. "Matilda, if he's having chest pains you should call 911."

"He doesn't want to call them. He took a Bayer aspirin and told me not to worry."

"Sounds like he's being stubborn."

"I'd agree. Now, I know you've only met us once, but well, I'd hoped you could help me convince him to head to the hospital."

Arthur's voice grumbled protests not far from the phone. "I'm feeling a bit better."

"Then why are you still clutching your chest?"

As they went back and forth, Tessa had already rearranged her schedule on the computer.

"Matilda, here's my cell phone number. I'm on my way."

Twenty minutes later, Tessa found the pair sitting on a park bench not far from 73rd Avenue.

The heat couldn't be the source of poor Arthur's sweating. She'd never witnessed a heart attack before, but she knew they shouldn't take things so lightly.

"How about we catch a cab to head to the hospital real quick?" she asked softly.

"And pay over a thousand for some quack to tell me to take an aspirin? No thanks," Arthur grumbled.

She'd had relatives like him. Bitter old men who had a switch you had to flip to ease their minds.

"I understand that you hate the hospital, but look at your poor wife. She's sick with worry."

Arthur pursed his lips. "It's not that bad, honey."

"Twenty minutes ago, you were in agony. It's time to go to the hospital." His wife crossed her arms and glared at him.

"Matilda only wants the best for you." Tessa took a step forward. "Who would take care of her if something happened to you?"

"How are you feeling, sweetheart?" Matilda asked.

"Like garbage, but I'll manage."

Rob's aunt turned to her. The woman's face scrunched as if she searched for the proper words. "Did you eat the clam chowder Rob gave you?"

"Sorry, I didn't have a chance to eat it. I took it to work to eat for lunch and my staff ended up eating it all."

Her face brightened with relief. "Good thing you hadn't. Arthur found out I accidentally substituted one of my herbs for a container of lovage. I was so glad you picked up the phone."

Tessa offered a shaky laugh. Good luck pot of clam chowder indeed. The hospital visit would've been the other way around.

Two minutes later, they were in a cab on their way to the nearest hospital. In all honesty, Tessa avoided hospitals like the plague. There were plenty of supernatural physicians available, in particular wizards who operated clinics in their homes, but they didn't come cheap or offer insurance plans associated with the majority of the employers in NYC.

The emergency room was comfortable, but left a lot to be desired. Most folks in New York told her not to go to the local hospitals. After hearing the receptionist, she wondered if they'd be issued pagers like they were diners at the local Bennigans.

"What's the emergency?"

Matilda squinted at the receptionist. "My husband's having a heart attack."

"Please go through the double doors and see the nurse." The receptionist droned the information like a telemarketer recording.

Rob arrived just in time. He stormed into the ER waiting room and spotted them. "How are you feeling?"

"Groggy, but not too bad."

He addressed his aunt. "My cell died while I was at work. I noticed the phone message while I ate lunch at home."

"I called Tessa and she helped us get to the hospital."

He muttered thanks in Tessa's direction while avoiding her face. She didn't want him to look at her either. To see her desire under the layers of resentment.

A nurse appeared with a wheelchair to take him through the doors. Rob helped his uncle until he was safely in the chair. Matilda followed close behind until the couple left into the ER. Rob stood there watching them through the tiny window of the closed door.

As she watched his wide back for a few seconds, images flooded her mind of his body on top of hers. His hands intertwined with hers as he made love to her. After a deep breath, she jarred herself out of her reverie. She twisted her eyes away from him and headed for the door.

A strong hand grasped her shoulder. "Wait."

She avoided his face. Somehow.

"Thanks for stepping in to help."

She nodded.

"You didn't tell them... about what I told you."

"No, I didn't tell them you were lying to them." She regretted the words after speaking them. They were the truth, but nonetheless she couldn't miss when he winced.

"I did what I had to do, Tessa. I was in a position to help, so I took a chance."

"That doesn't make being a liar any better. Your aunt and uncle are good people. They deserve the truth."

I deserved the truth, too.

"You saw my aunt. She's worried sick about ending up on the street." He tried to lessen the distance between them, but she took a step back. "I won't do that to her."

"You're gambling for a happy ending, Rob."

"I'm more than aware," he grumbled.

She turned to leave again, but he grabbed her arm. "I know you're mad at me, but I'm still willing to help you if you need it."

Their eyes locked for a moment. The pain from knowing things would never be the same hit hard.

As she turned to leave she heard him say, "If you're interested I can pick you up outside of your apartment when the time comes. Just give me a call."

Chapter 17

Dating Tip #8: When a matchmaker suggests someone for you, there may be ulterior motives: you need to date someone your own age for your own good or perhaps you conjure up ghosts every time you sneeze. Either way, I only make suggestions. You may already know what you need. The true matchmaker lies within.

Tessa had mixed feelings during the next repo mission with Rob. Maybe he knew her feelings left her torn and divided? Most of her past boyfriends never read her that well. Even if they had a rocky start, she'd fight tooth and nail to save her business. And that meant facing him whether she wanted to be in his presence or not.

His eyes brightened when she got into his rental car. She tried not to return his gaze and failed miserably.

After some time heading east, Tessa finally ended the silence between them. "Where are we headed?"

"A job in Long Island. Should be nice and easy."

From past trips to attractive spots on Long Island, she knew they had at least an hour of travel time ahead of her. Travel time where they'd be forced to talk.

The trip to Fire Island, their final destination, took under an hour. During the drive, he tried a few times to make small talk. She focused on the scenery instead. On a warm, breezy evening like this one, the Long Island coastline was pleasant and comfortable. The rows of beach houses reminded her of her parents' vacation house on Lake Michigan. They'd spend a few weeks during the summer relaxing on the water during the days that weren't stifling hot.

Their destination was a double-level beach house painted lime-green with white shutters. The house was dim against the neighboring houses with summer occupants.

"Are you sure they aren't home?" she asked.

"Clive was told by the loan holder that the owner is on a business trip in Europe. Should be an easy walk in and walk out job."

She nodded with a sinking feeling that easy should never be applied to doing repo work.

They approached the house from the back door facing the expansive deck.

"Do you want to try an unlock spell?" His attempts for conversation were persistent.

"I'm good."

Once inside, the deathly quiet house

beckoned. The motor within a large marine tank in the living room grumbled and buzzed. Above the tank a long bulb illuminated the space in a blue glow. The water's reflection bounced along the walls, casting strange dancing shadows. Something didn't feel right, but she couldn't put to words the feeling that they weren't alone. Rob crept ahead, checking around corners to make sure the coast was clear.

The flickering light drew her to the fish habitat where she peered inside to see what caught her eye. Floating near the bottom, a jar — one of those old-fashioned kind you used for preserving jams and such — had to be filled with what looked like snow. In a warm seawater tank? She took a closer look. A familiar marking on the container's side consisted of three wavy lines. A water witch's mark…

Now that's weird. But not exactly something she'd expect Rob to repo. She touched the tank's glass and waited for the water to whisper its secrets. Tingles from the jar vibrated into her fingers. None of them good — almost like the hairy tips from a spider's leg. What was even creepier was how the container slowly slid across the bottom in her direction.

Oh hell no…

Tessa took a step back. No need to lose what little common sense she had left. She should've asked Rob what they came here for. She could've sped up the process by assisting him in the search. Instead, she left the fish tank behind and looked for Rob in the living room. The furniture was so nice here. What she wouldn't give to be able to afford this kind of stuff. Like any other luxury beach house, the kitchen had marble counters with a deluxe chef's stove. She could almost hear the voices of a dinner party with sounds of banter and champagne bottles popping open. A bonfire on the beach would be seen outside the French doors. She'd be standing outside her home, rubbing elbows with the elite of New York.

And all of these riches would've come from *her* successful business—if she had one in the next year.

"Tessa, I found the earth witch's painting. It's in the basement."

She turned to Rob as the sounds of the beach party faded from her mind. Time to finish the job and find her scroll at last. The path to the basement was dark until they reached it. Large skylights lit the room, but the focal point that drew her eyes was a set of Victorian sconces above an ornate golden frame of an old French period girl with her small dog. On the other side of the room, a home theater had been setup with two rows of comfortable seating and a projection screen along the wall.

As she approached the painting, the hairs on the back of her neck rose. The palm where she stored the wand itched like hives.

"Rob, let's repo this thing and get out of here," she whispered. "Something doesn't feel right."

He froze as if he listened for something in

the silence.

A faint scent hit her nose. The house had been empty for months. Just a trace of fresh paint and cleaning products lingered in the air. But in this room, something familiar filled her with dread. A rainstorm during lunch. A man with a single name—Dagger.

"About time you two showed up."

Rob whipped around and pushed her behind him.

From the shadows on the other side of the room, Tessa noticed the brief flare of Dagger taking a drag of his cigarette, before blowing it into the air. The smoke trailed around him, then settled at his feet like an ominous fog.

"I expected you to come alone. But your lady friend is more than welcome to join in on the fun."

The painting behind them hummed. She couldn't tear her eyes away from Dagger as she fought to remember to breathe. A trap had been set, and they'd waltzed right in.

Rob stared Dagger down without blinking. "Let her leave. This is between you and me."

"It's much too late for that now. I promised my pet a chance to play." Another spark of his cigarette briefly lit the corner. "And both of you triggered his release from the painting anyway."

Slowly, Tessa turned her head to see the painting had morphed from its original form. In the place of the small dog with its brown coat sat a beast from hell. The girl had vanished, evidently smart enough to flee or maybe she'd been its first course. With bristly black hair and large orange eyes, the beast's drool dripped down the painting and pooled along the floor.

Oh, shit.

Tessa tapped Rob's shoulder.

"I know."

She tapped even harder as the beast in the painting grew in size as it approached the threshold of crossing into the basement.

"I know!" He shoved her toward the stairs. "Run!"

They scrambled up the stairs with Rob taking the lead. They dashed through the kitchen and barreled out of the French doors as the beast exploded out of one of the bedroom windows. It landed with a thud into bushes in the landscaping. The bushes rustled as it approached their position along the beach. They broke into a run.

The grunts of the beast urged them to run faster. Her chest started to burn as their sprint along the uneven ground tired her. The creature sprinted ahead to drive them closer to the water. They came to an abrupt halt as the hellhound jumped ten feet in front of their path. Rob pushed her behind him while reaching into his satchel.

"Do you have a staff?" she hissed. "Maybe a gun?"

Did he roll his eyes at a time like this?

"Do you think guns work on demons?" He searched his bag for something suitable as the monster ambled forward with a menacing growl. They backed up until water lapped at their ankles.

As the creature approached, its size had grown from that of a German shepherd to the size of a large horse with flames spitting from its nostrils. Its skin sizzled as the water touched its paws.

"Water now!" Rob pushed her into knee-deep water.

He pulled her deeper until they waded twenty feet away. She knew how to swim, but after ten minutes of avoiding the shore, her body tired. Rob tread water as if he did it every other day.

"Hang onto me."

She didn't want to touch him, but begrudgingly she wrapped her arms around him. He easily supported her additional weight as he continued to keep their heads above the water.

They had to be in the clear — until a tingling sensation hit her insides from the shore. Something was gathering energy, powering up like an engine revving. "What's that bright light over there?"

Rob took the words right out of her mouth before he pulled her under. "Oh, fuck me…"

From under the water a bright wave of light burst from the coast and spread toward them like lightning. The water rippled as the shock wave propelled them into the ocean's murky depths. She closed her eyes, her head rattling. For a moment she floated in darkness. Large hands touched her face, then Rob pushed her to the surface.

"Quick breath, another wave's coming," he belted out.

She did as instructed before another blast came at them from the beach. The vibrations coursed through the water sending them rolling across the bottom, farther away from the shore. All she could do was hold onto him and hope it all ended soon. Everything was dark. Not even the moonlight penetrated this deep.

Once the onslaught ended, Rob established a hold on a rock to keep them from drifting away while his other hand locked around her arm in a tight grip.

A few seconds later, the water settled once again. From the depths of the cloudy water, it was difficult to make out anything in the distance. The demon's overwhelming power lurked on the coastline, most likely pacing in circles.

She turned to see Rob staring at her. His face stiffened like stone, imploring her to hold her breath for a bit longer. His body was strangely relaxed. As a water witch, she should be swimming circles around him.

Suddenly she twitched, a subtle burning in her chest blossoming as her lungs burned for air. Her weary body strained against instinct to float to the top to freedom. Whatever reserves she had were depleted. She mentally prepared herself for what needed to happen next. Focus. Center. Harness the sea. She could do this to save them.

Rob's free hand rose, prepared to cover her mouth. Tessa grasped his hand as her magic built in her belly, swirling until the water around them folded under her command. With an audible pop, an air bubble materialized around them.

They released their breaths, collapsing against the confines of the barrier.

"Oh, damn," he panted, smoothing back his hair. He glanced at her. "Are you all right?"

"I'll be fine as long as you don't break my concentration."

Changing clothes was a snap. Converting a cup of soda from warm to cold could be done in a blink, but converting matter, then continuing to convert it for the purpose of providing oxygen was a *tall* order for a witch at Tessa's level of spellcasting.

"How long can you hold it?"

She squeezed her eyes shut. The strain deepened like someone adding another set of heavy books to a straining pile in her hands. The pile grew taller and taller. The pressure building each second.

Rob murmured a spell to offer light within their tiny space. Then he pulled his soaked satchel open. "Whatcha got, Harabeuji? We're in pretty bad shape here."

"Bad shape?" She coughed, causing the barrier to leak for a moment. "Ask him for a stick to hold the ceiling up!"

His eyebrow went up. "You still got that wand?"

Now that was a good idea. She called the wand to her hand and it poked out of her palm, perhaps aware of her dire circumstances. She touched the end of the wand to the surface of their protective bubble and the seal hardened considerably. With a boost from the water witch wand, they managed to hold out for an hour before heading back to shore. Thank goodness the beach was demon-free by the time they limped out of the water.

Exhausted, she plopped down in the sand, not caring about the wretched state she was in. Rob gently brushed a strand of her hair from one side to the other.

"You look beat."

Hair spray with a gob of mousse couldn't stand the force of a warlock on the warpath. Her hair and clothes were a mess, but she didn't give a damn. Rob gave her a few more minutes of peace as he snuck back into the house to see if he could snag the painting.

"Never head back into a house with the knife-wielding murderer!" she called out to him.

No *money* was worth what they just experienced.

"Even if the painting was a trap, I can't return to the office without it," he growled. "If there are issues related to the validity of the repo'ed property, then the Supernatural Municipal Government will have to deal with the mess." Rob took his job way too seriously.

After a bit of time, Rob left the house with the painting in hand. The girl and her dog had been restored to the front like before. She shivered thinking of the altered picture from not long ago. A breeze from the ocean made her damp clothes uncomfortable so she wrapped her arms around herself.

Rob opened the portal and tossed the painting inside.

"Do you want to pass this time?"

Standing was difficult, but she managed to reach the opening and peek inside. She had the wand now and an opportunity. Time to make use of it before she left the valuable tool inside.

Tessa whipped out the wand and let it pull her toward the scroll. She made squishy noises as she waded through the piles of magical items.

Rob laughed from the edge of the open gateway. "You ever thought of trying to teleport using the wand?"

"I wouldn't even know where to begin," she bit back.

Rob sauntered to her side after checking his watch. "We got extra time today—about eight minutes."

"Ok, so within eight minutes I need to learn how to teleport using a wand I've yet to master."

"Do you want to find your scroll or not?"

Briefly, she remembered that his deceit had sparked her anger. "Yes, I do."

"If a wand attaches itself to an owner, then you have a bit more leeway with spells." He tested her grip on the wand. "Now hold onto it tightly and imagine we are standing next to your car."

She closed her eyes.

"Imagine *your* car," he cautioned. "See it in

your mind so you don't teleport yourself to the wrong car."

Before she casted the spell he interrupted her again. "Stop."

"What is it now?" She followed his eyes to the portal entrance a few feet away. To her horror, she saw Dagger standing at the entrance with a triumphant smile on his face.

Rob's mouth formed a hard line and he cursed under his breath.

Dagger took a step closer to the portal. "It appears you put yourself in a precarious position."

"Look you piece of sh—"

"Save it. You know what's about to happen. If you would've stayed out of my affairs this wouldn't have been a problem. Perhaps a few years in Limbo will be a valuable lesson. Don't interfere again in my affairs again or I will end you."

Tessa gasped and stepped back from the rapid rise in temperature of Rob's skin. His face turned ruby red. He clenched his fists to the point where veins pulsed under his skin.

"Have fun with your little pet." His face turned to Tessa. "That is, unless you would like to come with me? You can always keep me company."

At the moment, the prospect of eternity with Rob fared better than fifteen minutes with this crazed lunatic. She'd even choose the leprechaun pimp. "Not interested."

He shrugged. "So be it."

With a whoosh, their means of escaping

closed, leaving them trapped in the never-ending hills of Limbo.

After twenty minutes of cursing and muttering, Rob plopped down beside Tessa and stewed.

"If I get out of here..." he grunted.

As she stared at the mounds and mounds of magical objects, she tried not to think about the obvious: she was trapped without food or water. Even with all these things scattered about to the far horizon, rescue wasn't eminent. Rob couldn't get them out.

Numbness gripped her hands, and she shook them, trying to calm her breathing. Everything would be all right. She wasn't alone. Hell, she was with a Navy SEAL. A Navy SEAL who cursed and gestured wildly like he'd beat up anybody who said the first word to him. She turned away from him, continuing her breathing exercise.

In such a barren space she closed her eyes and tried to "reach" for water. If there were any bodies of water within a few miles of her position they were miniscule and difficult to detect. The powerful magnet of the Atlantic Ocean was gone.

Nothing left to be done now but sit and rest. She found a discarded black cloak and laid it on top of the "ground" to create a marginally comfortable place to sit.

"I wouldn't use that," Rob said

nonchalantly. From a spot a few feet away from her, he tossed a book at the cape. The book fell through the garment into nothingness.

"Hmmm. That isn't good."

"Yeah, there's too much dangerous stuff around here. Ask me before you pick up anything."

She needed to rest and that required something to lie on instead of piles of lumpy books, shoes, and wooden chests.

"How about that purple and pink striped cape over there?" she asked.

"Will transform you into a horse without the matching medallion."

She pointed to her left. "And the golden cape?"

"Turn you into stone."

She groaned. "Ok, then what can I use?"

"Weren't you educated in magic?"

"I had a standard education which apparently didn't include hours of instruction on freaky magically imbued stuff."

Rob sighed. With a frown he searched through the closest piles. He shifted through the mess, tossing a garden hose, a rusty old saw, and the head of a Barbie doll. From the bottom of the hole he created, he pulled out a vermillion blanket with tasseled edges.

"Now this would make a perfect blanket."

She approached and fingered the silky material. "What is it?"

"It's the reading blanket of a sorceress whose name is too difficult to pronounce."

He laid the blanket across the piles, leaving a bumpy, pointy surface. With three delicate taps, the blanket stiffened to create a comfortable surface free from lumps.

Tessa kneeled on the blanket and stroked the smooth surface. "Now that's nifty."

Now that she'd found a place to relax, she set about taking off her soggy shoes and socks. Limbo was neither hot nor cold, so she left her shirt and pants on.

She laid her head down and tried to rest.

Rob was close by, alert and silent. Did he fear something here in Limbo? Were there others lurking among the junk?

"Could another repo man open a portal nearby for us to escape?" she asked.

"Possibly, but usually the amulet's magic prevents us from colliding on top of one another."

"You mean the amulet you have right now would prevent others from opening a portal close by?"

He grunted. "That would be a real problem if I hadn't left the amulet on the beach."

"Oh, sorry." She knew the trinket had value. It must've pained him to know he left it behind.

"Couldn't you have brought it in with you?"

"No, I had to leave it behind to hold the door open. The magic doesn't work that way."

"One-way service, huh?"

"Precisely." He picked up an old ale mug and threw it like a football. The sounds of glass shattering as it impacted something echoed back.

A tiny toy five feet nearby caught her eye. A tin solder with his musket appeared dented with chipped paint. It was so hypnotizing. As drowsiness hit, her eyes slowly closed to the tin soldier raising his musket to the pink sky.

Rob watched her sleep. She had a slight snore he hadn't heard before. He chuckled when she turned over and started up again. She probably only did it when she was really tired.

The urge to lie down and wrap his arms around her was strong, almost instinctual. He wanted to be with her, but doing such would just push her further away.

Let her stew for a while. She was pretty mad the other night. Maybe she'd forgive him before he had to go back. He sighed.

Would it be so bad if he scooted closer?

Then she woke up, so he looked away. Without a word, she rose and stretched.

This place was quiet, too quiet for him. He preferred some kind of sound to keep his mind from thinking the worst: they were trapped here without means of escape. All alone.

He sat less than a foot away, shirtless. He'd long given up on the spell masking his injury. Might as well conserve what energy he had. She looked at the tight white bandages wrapped around his torso, holding his middle tightly. A few of the bandages on his right side were stained from the ocean.

"Why haven't you redressed your bandages?" she asked him.

"I'm resting."

She took in the view. "How long have I been sleeping?"

"For about three hours. Are you hungry?"

"I'm peckish, but I'll be okay." She sat down Indian-style and stared at her hands.

She'd looked up again, and he hid a smile. *Liar.* That woman really needed to work on her body language.

"According to Harabeuji, we have a sixty-four-ounce water bottle, a sandwich, and an energy bar. We'll have to stretch them until I find something that makes food."

Most people would think casting a spell to create food would be simple and easy. Hell, he opened portals into Limbo, but the rules governing their spell-casting threw food into a higher level of ability. It was based on the theory of creating something from nothing. Or, in this case, creating something edible from thin air.

"I guess that means you know every unlock spell, but your food spell-casting skills aren't too hot," she said.

He chuckled, unable to hold in the wince as he held his side. "You wouldn't want to eat what I would create. Casting food spells is a lot like cooking."

Silence prevailed again between them. What was there to discuss? The weather, or lack of it. The tension between them was palpable. Every time he took in her face, he was forced to think about his mistakes. He asked the first question that came to mind.

"How do you choose the right woman for a man?"

She turned slowly. "What kind of question is that?"

"You have something better to do?" He gestured around him.

"Well, that's a difficult question to answer."

"Precisely why I asked it."

"Most often the right person isn't what the client expects. They have this pre-built conception of what's right for them. They either want some educated chick with big boobs or a brainless amoeba with big boobs."

He offered her a sly smile and tried to not to peek at the shirt stretching over her breasts. She'd said the "boob" keyword too many times.

She continued to speak. "I've had so many conversations with men who have unrealistic expectations. They say they want a powerful woman with a great personality, but in the end they're thinking with their lower-hemisphere brain."

"So all men are like that, huh?"

She rolled her eyes. "You know that's not true. I'm saying most of my clients are like that. The ones with millions of dollars who are surrounded by women who want to be a trophy wife. They're dying to stand on the sidelines holding his wallet."

"Magic-magnets. Is that what you want to be, a trophy wife?"

She flashed him a wry expression. "That's not funny. You know I'm not like that. And no, I wouldn't be truly happy."

Based on the thoughtful look on her face, he wondered if she had wanted that before. She was a classy lady, but she didn't flaunt it. It was more like she exuded it. She had connections and money and all, but could he be a part of her world?

"Was Dagger setting a trap for us the whole time?" she asked.

He sighed, none too happy about the obvious. "Pretty much. I have a feeling I was repossessing exactly what he needed."

"Like the tainted wand stuff Harry talked about?"

He flicked a gaze in her direction. Until he'd seen the fire witch's painting he didn't have any evidence to back up what Harry had babbled about, but it was all there: the cursed water witch's snow, the fire witch's painting, and the earth witch's damned piano. That left one element though he had yet to see: wind.

"Yeah. I didn't think any of it was true until I saw the painting." His voice grew thoughtful.

"Didn't we mess up everything when you took the piano away?"

If only magic were so simple. "In most cases yes, but if he determined the source of power in the instrument and plucked away a sizable piece—we didn't accomplish a damn thing."

His head slumped forward a bit with fatigue.

"How did you get hurt?" So she tossed the ball back in his court with a personal question.

He briefly stretched, holding his side. The ache wasn't going away. "During a rescue mission I made a mistake a soldier should never make."

A long pause. "And what's that?"

"I stopped listening for danger. I became complacent in my abilities, mostly the magical ones."

"I thought you were good at what you do."

"I am, but sometimes even good people make mistakes and get comfortable. After getting hurt, I told myself I'd be more careful and less reckless. I'd run once in a while if I had to protect others." He winced again—the pain turned into a persistent stab every time he inhaled. Damn, he should've let that wizard work his magic on him.

"You need to change your dressing. Do you need help?"

"I'm holding out just fine." He'd pushed himself way too far. Every damn word he spoke hurt like hell.

"Can the tough guy routine." On her knees, she crawled toward his satchel and opened the flap. "Harabeuji, do you have a first aid kit in this bag of tricks?" She peered inside then turned to Rob. "Is there a spell or something to trigger the hidden compartments?"

"It tickles when she checks my pockets," Harabeuji chuckled. "She has soft hands."

"I think he just said something." Tessa glanced up. "What did he say?"

"Nothing important." If Tessa ever learned Korean, Rob might have a problem on his hands. He swept his fingers across the Korean letters on the inner fold. The magic hiding the deep pockets disappeared.

"Behave," he said in Korean to Harabeuji.

"Now we're cooking!" Tessa said with a grin. "You could've packed a four-course dinner in one of these."

"I didn't...plan on being trapped in...Limbo." He shifted uncomfortably.

"Be quiet while I look," she shushed.

Eventually Tessa pulled out a white plastic container with the first aid symbol. She fished out a roll of gauze with scissors. Then she set about the task of changing his dressings.

"Can you point to where I should cut it first?" Tessa looked over the folds of gauze, a look of puzzlement over her face. Perhaps he should supervise?

She picked a spot and started to cut the old dressings.

"Be careful with those scissors," he growled.

"I'm doing my best. How the hell do you do this yourself?"

"I don't hold scissors like that...Ouch! Give me those things." He grasped the handle. "Where did you learn first aid?"

"Here and there. Kind of through observation on the lacrosse field sidelines."

He cut into the dressings. "You played lacrosse? I can't see you running over people."

"I didn't try out for the team willingly. Danielle won a bet, and I was forced to try out. The coach thought I was good enough to play as an attackman on the team."

As he removed the bindings to free his ribs, the pain became hard to bear. He tried to control his breathing, but it didn't help much. "I can't imagine you..."

She placed her index finger on his lips. "Don't talk."

She gently took the gauze and started wrapping the material around his waist. The close proximity to her body was unnerving, even through the pain. He tried to think of her as a nurse instead of a former lover. This was rather difficult in their current position. The bindings she made had to be tight, but not too tight to cause pain and prevent breathing.

Once she finished binding him, she found the clips and tape to hold it in place.

By the time they completed the task he wanted to pass out. Waves of never-ending pain coursed through him. He closed his eyes and focused. *Breathe in deep through the nose and out through the mouth.*

Within the haze, someone offered him some pills. He swallowed them with gusto.

"Are you all right?" A warm hand touched his shoulder. He wanted to lean toward her but stopped himself.

"I need a few minutes to rest," he murmured. "Then I can help with the binding with a spell."

Gentle hands grabbed under his shoulders and urged him to lie down. Every inch he moved made the ache worsen, but eventually he managed to rest. What had she given him besides a painkiller? Sleep pulled relentlessly at him. A palm touched his cheek. The fingertips brushed against his hairline in featherlike strokes. He kept his eyes closed, and his body relaxed further.

But his mind fought to stay awake. As his consciousness faded away, he heard footsteps walking away. The heat from Tessa left with it. He was too tired to go after her, too tired to tell her not to look for her scroll.

Damn, stubborn woman.

Chapter 18

Dating Tip #11: Show confidence and leave the skeletons, both summoned and metaphorical, in the closet. Women don't want to hear about your failed escapades or 1,001 nights of passion with past liaisons.

Limbo's wide expanse beckoned Tessa with a rolling prairie of junk. For a few minutes, she memorized the distinct objects around them to use as a place marker for later. Large green urn, bright red staff standing up, immense mound of books with blue covers... Once she filled her mind to the brim, she called the wand to her hand. The bristly stick barely registered as weight in her palm.

She imagined her vehicle with the scroll inside. Could the wand take her there? Instead of teleporting her to her destination, the wand drew her forward. Like a wandering water stick, the wand pulled her along over the wasteland. Once in a while, faint slurping noises ended the silence. Someone opened a portal and tossed in repossessed property. They were so far away. A spark of light followed by a moving speck.

Her stomach grumbled after a mile or two. Could the wand create food? Did she dare try it? She tapped her hand with the wand while imagining some chocolate cake.

Why not go for the good stuff on the first try?

The wand twitched, then slapped a gob of wet mud in her palm.

"Eww." There went that idea. She used the end to scrape the top layers off. They landed with a soggy plop onto an expensive-looking tea service set. She stared at the gleaming white teakettle, horrified that she'd marred its smooth surface. The reflection looking back was full of warts and green splotches.

Don't touch anything! she could practically hear Rob snap.

She pulled back, checking her skin. She was free from any blemishes; the flaws were only seen through the tainted magic in the teakettle.

Her left hand was still covered in mud. Sadly, she didn't expect to see an enchanted roll of paper towels or box of wipes, but she did look around for a few minutes. She wanted to wipe her hand off on a torn cape nearby, but she'd learned her lesson. Best to leave it be. Might be as cursed as the china set. This place was so off the wall. The whole thing resembled a magical yard sale after a hurricane had plowed through.

Stuck with a soiled hand, she used the

wand again to find her scroll. She didn't see an end to the horizon, only hills with a pink sky overhead.

She needed to make some progress before Rob woke up and found her gone. She willed the wand to move faster. The pull turned into dragging. The twig yanked her forward with rough jerks. *Ouch!* She gripped the end tightly, hoping it wouldn't shove her into something sharp or jagged.

Tessa climbed over one mound that continued to go up and up. Her lungs ached with each step. It didn't help that her perch was precarious to begin with as she climbed over books and even an old iron bedpost. Once she reached the summit, she wanted to breathe a sigh of relief—until at the crest it pulled her forward—toward a sheer cliff into darkness. She tried to turn back, willing the wand to stop. It relentlessly tugged her toward the looming expanse. On the far side, mounds began again. Objects on the far edge would shift slightly, then the heaviest item would roll down a pile into the foggy depths of the chasm.

Damn it all to hell.

To keep herself from falling over the edge, she held on for dear life as the wand continued to float over the edge. "Stop! Damn it!"

The wand stopped in mid-air. With legs flailing, she tried to swing back.

Don't look down! Don't look down!

"Reverse! Reverse!" she screeched.

The first jolt backward made her unstable grip loosen, but she managed to hang tight while the wand returned to the edge. Finally, her feet found solid ground. The wand continued its progression backward—back the other way toward the edge of the hill.

She tried to release the troublemaking twig, but it stuck to her hand. "Let go!" The wand let her go, but it was too late. Tessa plunged down the hill she'd climbed not much earlier. During her painful descent, she emitted every curse she knew, maybe a few she'd heard Rob use as well. This was between grunts and screams of pain. On the way down she hit two staffs (ouch!), broke a vase (her back!), and finally came to rest by hitting the side of her face against another tea set (revenge from the previous pot she'd soiled earlier with mud).

Tessa rested for a moment, waiting for her heart to slow its rapid beating. The jabs into her back ached. She stared up the hill, wondering why pieces of it were coming at her. The avalanche started with a few smaller things, but she couldn't shake the deer-in-headlights feeling as more junk approached. She closed her eyes as another body covered hers.

Something shifted above them. She had a small pocket of air tucked in the safety of Rob's arms. From her position underneath him, she didn't know if he had air to breathe.

"Rob?"

The weight continued to roll off them bit by bit. Hands pulled Rob off her. In a haze, she saw the concerned faces of people she didn't know. Three men took Rob out of the hole, while a woman and man freed her legs. All of them were warlocks.

One of them stood out from the others. He was short with white hair and grumbled about how his day had been ruined rescuing his employee.

"Are you bleeding?" one of the men asked her.

"No, it's Rob. Someone check him for injuries," Clive said.

There was *blood* on her? "Rob?" she croaked.

When she tried to see Rob, a warlock pushed her down. "Stay still."

From her angle, she watched three warlocks assess Rob. One of them stepped away to allow the other two to work. She glimpsed a wand protruding from Rob's shoulder. Didn't she release it before falling down the hill? She flexed her empty hands. He'd saved her, and in the process the wand in her hands stabbed him as he covered her body with his own.

"He's breathing, Tessa. Stay calm, we're getting you two out of here." With ease, one of warlocks lifted her.

"How did you find us?" she asked Clive as they headed for a nearby open portal.

"You two nitwits have been missing for three days. While you were gone, one of my competitors spotted you two lumbering around in Limbo. All the repo men in New York coordinated an effort to find you."

Three days?

They crossed the threshold into a subway restroom. She peered back into Limbo where Rob and her scroll remained. Thank goodness at least Rob would be returning with her.

Two days later, with aches and bruises, Tessa ventured to Rob's house to check on him. His aunt answered the door and greeted her with a brief hug.

"He's upstairs," Matilda said softly. "I left him some hot tea a few minutes ago."

With effort, she climbed the stairs. She knocked gently on his door while prying it open. He sat against the headboard, bare-chested with hair tousled from sleep. He had a fresh white bandage around his shoulder and body. She swallowed the welling of desire as she took him in.

She took heart in the fact that his injuries were preventing her from acting on her desires. She didn't want to hurt him further.

From his nightstand, he tossed her wand onto the far side of the bed. The wood twitched as if it sensed her presence. She offered her right palm face up.

"Come to me," she commanded.

The troublesome stick rolled across the bedspread to her hand. Rob didn't say a word, merely pulling back the covers on the other side. *Her side.* He resumed his position with icy brown eyes boring into hers.

Did she want to take him back?

Forgiving someone's mistakes was so hard when the pain they caused was such a familiar one, but she missed him so much. His gruff manner, the smile he only revealed once in a while at the perfect moments.

Wasn't love about taking chances?

She closed the door softly and lay down next to him.

Chapter 19

Dating Tip #9: Witches are like regular women who want all of your attention. Don't take your lovely lady to a gentlemen's club. When there's more eye candy than in a confectionery store, the date will go downhill – very fast.

Having Rob back in her life was welcomed. They'd have time to right the wrongs in their relationship. But now all relationships in Tessa's life had been fixed so quickly. Some took years.

Guilt was a powerful thing, especially for Clark Dandridge. Every spellcaster had to pay the price for what he conjured – or what he did in real life. The same went for Tessa's dad.

Of course, that didn't mean Tessa's mom didn't force him to redeem himself at every opportunity. Case in point, every fall and spring he took her mom to New York to let her shop or experience fashion week. During this visit, she was pretty sure her mom went through every department store in Manhattan looking for the perfect dress for bridge club. Her small apartment wasn't meant to host lavish affairs, but for a quiet dinner with her parents the place worked nicely.

The couple arrived not long after the deliveryman from the Italian restaurant dropped off the food. Her dad had called ahead to warn her that Mom was tired of Asian food and balked about not being able to enjoy a nice Italian meal. His office in Chicago ordered the food ahead of time to save Tessa the time and expense. She about passed out when she saw the bill.

At least she didn't have to worry about her apartment.

As she recovered from her injuries, her best friend had gone through her place from top to bottom.

"You're too messed up to stop me," Danielle had joked, "so I'm going to clean up."

"I have a maid for that."

As the witch left her bedroom, Tessa heard her call back, "She sucks. She doesn't feed the cat either."

Kiki rubbed Tessa's legs as if on cue to interrupt her thoughts.

"You hungry, sweetie-pie?" Tessa reached down and rubbed the cat between her ears, her favorite spot. Tessa glanced at the spot in the kitchen where the cat bowl had been tucked into a corner. The bowl was pretty full. *Take that, Rob*, she thought with a grin.

After some time, the Persian strolled away, off to handle business far more exciting than watching Tessa prepare dinner. With a swish of her tail, Kiki plodded back into the bedroom. Perhaps a nap was in order.

Tessa placed her best plates on the table alongside the silver from her grandmother. After adding the napkins, the doorbell rang.

After she slapped on a cheerful smile, she answered the door and ushered her parents inside. Her mother wore an elegant lime-green dress with an empire waist, while her dad appeared as if he'd recently come home from work. The man must jump out of bed wearing his suits.

"You look fabulous as usual." Her mother kissed her on the cheek.

Her dad greeted her in a similar fashion. The two of them made a nice couple, even if from afar they appeared to be opposites. Her mother was outgoing and ambitious, but only within a social context. Her father was gruff. All the time.

Tessa fetched a tray of drinks from the kitchen. "Is anyone thirsty after a long day in New York City?"

Her father gulped the vodka and tonic she offered him in a single gulp. Whoa! Must have been a crazy morning with mom.

"I had a great time at this one shop. You'd love the place, Tessa."

"I'm sure." After she donated an organ or two on the black market, she might afford to splurge on clothes.

"Is the food here yet?" her dad asked.

"I've already laid out the silverware and plates. We can eat any time."

He made a beeline for her small table and sat down.

"Are you forgetting your manners?" her mom asked.

"You two should know by now my civilities go out the door when I'm hungry," he said. "You don't want my blood sugar to get too low."

Her dad used his blood sugar as the excuse for most of his poor behavior. The man was an avid tennis player, yet according to him he was on the cusp of major diabetic shock every couple of days.

He winked at her mom as she sat down with a grin. It always felt good to see they were happy together these days.

Steam filled the kitchen as she opened the boxes of food. Her stomach growled. Decadent veal parmesan, creamy fettuccine alfredo, and a generous salad for six people.

She gathered the food and placed it on the table while her father droned on. "I'm about to pass out here."

Before she had a chance to lift her hands away, her father served himself a portion of veal.

The doorbell rang, and she froze.

Were her parents expecting company? She slowly approached the door and glanced through the keyhole.

A choked gasp scraped her throat.

Two men with brooding expressions waited outside the door. Dark magic slithered around them and bounced against the walls. The loan sharks had come for her. They'd told her she had three months.

Larry and Erwin meant only one thing: whatever time she thought she had was officially up.

A million reactions came to mind, but Tessa stood there instead, fighting to slow her fast-beating heart.

"Answer the door," her dad grunted. "My blood sugar is getting low just waiting for you."

She couldn't just ignore the loan sharks.

Her fingers settled on the doorknob, only to give her a moment to collect her scattered thoughts before she opened the door. With a straight back she looked them in the eye. No matter what kind of warlocks they were, this was her domain—her home. They'd better respect it.

She hoped.

"Tessa?" one of them asked.

"Can I help you?" She could've said hundreds of things like "Could we do this another time?" or "We have enough food for six people. Want to eat?" But she knew very well what the heck was going on, so avoiding the overflowing cauldron wouldn't change a damn thing.

"We have some business to settle with you," the first man said. "Can we come in?"

"Yes."

She moved out of the way, and the warlocks strolled into her living room. They didn't sit or join her parents in the kitchen. Thank goodness.

The first warlock, dressed in a black suit, eyed everyone with a pale face that could best be described as expressionless. He simply looked around, taking it all in as if something bad would leap from behind Tessa's couch and tackle him.

The second warlock, also in black, had a mighty kung-fu grip on a wand strapped to his belt. Between the two, he appeared more badass. The guy had a bald head and impossibly wide shoulders. Even his rear end had an intimidating girth.

"I don't have any money," Tessa said. *Why not get to the point?*

"Tessa?"

All three of them turned to see Tessa's mom and dad standing in the doorway between the kitchen and the living room. Her mom's frown was disheartening.

"What's going on here, Tessa?" Her father crossed his arms.

Tessa's stomach clenched painfully. Things just couldn't get any worse.

Naturally, the door knocked again. Everyone's heads turned toward the sound.

"I don't want to repeat myself again. Tessa, what are they doing here?" her mother hissed at her.

Reluctantly, Tessa opened the door. New dinner guests shouldn't be a surprise anymore.

It was Rob. He wore a cocky grin and had a bouquet of roses. She tilted her chin toward the heavens.

Somebody kill me now.

"I thought I'd surprise you with these. Especially since you say I don't know how—" His voice trailed off as they heard her mother began to question the loan sharks.

"My daughter owes you what?" her mom spat.

"This is kind of a bad time." Tessa held the door open to the tiniest crack.

Rob's lips formed a straight line. He pushed against the door, but Tessa didn't budge.

"Could you come back?" she begged. Trouble and Rob seemed to be constant dance partners.

"Out of the way, Tee." Tessa expected his words to be coarse, but this time they were gentle.

"You promise to behave?"

He nodded and offered his hand. It seemed innocent enough.

Tessa's mother still wasn't done yet. "When my daughter gets back in here, there might be nothing left for you after I get done with her."

"We don't mind waiting," said the quiet, baldheaded one in a creepy way. "This is rather fun."

Tessa returned with Rob into the living room and wished a black hole would appear to swallow everyone. "Mom, calm down. I needed some money for operating expenses. Larry and Erwin are here to check up on me. They're expecting payment in a few months."

"We've been told your time had to be reduced," Larry said.

Tessa avoided her parents' face. "The truth is I have nothing to give you. My Smythe Scroll is missing, and if I don't find it I won't be able to pay anyone back."

Her mom gaped her, mouth open wide. "What?"

Even her dad mimicked her mom's shocked expression.

"There is no money to give." To say those words made her stomach ache even more.

Rob's jaw twitched then he turned to Larry and Erwin. "I think you've had your say. It's time for you gentlemen to leave now."

She closed her eyes, tried to think of anything she could do. All she had was $300 in the apartment. And all of it was a ten-dollar bill here, a twenty there—a far cry from the thousands that were necessary.

Why did this shameful thing have to happen in front of her parents? And Rob, too.

Dad spoke up. "I think you gentlemen should do as this man says and leave."

The pale one flexed his long fingers as magic gathered around him, sending a strong haze of cinnamon into the air. "We've been told to collect what is ours from her."

Rob cocked a grin. "You come try to take the money and see what happens."

The larger warlock laughed. Rob's hand drifted toward his satchel. "You'll never outdraw me in a fight with your little man-purse there."

Everything happened too fast. Black wands materialized in the warlocks' hands, and Rob's hand slipped into his satchel. From a pocket he pulled out a white wand.

Tessa's mom jumped back, apparently dumbfounded that things had progressed this badly.

Her father, though, had other things in mind.

"You guys take an American Express check?"

Ten minutes later, four people—her parents, Rob, and herself—sat at Tessa's tiny table.

Even though there was plenty of food to eat, no one really seemed hungry. From under the table, Rob took her hand and gently squeezed it.

"Your name is Rob, right?" her mom asked quietly. "Tessa never told us about you."

"I see." Rob kept his gaze focused on her, almost as if he expected her to speak.

"I'm sorry you had to get in the middle of her mess." Her mother took a sip of her wine, her hand gripping the handle tight enough to break the stem.

Her dad coughed. He should've made some joke about his impending low blood sugar, but he merely scratched his chin.

Rob finally took a bite of his food. The tension in Tessa's shoulders eased with each of his movements, yet her face still reddened with shame. Rob had told his family about her, but she hadn't done the same.

"These kinds of things happen to good people," Rob said. "I hope Tessa does the responsible thing and takes care of her debts."

"That's all we can expect," her dad added.

"Rob, these are my parents, Gertrude and Clark." Better late than never, right?

Her mother's eyes formed slits. An unavoidable, private conversation about money was coming in a few days. "I think introductions have already been covered."

Rob's grip on her hand tightened. With him staying strong at her side, Tessa thought she was done feeling disappointed, especially in herself.

Chapter 20

*Dating Tip #14: Intimacy in a relationship is a
natural progression. I highly recommend that two
consenting adults establish a relationship so that
you don't ruin things when you realize the spot on
the nape of her neck isn't a mole but a magical goiter
that talks back if you poke it.*

Rob was silent for several days. Far longer
than she'd preferred.

During the time her quiet apartment left her
wary, especially after Dagger had left them in
Limbo. She got a text message out of the blue:
*Back in town, want to see u at the diner near
Central Park.*

At first she was irked. Hell, he'd been so
supportive back at her apartment when she'd
gotten into trouble, but disappearing for days at
a time without so much as a phone call was
rude. If he was at the hospital or doing work for
the military, a short message would've been
welcomed.

It was rather hard to hate a man like Rob,

doubts aside. Especially when he looked so good leaning against the counter. He was chatting with Lindy when she arrived.

The waitress smiled. "Nice to see you again, Tessa."

"Likewise." She scanned the busy diner with patrons in all the booths. "Looks like you've been busy."

"Dinner time is always like this. I have to check my tables." She kissed Rob's cheek then whispered something in his ear with sad eyes.

Was something going on with Lindy? Or with *Rob*?

After leaving, they decided on a movie, but not before she bought another pair of stockings. She'd ripped hers on the way to the diner. Normally, she would've gone bare without any, but she didn't feel the outfit worked without it.

"You don't need panty hose."

"Yes, I do. You're not qualified to make these kinds of decisions."

"I'm qualified when it means I get easy access without those things in the way."

"As if that would stop you from tearing through them anyway," she said with a laugh.

He wrapped his arms around her and dazzled her with a devastating kiss. Right there in the middle of the busy sidewalk as pedestrians walked by. The kiss felt like it never ended, leaving her hungry for the night ahead. She'd never been kissed in public like this. And after an episode like that, she didn't mind the minute-long show they provided.

"Are you sure you want to go see a movie?

We could always practice making one." His finger ran along her chin, before he planted a kiss on her cheek.

"We have all night and I want to see this movie. Danielle told me Ursula's been raving about it all week." She pulled him forward. "We're almost to the convenience store. I could use some quality time with my boyfriend."

"So I'm your boyfriend now, huh?" He flashed a grin.

His reply brought a blush to her cheeks and made her bite her lower lip. Was this how real relationships outside of matchmaking went? "Don't tease me, Rob. I'm serious."

"I know you are." He placed a peck on the back of her hand. "I'd like to spend time with my girlfriend, too."

The convenience store had a few customers. Some of them browsed the liquor aisle for their next fix.

Rob followed her with their hands intertwined. The selection of panty hose in the third aisle wasn't the best, but a cheap pair would hold her over until he destroyed them back at her place. She grabbed a pair and made a beeline for the cash register. She almost made it. She shouldn't have passed the candy. With a gentle yank, he pulled her back.

"We can get candy in the theater," she protested.

"With those prices, I'd rather donate a body part to science."

She needed to renew her mood with a sappy romantic comedy, and Rob wanted to

spend the next two hours scouring the candy
rack as if the national security of the US
depended on it. The line for the checkout was
nonexistent so Tessa left his side and tossed the
panty hose on the counter. The tall, lanky clerk
with a large nose ring smiled briefly before
ringing up the purchase. If Rob didn't hurry up
they wouldn't make it on time.

The clerk frowned. "It was declined. You
got cash?"

Declined? She tapped her fingers on the
counter. Remain calm, a simple error. "There
has to be some mistake. Could you run it
again?"

He tried again and shook his head.

"Here." She fished in her purse and pulled
out her corporate bank card. If this was empty,
she'd seriously drop dead in the middle of this
convenience store. Especially after the episode
with the loan sharks.

An impatient couple behind her with
handfuls of chips and beer huffed.

"Sorry," the clerk said. "No good either."

Tessa didn't bother taking the panty hose
back. The store faded away as she shuffled to
Rob. There had to be a mistake. A bank error. A
robbery based on a fake identity attempt.
Didn't she hire an accountant to track her
money… She could hardly breathe as the
realization hit: something had happened to
what little money she had left. And now she
had *nothing*.

He turned to her, his hands stuffed with
candy bars. He glanced at her empty hands.

"You need some cash? I got a few bucks."

A few bucks and some change was the least of her problems right now.

She glanced at the cash register and froze. A man wearing a skull-cap pulled out a gun and jabbed it at the clerk.

"Open the register and gimme me the money!" the robber spat. The clerk's arm jerked as he pressed buttons on the register, his eyes never leaving the barrel.

They were a few feet away. Close enough for Tessa to smell the guy's overpowering aftershave. Her left leg moved back. She was in mid-step when Rob's hands locked on her waist.

"Don't," he warned.

The gun twisted in their direction and her mouth popped open like mailbox. Her heart thundered in her chest. Using magic right now in front of the clerk, robber, and all the patrons wasn't an option she could risk.

"Don't even think about moving." The thief turned to the man frantically grabbing the meager amount of bills in the register. "C'mon, I don't have all day!" Once the money was stuffed into his pocket, the thief bolted for the door. She expected him to flee, but he stopped in front of them.

Dark eyes flashed to her purse.

He reached out and tried to snatch it from her hands. For some reason, her stupid fingers disobeyed and they locked on the expensive handbag as if it were a precious child. The man's face contorted in rage as Rob's voice was

heavy and angry against the back of her head.
"What the hell are you doing? Give it to him."

She released the purse as the robber
pointed the gun at her shocked face. The
handbag fell to the floor. The sound of the
released safety echoed in her ears. The instant
tried to fire, Rob shifted behind her, reaching
forward with his right hand to touch the barrel.

"No," Rob whispered.

A surge of power coursed from Rob's hand
like a missile into the robber's firearm. The
burst of magic raced along the gun into the
thief.

The snarl on the man's face faded as his
eyes drifted upwards and his body collapsed on
the floor. Dumbfounded, the clerk leaned over
the counter to see the robber knocked out.

This day wasn't getting any better.

Rob snatched the purse off the floor and
grabbed her wrist. He pulled her out of the
store. "Don't look back and keep moving."

As they ran from the store, her heartbeat
fluctuated from troubled to furiously pounding.
One block down the street turned into many.
She didn't even pay attention to the street signs.
Anger blanketed her fear as they slowed down
to stop at a busy intersection.

His released her wrist touched her face.
"You all right?"

"I wish I was."

Not only had they witnessed a robbery, but
her business bank account was empty, too. That
meant one person was behind all this.

She tore through the purse, tossing out

anything that kept her from finding her phone. Her hands trembled as she flipped it open. She should've called 911. Her aunt was gonna need an ambulance after she was done with her.

Rob turned to her with a frown. "Tessa, what's wrong?"

Her mouth struggled to form words. "That vindictive…" *Aunt Daisy*.

When the light turned green, Tessa darted across the street and dialed the number for the twenty-four hour line for her corporate bank account. As the electronic voice gave her balance—a negative one—her heart dropped to the pavement. When she switched to her personal account, she knew what was coming. The blow wasn't physical, but her gut twisted when she heard the words every person dreads: *You have insufficient funds in your account. Please contact customer service to take care of this matter. We thank you for being…*

Rob's phone rang and he stepped to the side to offer her some privacy. She glanced around, not realizing she'd stopped in front of a storefront. Another call needed to be made and she might as well do it right now. She pressed the buttons on her iPhone screen hard enough to hurt her fingertips. Her aunt's office line rang and rang. She wouldn't be in, but who knew when bitter family members who stabbed others in the back put in their hours.

Aunt Daisy's cell phone went to voice mail on the first ring. Her cheerful voice echoed through the phone, sending Tessa spiraling into a pit of fury.

"Daisy Kilburn, whatever did I do to you?" she spat. "Call me tonight. Not tomorrow. We need to resolve this once and for all." She ended the call. It took every ounce of willpower not to throw her iPhone into the street.

A warm hand touched her shoulder. "What's going on?" Rob asked.

A tear slid down Tessa's face. Her voice broke. "The shit's hit the side of the cauldron pot. I'm broke."

Twenty minutes later, a text message from Daisy read: *In town, meet at the Café Du Monde in Midtown*. She was in town? Well, won't that make the happy family reunion even better?

Rob asked Tessa multiple times if she wanted him to accompany her to meet Aunt Daisy, but she declined his offer with a heavy heart. She wasn't sure what the outcome would be tonight, but afterward, she had a feeling her mood would be too sour for anyone to endure. And, anyway, Tessa might need somebody to bail her out of jail if she got arrested for *assault*.

Not long after trying to calm down, Tessa walked into Café Du Monde, an upscale coffeehouse. The place resembled a luxury Starbucks for clientele who desired cups of coffee from organic farms in exotic locations. A rather nice place to visit, but not in her current mood.

Tessa spotted her aunt at a booth reading a Danielle Steel novel. It was rather hard to miss her—she wore a wrinkled sundress that was two sizes too big and a misshaped hat to cover her over-processed curly blonde hair.

After she slid into the booth, a waiter stepped up to the table to take her order.

"I'd order something, but I don't have the funds." Tessa's eyes never left her aunt's. "Could I have a glass of water please?"

"Of course." The server slowly backed away.

With fingers gripping the table to prevent curse words from jumping out of her mouth, she spoke. "Interesting to see you here in New York as this went down."

"I had vacation time coming," her aunt replied sweetly. "You picked the perfect time to call."

She shook her head. "Cut the bullshit. If you have ruined me, I will sue your ass so fast…"

"I haven't done a thing to you. You shouldn't send invoices you can't pay."

"Then it's your responsibility to handle my bills. I review the reports you send me every quarter." Tessa's voice began to rise. A few heads turned her way, so she lowered her voice. "There weren't any discrepancies."

"Well, there were those invoices from early in the spring. And then there were those bills from when I went on vacation for those two weeks in Hawaii. Hawaii was lovely that time of year, especially compared to Chicago in the dead of winter. Did I show you the pictures?"

Her right foot tapped the floor in a nervous fit. "Aunt Daisy, what bills?"

"Oh, yeah, there were just so many that I put them in this box. Here. I didn't have the time to enter them all."

With a thud, Daisy placed a box crammed to the hilt with bills on the table. A firebomb could have gone off in this establishment, and Tessa wouldn't have left the seat to rush for the door.

"How could you?" Her shaking hands touched the bills as the feeling of lightheadedness steadily increased with each unpaid invoice.

"These things happen all the time with larger firms. A missed bill here, a mislabeled file there. I mean, with my firm handling two Fortune 500 companies, a slip-up here and there usually gets caught during the audit." Aunt Daisy sipped her coffee. "I wonder if you'll survive until that point."

"You can't do this to me." Her voice rose again. "No matter how you feel about what Grandma did to you, doing this kind of thing to people is..." She reached for the words. "Fucked up."

"It's done and over with now. You need to start liquidating your assets and handling your business as you prepare to close it."

Tessa couldn't believe this raving lunatic was droning on as if her aunt hadn't had a hand in Tessa's downfall. After a huff, she stuffed the bills she'd pulled out back into the box. "This isn't over by a long shot. You're going to pay for this."

The older witch laughed before slamming her empty cup to the edge of the table. "What will you do?" Smugness oozed across the table. "Ask for help from my mother?" She snorted. "Perhaps she'd love to know how you squandered her money and couldn't cut it in New York."

"No thanks to you."

"Sweetheart, I prolonged the inevitable. You can't manage a business, nor can you assume the role of the perfect girl for my mother. Welcome to reality, sweetie."

Wow.

Anger pulsed from her legs up to her arms.

She whipped out the water witch wand and pointed it at her aunt.

Normally she wasn't prone to violence, but after realizing her aunt had rendered her penniless, she couldn't escape the driving need to scare the shit out of her. With the power of the wand trembling in her hand, masking their encounter would be easy.

Aunt Daisy's eyes widened as if she pointed a loaded gun.

"What-what's that?"

The wand wavered in her hands. "You've never seen a water witch wand before?" With a flick of her wrist, Aunt Daisy's cup flew across the table from the edge to teeter on the opposite side on the handle. Then with another flick, the cup bounced across the table before landing inches from her aunt's nose.

Aunt Daisy recoiled, her mouth wide. "Don't."

"I could hurt you right now as much as you hurt me. But then what would I get? I'd be as miserable as you are." Tessa's fingers ached from her iron grip on the wand's sharp knobs. "Look at you. Sitting there alone with no one to love, a dead-end job you hate, and no aspirations for something better." Her voice broke as her aunt gulped. "I should hate you, but instead right now I feel sorry for how much of a loser you are."

The coffee cup drifted back to the table as she withdrew the wand. With as much dignity as she could muster, Tessa picked up the box and left the café. Her aunt sat silent in her seat.

Chapter 21

Dating Tip #16: Your date should never refer to you as "Sugar Daddy." Anyone using the phrase values how well you can pay the bill for dinner and not how well you can be a lifetime partner.

Rob's time was up. Kaput. The fat lady had sung her last tune, left the stage, and now the janitors swept the floor. He'd accomplished what he'd wanted to do though. The debts had been paid and now his aunt and uncle could rest easy. But other things had come up. Like Tessa. She had pain he wished he could take away.

A day had passed since his failed date with her, but a problem even bigger than money bothered him. He stared at the cell phone in his hand. He'd been sent a brisk reminder to report to base. Since he'd been cleared, he'd be sent overseas immediately. So he had to finalize things. It should be simple. Just call up Tessa, tell her to meet him for dinner and say his goodbyes. In a perfect world, he'd tell her he would come back soon, but life was never that simple. Not with the way their relationship had progressed. Could their relationship endure with potentially thousands of miles between them?

He didn't want to let her go like this.

He dialed her number. Part one done.

"Hey, Rob. What are you up to?" she asked.

He swallowed. "Nothing much."

"I just met with my staff to tell them I'm closing the agency." She tried to sound like she wasn't hurt, but her pain swam just below the surface. "Not the best news so I used happy hour to let them down gently."

"I'm sorry about that." He sighed, trying to form words that would get things moving. *Dinner. Dinner.* Ask her out for dinner. "You interested in another trip to Limbo?"

He rubbed his forehead. *Epic fail.*

"Where do you want to meet and do I have enough time to take a shower?"

"I'll text you the address in East Village. Take all the time you need."

Surprisingly, she didn't take much time at all. She appeared all too eager for another chance. It hurt him even more to see her that way.

"This'll be an easy job," he said. "Matter of fact, I've already contacted the party and they want to give it to me."

"That's a new one."

Rob chuckled. "I'd be out of a job if everyone turned in what they owed."

"I think with the world swarming with

people like my aunt and Dagger you'll never run out of folks trying to screw over others."

"This will be a quick trip. No crazy people, no spellcasting, and under no circumstances, diving into the ocean to hide from demons."

Tessa followed him to the apartment. Rows of high walk-up apartments and townhouses dotted the street.

"Please tell me our destination is on the second floor," she asked.

"Exercise is good for the soul. We have five flights of stairs. As if you have room to talk, your apartment is on the third floor."

"And I bitch and moan for each one of those steps."

He grinned. "Well I like the results." He smacked her butt.

They didn't have far to go. The fifth floor was well-lit with white doors and numeric labels on the sides. Rob knocked on 5C.

The door opened to something quite unexpected. The man behind the door looked at Tessa with surprise. "Tessa?"

"Hi, Paul."

"You know this guy?" Rob asked.

His target moved out of the way so they could enter.

"Yes, I see him most mornings on the way to work. He's a clerk at Starbucks."

Paul's apartment was a matchbox — like most places in New York City. The living room served as both his bedroom and dining room. A galley kitchen large enough for one person was directly off the living room. As Rob expected, there were no crazy people jumping out of corners.

A nice and easy repo for their last trip.

"Have a seat while I get what you came here for." Paul entered the kitchen as they sat down on his sofa bed.

Rob glanced around again. Paul didn't have much. Scattered on his coffee table were newspapers with acting gigs circled here and there. Drops of coffee and the remnants of where cups had lain stained the papers. A single closet and dresser hid clothes stuffed into them on the opposite side of the room. His target was just another starving actor trying to survive.

Paul returned holding a small jewelry box. His eyes appeared forlorn as he sat down on the rickety chair across from them.

"I'd hope to make some money to be able to keep it, but with two jobs I couldn't make enough." He opened the box to reveal a silver ring. After placing it on his palm, they watched as the jewelry shifted, attempting to roll onto a finger. With a sigh, he offered it to Rob.

"What does it do?" Tessa asked.

Paul scratched his ear. "The wearer receives confidence and beauty. I wanted to use it to…you know, get some jobs on casting calls."

She nodded.

"I managed to secure a job as the understudy for the Broadway play *The Death of a Salesman*, but they never called me in to perform," Paul said.

"That sounds good. Really, it does." She

tried to hide it, but the look on her face spoke volumes: regret. He had to make this quick before she said something. He'd been down this road too many times. But the truth was the truth. *Never play unless you have the money to pay.*

Rob took the ring and stood to leave.

Before heading back downstairs, they said their goodbyes.

"Rob, do you ever regret any of your repo missions?"

He sighed as he descended the stairwell. "Not particularly, but I did feel a bit bad after I understood your circumstances."

"So why did you take Paul's ring?"

"Tessa, we all have responsibilities. Whether Paul is a starving artist or homeless alcoholic he needs to pay his debts like everyone else who writes a check every month."

She rolled her eyes and he couldn't help smiling. His lady had a good heart. And he didn't want to break it.

"Where will we open the portal?" she asked.

"We'll do the jump into Limbo from your place."

When they arrived back at Tessa's apartment, she waited for Rob to toss in the ring.

At last, a final effort to locate her scroll. With little time left, she bordered on desperate.

They prepared space for their trip by moving the coffee table out of the way. Once the portal opened, she leaped through the entrance and crashed onto an old sled. The rotted wood caved under her weight, leaving a sharp pain running up her back.

"How about you slowly find your scroll?" Rob said with a smirk.

Like he had room to talk? She wasn't the one doing repo missions with a rib injury. She made a rude gesture in his direction.

Tessa whipped out the wand. No more games. This thing needed to do its job and that was for it to obey her commands and teleport her where she wanted to be taken. No more casting spells to plant mud in her hands or pull her along until she reached a chasm of doom.

"Seven minutes, Tessa. You can do it."

With confidence, she held the wand firmly and pictured her car in her mind. From its champagne color to its leather interior—even the small coffee stain on the floor of the driver's side to CDs scattered on the backseat. The wand jerked as power surged from one end to the other. The air around her folded with a whoosh as the wand teleported her to the vehicle.

She expected the landing to be smooth, but the wand lived up to its crazy antics. One second she was in front of the portal, and the next she was in mid-air dropping ten feet to hit the hood of a car. Her car! After a choked cry from hitting the top, she rolled off the side onto a pile of dusty statues. The bulging eye sockets of one of the bronze figures stared back at her. Eww.

Tessa held her sore back as she limped over the vehicle. Had to move. Not much time.

She grasped the handle only to find the door locked. *Damn it.* She slapped her forehead. All this time, she had never thought to bring the damn keys. Screw it! She tapped the driver's side window with the wand. The glass shattered and littered the driver's seat. A couple thousand dollars in car repairs was nothing compared to replacing the scroll. Anticipation filled her. She could see it in her hands, smell the old parchment. All her efforts led to this moment. She wrenched open the door and scanned the floor. Nothing.

She checked the back seats, looked through the glove compartment box, and waited for that *aha* moment where everything wrong could be made right.

Her car was empty. Someone had been here and taken the scroll. The GPS unit was missing from the dashboard. Had thieves taken her property? Anger heated her face and spread into her chest. A growing need to ram her fist into the seat grew.

There wasn't any time to debate this. She had to go!

Tessa closed her eyes and focused on the power vibrating in the wand. Everything around the portal was easy to recall—from the three-headed marble statue to the floating bookcase with tomes that smelled like bleu cheese. The wand obeyed her command and threw her in front of the portal where Rob was straining to keep it open.

She hopped through the portal before he collapsed on the floor. The amulet rolled from his hand, plopping to the floor. Smoke rose from the jewelry, leaving a stench of burnt wood in the air.

Tessa checked his hands. "Are you hurt?"

"Naw." Sweat dripped off his brow, running onto his damp shirt. "I told you seven minutes. Not eight. Not fifteen, but seven minutes."

"How long was I gone?"

"Long enough for me to have to move heaven and earth to keep the damn door open."

"I'm sorry. Either way, it doesn't matter." Her voice cracked as the empty car flashed in her mind. This wasn't fair. "My scroll is gone."

Rob tugged her close. "What do you mean gone?"

"The car was empty." A single tear fell, but she quickly wiped the wetness away. Crying wouldn't fix this mess. "Some asshole took everything."

Rob placed her head on his shoulder. The spot was firm, yet at the perfect height for her relieve her burdens. She let every inhale and exhale come and go, hoping the pain would ease. But the wound persisted like all disappointments in her life.

Warm lips kissed her forehead. She leaned up to look at his face, searching his eyes. "I don't know what I'm going to do now, but we'll figure out something together, right?"

His mouth formed a straight line. The pause before he spoke again set off alarms. What was he hiding this time? "I wanted one last time with you…before I go."

"One last time? Go?" *No. No. No.* All of this wasn't happening. Not all at once.

She couldn't miss the disappointment in his eyes. "There's something I need to tell you."

Chapter 22

Dating Tip #10: In magic, what goes around comes around. Relationships are the same way. Be careful what webs you weave to catch that someone special. You may find that the mistakes of the past come back to haunt you. For real.

Tessa stiffened as he continued. "I already told you I was injured while on active duty."

She nodded—suddenly feeling the need to steel herself for what was coming.

"All I've wanted is time and money. Just a small piece of the pie while I kept up the ruse of an injury to the hospital."

Right then she knew what was coming and her grip around his waist tightened.

"My time ran out a few days ago. I got my discharge papers not too long ago. I have orders to report to Fort Briggs tomorrow."

Tomorrow. She couldn't swallow the word without wanting to cry.

Twenty-four hours from now she'd stand here alone. This warm feeling, this steady wall she'd come to depend on would go away for a while.

Her fists clenched as her throat tightened. She blinked and the world blurred with her tears. Why did she have to let go of one of the good things in her life?

"Tessa, look at me, baby." He tried to gently move her chin, but she wouldn't budge. "I'm really sorry I didn't tell you the truth."

She wanted to be angry, but she let the bitterness go. What could she say when he planned to serve his country? Wouldn't he come back? Finally, she found the words to speak. "I don't know what to say." The words came out as a choke, her voice hoarse.

"I will have shore leave, and I'll be back to New York to see you."

A feeling of exhaustion seeped into her so she tried to pull out of his embrace, but he held her tight. "Let me go, Rob," she said softly. "I need some time to absorb this."

Focus became difficult as she struggled to hold herself together. *Do something, make your hands busy!* Two of her neglected delivery boxes drew her eyes. She grabbed the larger one, trying to maintain her composure as Rob remained silent behind her. She tore at the flaps, not caring if she damaged what was inside.

A fleck of cream-colored paper caught her eye from within the box. *No, please no.* With unsteady fingers, Tessa pulled the remains of her torn scroll from the box. The cardboard container dropped from her hands as she grasped the broken scroll. Portions of it were torn to shreds, the magical runes no longer visible. Within the folds of ripped paper, a note: *Special delivery, my sweet. Dagger.*

Rob stepped in front of her.

"That motherfu—" A sob clenched her gut, tighter and tighter. She collapsed forward, unable to hold it in anymore. Rob took the pieces of scroll from her hands. He tried to tug her back into his arms, but he didn't bring her comfort.

All those repo missions: pissed off wood nymphs, crazed warlocks, a fight in a wizard's bar—all of it for nothing. Property formerly worth a couple hundred thousand dollars sat lifeless in her hands.

Anger pooled in her stomach. "If I had the power, I'd call the ocean to come *swallow* Dagger whole."

Rob's jaw hardened, but he didn't let her go. His hand caressed the back of her head.

"There's no rescue, no happy ending. Archibald Cramer is in the fifth dimension expecting me to call him about the arrangements. He was my last chance for a big payoff."

"Tessa, I—"

"Unless you have a cell phone with fifth dimension service there's nothing you can do." She pressed her lips together as the dread of the days ahead clawed at her. "I guess if you get shore leave, you'll have to come to Chicago— the final resting place for matchmakers who can't hack it in New York."

Chapter 23

Dating Tip #18: Everyone wants someone to listen to their hopes, dreams, and aspirations. Be an active listener. Don't send a clone during your date while you are casting spells in a haunted bog off the shores of Scotland.

Grand Central Station was a blur for Rob. A mob of strangers bumped into him as he took each painful step to leave town. The memories from the last twenty-four hours carried him to his seat on the train. His aunt and uncle had fed him a feast meant for kings last night, but he left in the early morning before they got up. He didn't want to bring any more pain to his aunt. She'd cried during dinner.

Also, his aunt hadn't taken it well when he confessed he was leaving. Seeing her saddened face stabbed at him. He was a damn fool for hiding it so long. He only wanted to protect her.

After their quiet dinner, she placed a folded, peach-colored handkerchief in his hand.

"Take this with you," she said softly. "I forgot to pass it along when you left for basic training."

Something fragile lay within the folds. "It wasn't mine to take. It's my dad's." *But his dad was dead now.*

His aunt had tucked a familiar black-and-white picture inside. "It's your birth-mom, Minho. It's always been yours."

How he wished he could share this picture with Tessa. His gaze flicked to the empty seat beside him. He placed his hand on the cold cushion. He could almost see her sitting here, leaning her head against his shoulder, smiling up at him while he read the words on the back of the picture. He'd never taken the time to sneak a peek at the Korean words: *my most precious treasure. My wife and son.*

He sucked in a breath. So his dad had taken the picture. He never bothered to ask before. Talking about his birth-mom always made his dad clam up. A tear dropped on the photo and he quickly brushed the spot away. He forced a smile on his lips.

This was a good shot. Love was locked into each detail. In the way the mid-day sun shone through the nearby window. In the way his mom smiled at the camera as if to say 'I love you.' In the way his mom tucked him close like she wanted to protect him from the world.

Why did his parents have to pass away and leave him behind? The pain from loss ran deeper than any injury he'd ever had. He didn't want to be alone anymore. Especially after meeting Tessa. He tucked the picture into a satchel pocket.

His hand lingered on the empty space for a bit longer.

Reorienting to his old life came quickly. Far too quick for Rob's liking. Twenty-four hours after arriving in North Carolina he'd been told his deployment orders were ready. Most likely he'd join a SEAL team already in the field. He wanted to shift in his seat outside of Commander Fry's office, but he refused to so much as twitch. The day of reckoning had come and no matter what assignment he'd been given — or what punishment for taking his time returning to base — he'd face it like a man instead of a punk.

"Sir?" Rob glanced up to see an officer standing no more than a few feet away.

"Yes?"

"I have orders for you to accompany me to meet Admiral Hurst," the man said.

Rob's eyebrow rose. He'd never heard of the name before. "What about — "

"That has been taken care of."

The man quickly left, so Rob hurried to follow him. As they weaved through the hallways, suspicions pecked at him. Had someone found out about what he did on the side? Was he in trouble somehow?

Admiral Hurst's office was at the far end of the command administrative building. In an area Rob never had authorization to visit. His escort reached the end of a quiet hallway and opened the heavy wooden door for Rob.

"Go inside, Sir. Admiral Hurst has been waiting for you."

Rob nodded and ventured into the dim room. He looked around, expecting a well-lit, not dark, space. Making out the furniture at the other end of the room was damn near impossible.

"Have a seat, Shin." The deep voice came from behind him.

Rob froze. A shorter man walked around him with a stiff gait. Bushy eyebrows almost obscured light blue eyes. He could've sworn he saw the admiral, yet he didn't feel him or smell him. No aftershave or even the sound of footsteps on the dark-brown carpet echoed through the room.

Usually, there'd be a change in the electric charge in the air. A rising intensity with the spellcaster's strength.

"I prefer to stand, Sir. If I may." This guy had to be either a warlock or wizard of some kind—which meant Rob couldn't tell the difference. Not a good sign.

"Fair enough." The man flicked the thick fingers on his right hand and a black leather chair materialized behind him so he could sit. A single light illuminated the center of the room, leaving the rest in murky shadows.

Admiral Hurst rested his hands in his lap and stared at Rob for a moment. "Keeping rogue spellcasters under control has been an issue for thousands of years. We've had to face warlocks who helped the Mongols to the spellcasters who manage to unknowingly start wars among the humans. Even the wizards protecting the Crusaders were a bunch of rowdy bastards we had to corral." He paused. "But you're something entirely different. You're both a warlock and a soldier. We've been keeping an eye on your activities and find you honorable."

"May I ask who 'we' refers to, Sir?"

The side of his mouth tilted into a sly grin.

"Who we are doesn't matter. What is of the utmost importance is that you can go where we *cannot* and you've already taken the steps to clean up a few messes."

So he was in the midst of a *wizard*.

'"How do you know who I am, Sir?"

"Once a few other associates spotted you with Harry, we took the time to check your background and look into your repossession activities. We think we have an opportunity to take care of a growing problem."

A few associates? Rob frowned. Most likely the guys who had been drinking it up and playing cards at the bar had been high-ranking wizards.

"We sent in a few wizards to intercept Dagger to determine if he was the source of tainted wands, but all of our men were annihilated after their weapons were drained of power."

Oh, fuck. Rob tried to not let the sour feeling sink in, but it had: that rat son-of-a-bitch had figured out a way to combine all of the cursed elements to taint wizard wands.

"How capable were the men you sent?"

Admiral Hurst shrugged. "They didn't have your military training, but they were armed with the best weapons."

"Which were rendered useless by Dagger."

"Yes." For the first time, a tinge of anger lined the man's words. "What we need you to do is find him and eliminate him using a warlock's arsenal. Due to the work you perform, we notice you haven't chosen the side. You have a brilliant record in the military and you've worked hard for your country."

Rob had heard all this talk before. Wizards like Harry tried to present their side of things like their shit didn't stink. Even if they couldn't cast dark magic, that didn't keep corruption, embezzlement, and bribery from within their ranks. At least when Harry tried to bring him over to the wizards' camp, he offered Rob a drink first.

"I'm not doing this for you," Rob finally said. "I'm doing this because it's the right thing to do, Sir. Like you said."

A shimmer of light danced in the wizard's right eye. "Fair enough. I didn't expect you to choose a side."

They stared each other down. Usually Rob kept his gaze square on the wall above a higher-ranking officer's head, but this guy gave a different vibe. Almost as if he wanted Rob to step up to the plate and say something. As much as he'd like to take out Dagger, he had a job to take care of from his superiors. "What about my orders from my human commanding officer?"

"I'll take care of that. Don't worry."

Rob didn't doubt it. The wizards probably carried weight around here. Maybe in a few other branches of the military.

The wizard continued to speak. "We could use someone dedicated like you."

Here we go. Rob would go where he was asked to serve his country, but when it came to the world of magic, the game wasn't the same. "I like…my current assignment, Sir."

"Every man has something he wants to fight for," the wizard replied. He tapped his fingertips together and power pulsed with each contact. A reminder of what he could do. "Is there anything I could do to change your mind? Is there something you want or someone who needs healing?"

His lips parted. Rob didn't like the wizards paying him for anything, but this was one favor he didn't hesitate to collect. If he never saw his lady again, he could do this one thing for her. "There is someone I need help to contact."

Chapter 24

Dating Tip #25: Last-minute decisions often result in the most spectacular dates, but that doesn't mean everything should be left to chance. If you're a necromancer, don't bring your summoned zombies if you can't find a babysitter.

No boyfriend, no scroll, and now no hope for the approaching deadline. After Rob left her apartment that day, Tessa spent the evening into the early morning at her desk trying to figure out what she could do. The deadline loomed with Cramer.

Before he left he made her promise she wouldn't give up. As they parted in front of her door, he looked her in the eye and made her swear. "You're not going to go gently into the good night."

"You're trying to use Dylan Thomas on me right now?" She wasn't feeling rather poetic at the moment.

"I'm serious, Tee." He gripped her

shoulders so she couldn't look away. "The minute I leave the city you're on your own. The woman I fell for wouldn't go down without kicking some ass first."

So she tried. Financially, she'd backed into a no-win situation. Tessa was past the cancellation stage for the venues. She'd already made a down payment, but all of them expected the rest of the money two weeks before the event. And she didn't have a dime to her name.

She'd pressed her face down so long on the ADDITIONAL LOAN REQUESTED DENIED stamp from the Dwarves First National Bank that she wouldn't be surprised if she had a new facial tattoo. Her request to buy a new scroll had been denied. She wasn't shocked. A couple hundred grand to buy a replacement scroll, which now sat useless in the recycle bin, wouldn't come from a business arrangement.

A quick trip to the pawnshop earlier in the morning to sell a few things also didn't go as planned.

"I'll take all that other stuff you got, but well, the wand doesn't want to be sold." The young wizard from the pawnshop in East Village tried to pry the stubborn twig from her palm, but it wouldn't budge. Yes, it didn't belong to her in the first place so it served her right for trying to sell it.

She kept hearing Rob's words, her heart tugging each time, but her supposedly productive, rage-against-the-dying-of-the-light morning turned into a depressing afternoon with ice cream while watching a few Meg Ryan movies. She cried like a baby watching the unrequited love between friends in *When Harry Met Sally*. Then Tessa cursed Tom Hanks' character as he took away her tiny bookstore business in *You've Got Mail*. Not the best movie to watch. She should've known better.

Probably by this time, Rob was likely heading to a military base. He left her a text message that he'd contact her when he could. Wasn't that a silver lining?

It didn't make her feel any better.

By ten o'clock p.m. the local news came on, interrupting her movie fix. A full day wasted feeling sorry for herself.

Something shifted her coffee mug on the counter of her kitchen. *Was that Kiki?* Hell, with all those ghost cats roaming around, she shouldn't be surprised if a cat or two jostled a sugar bowl.

One of the ruled out suspects lounged on a chair across from her. Kiki meowed.

n elderly voice whispered, "Tessa? Are you home?"

"I'm home," Tessa called back.

Her grandmother floated into the room, saw her attire, and harrumphed. "You look as if you sat here all day." She glanced at the huge bowl of popcorn and five empty cans of diet soda.

Tessa avoided her grandmother's face, unable to tell her what happened. She'd cried all day today, and there weren't any tears left, only the raw feeling of defeat.

Grandma Kilburn sat down next to her. "What's wrong, sweetheart?"

"I failed."

"Oh, every client's different. I had a few doosies myself once in a while. But today's another day."

"It doesn't matter. I'm leaving New York."

Her grandmother frowned. "Why would you say such a thing?"

Tessa sighed, wishing Grandma Kilburn's form was corporeal so she could experience the warmth of a grandmother's touch, smell the sweet scent of her lavender oil.

She told her grandma of the lost scroll as well as her adventures with Rob. She left the worst news for the end.

"I'm bankrupt."

"Have you spoken to your parents? Why aren't you fighting?" Grandma Kilburn's face was stern, her shoulders pulled back.

"It's more than that. I have a client I worked for months to secure and nurture, and now I'll lose him." Tessa felt so ashamed to reveal this. The one person she wanted to impress knew her failure now. She couldn't survive as a matchmaker.

"That's one client." Her grandmother's hand brushed against her hair, going through the motions of smoothing it. The very gesture sent a strange chill down her spine.

"He is the one client who owes me the most money and has connections with the Supernatural Council." She laughed softly. "I don't even have enough money to pay for the venues I secured a few months ago."

"Oh. That is unfortunate." Grandma sat back against the couch, for once silenced.

Then she sat back up, revitalized once again.

"But that doesn't matter." Grandma Kilburn stood and then pointed her finger at Tessa. "Take off that housecoat, girl. You're going with me for a walk."

"To where?"

"Hush your mouth and do as you're told. While you get dressed, I need to gather some reserves for a powerful spell from the beyond."

Twenty minutes later, in a T-shirt and pants, Tessa left her apartment with her grandmother.

"Where are we going?"

"Don't you listen when your elders talk? You'll learn soon enough."

They secured a cab and drove northward to the Upper West Side. Their final destination was a high-rise apartment building nestled next to the Trump Towers.

Her grandmother floated out of the cab ahead of her. They entered the building lobby, but Grandma Kilburn stopped her before she approached the concierge.

"Close your eyes, Tessa. I need to mask you."

The chill from Grandma's fingertips caressed her forehead down to her belly. When Tessa opened her eyes, the world was painted black and white.

Amazing, yet peculiar like a movie from the

1940s. Tessa gazed at the dark shadows along her hands.

"Don't get all nervous on me. It's one of the side effects I could never prevent. Your great-grandma Greta Kilburn could cast this spell with her knickers on backwards." Her grandma floated toward the elevators, forcing Tessa to follow.

They exited at the 35th floor and then headed toward one of the townhouses. Tessa raised her hand to knock, eliciting a scolding from her grandmother.

"You're masked! What are you doing?"

"I forgot already."

Grandma Kilburn rolled her eyes. "With all that work you've done repossessing people's property, you should know you don't march into people's homes."

A cold hand slid around her wrist, chilling her skin. Slowly she was pulled through the door. The process of flowing through matter was jarring. Once through the door, they entered the foyer of a beautiful home with ten-foot-tall windows and oak floors. Gleaming white walls with modern fine art dotted the walls.

The chatter from a couple emerged from around the corner. Grandma Kilburn led her forward toward the voices in the living room. For a moment she wondered if her eyes deceived her, but there was Liam with the woman he had chosen during the party. The older man sat cuddling with his auburn-haired lady while she read a book.

"Liam, why don't you want to go to Europe this summer with me?"

"We can go to Europe, Lemondrop. I'd just prefer to vacation in Aruba."

Lemondrop?

The woman smiled coyly, turning to plant a quick kiss on his cheek. "You always give in to me eventually, don't you?"

"Rather hard not to give in," he grumbled with a grin.

The woman continued to read as Grandma Kilburn stepped forward. "I'm sure you recognize this man."

"Of course, my client Liam Pershing."

"Don't you see what you've done for him?"

"Well, of course, he's still dating the woman I matched him with."

"Look closer, girl, like I taught you. There's more to this scene."

Tessa scanned, shaking her head.

"Is this the same man who walked into your office for your services?"

This Liam was clean-shaven with shorter hair and less creepy clothes. Elena was the same woman, with her mousy lime-green glasses perched on her nose. Liam had flocked to the younger witches during the party, but this woman stepped up to him and told him he'd dance with her when the music came on. From that moment, the other magic-magnets didn't have a chance. Her assertiveness and aged beauty won him over. Little did Tessa know how things had changed so much since their date several weeks ago.

And Elena's hand! A dazzling engagement ring blinked at Tessa from across the room as Elena held her book. Old Liam had popped the question.

Tessa pumped her fist in victory.

"Do you see now?"

"Yes, Grandma. I see now."

"Look at the wonderful things you've done. C'mon, it's time to go." Grandma left the living room.

"Back home?"

"No, we need to make another visit."

Their journey took them across the Hudson River into Jersey. Who would she see next?

After a forty-five minute cab ride, they reached the outside of a sprawling mansion. With its gothic columns and quirky spirals, the place stood out against the modern, gated mansions along the road.

Once outside the cab she asked, "How do we get in?"

"The same way as before." Grandma Kilburn took her hand and led her through the fence. They walked up the flagstone path to the ornate double doors with sculptures of cherubs carved into the dark wood. She peered at the door, wondering what lay behind them. Was this Cramer's house? Did her grandmother find him?

With impatience, Grandma yanked her through the thick door, cursing as they stormed through an incantation protecting the entrance.

"I remember back in the good old days when locks were enough to protect homes.

Now people need spells to protect stuff. Your Aunt Lenore put a protection spell on her recipe box." She harrumphed. "As if anyone would want to steal a recipe for dry and hard pumpkin cookies."

Once through the doors, they ascended a grand staircase. Twenty-foot windows offered a view of a sprawling front yard beyond the door. At the top of the stairs, the tinny sounds of a harpsichord could be heard from the room at the end of the long hallway.

Tessa followed her grandmother into a room—the music room. There were two rows of seating for guests, along with rows of cabinets for sheet music. Along the far walls, built-in shelves were filled with old books. Once in the middle of the room, she could make out the couple that played. With jovial faces, they danced over the keys. They battled as they played, with one jumping back and forth between the first and second row.

It was her first client. A referral from her grandmother to get her started. Lionel Singer sat with his wife Amelia and continued to play as they watched. Tessa took a step closer to see that Amelia was expecting. After three years, their relationship had moved from marriage to now a pregnancy. Her heart swelled with satisfaction.

She did this. She made this happen. And all of this from introducing two people who very likely would've never met. Amelia worked in Long Island as a waitress while Lionel was an overbearing classical pianist out of Jersey.

"You've done great work here, Tessa. Do you see the true magic in this room?"

"Yes, Grandma. I do."

"Good. Then it's time to get to work." With a swish of her transparent hands, their mask of invisibility fell. "Good evening, Mr. Singer. My granddaughter needs your help."

Tessa expected any normal warlock to show shock when someone pops up out of nowhere in his home. Lionel took it very well.

"You could've knocked, Mrs. Kilburn. A door, to be precise."

"Nonsense. I listen to you and your wife playing all the time. No need to bother you two."

Amelia reddened. Tessa sure hoped Grandma left when they decided to do a little something extra on the music bench.

He offered a stern face as he stood and offered them seats. "How may I be of assistance at this late hour?"

Her grandmother briefly went over her tale while Lionel and Amelia nodded at the appropriate moments.

"I wish I could help in regard to Archibald, but I'm afraid I'm not part of his circle of associates."

Grandma nodded with a slight frown.

Amelia joined their conversation. "But that doesn't mean we can't try to set a plan in motion in case we find someone who can contact him. I think I have an idea."

Amelia made a clever event planner. Within a half-hour, she had a plan to hold the party at their home. She'd handle hiring a formal event planner to secure the seating and decorations. Lionel's quartet would provide music for the evening. Tessa couldn't have been more pleased. All she needed was to secure the food and move heaven and earth to find someone who didn't want to be found.

Twenty-four hours had passed since Tessa's grandmother had offered a helping hand. But the clock was ticking; tomorrow the party was expected to take place.

Tessa called Ursula and Danielle to meet at them at her apartment for an emergency meeting. They went over the list of clients to determine if any of them would cater the event or donate their time to help.

She struggled to humble herself and ask for help. Losing the scroll was hard enough to endure.

"Don't worry about calling them, Tessa," Danielle said. "I have a way with words."

"I may not want to do it, but these are my clients. I need to step forward and ask." She glanced at the list with notes scrawled after the names. Who'd agree to cater an event twenty-four hours before it took place? "Have we decided who'd be crazy enough to help us?"

Ursula tapped the fourth and seventh name

on the list. "Kent Gilmore and Quincy Harper would be our best bets. Kent owns restaurants out of Chicago, and Quincy is a head chef here in Manhattan."

She picked up the list and headed into the kitchen to make the calls. Her hands shook as she dialed the numbers. Kent wasn't available, but his secretary took her message. Quincy picked up the phone on the second ring.

"Quincy, how are you?"

His pleasant voice echoed a greeting and then he asked why she called.

"I'm in a bit of a bind. I have a last-minute party tomorrow and I need some help."

"I know a few caterers who might be able to do a last-minute gig. But it'll cost you plenty."

"Yes, I know." Her foot tapped against the floor. She bit her lower lip. *Just say it. Tell him!* "Look, I'm about to hold the largest event of my career and I don't have a dime to spare." Her voice caught for a moment, but she held on. "I would owe you big time if you could step in to help."

A long pause. The noise of papers rustling on a desk. *He'll say no.* She'd asked for too much. Said too much.

"It's your lucky day! Not only do I have extra fish, but I have some culinary students who are coming in tonight. We could whip you up some hors d'oeuvres for your bash tomorrow."

She nearly collapsed on the floor with joy. "Thank you! Thank you!"

"Hey, everybody has hard times. My life

has definitely taken a turn for the better with Melanie. But I hope you'll survive this and come out squeaky clean."

"I will, thanks again."

They finished their conversation with how Amelia Singer's event planner would contact him. She was about to leave the kitchen when her iPhone beeped with an incoming message: *T, I pulled off the impossible through a wizard commanding officer. A.C. will be back in town tomorrow. Be ready. Rob.*

Another message followed with the address of a penthouse in Midtown. Cramer's home.

Tessa's hand covered her mouth to stifle her squeal. Holy shit, Rob did it!

Ursula bounded into the kitchen with Danielle not far behind. "What's going on?"

When she caught her breath, Tessa said, "Not only do we have a caterer, but we have the guest of honor coming as well."

Chapter 25

Dating Tip #1: One of the most important things to remember is that the rules of engagement do not apply to all couples — whether they are werewolves or fairies — one size doesn't fit all. Use your heart and you may find it leads you in the right direction.

The next morning, Rob arrived back in NYC to complete his mission. The minute he stepped into the Coney Island neighborhood, he sighed. Coming back here should've included the prospect of seeing Tessa again, but that wasn't meant to be.

Right off Surf Avenue, he took in the sounds of amusement rides, busy shop fronts, and mobs of plucky tourists. A place meant for fun and relaxation hid a darker side. One of the most iconic places in American culture was the NYC hotspot for warlocks. Go figure.

"I love Coney Island!" Harabeuji spouted from Rob's hip. The bag spirit haggled him to no end to get on the roller coasters.

No more than a hundred feet away, on the

other side of the street, Rob flicked a glance at a man with a younger kid holding a stuffed toy. The guy broadcasted his abilities loud and clear as a wizard—yet even with his powers, he didn't take a step to cross the street toward the amusement park. Such was the collective power of the warlocks to fence off three city blocks and keep the white magic spellcasters away.

The poor wizard scowled then pulled his kid away. He probably was pissed he couldn't visit Nathan's Hot Dogs. Rob considered that a crime in and of itself, but there wasn't anything he could do about it. Just another reason for everybody to want to piss in the other camp's backyard.

Rob kept going toward the exhibits along Jones Walk. The late April breeze from the Atlantic Ocean touched his face and made him smile. Tessa would've liked this. How come they'd never taken the time to visit a place like this? With her refined nature, Tessa seemed better suited to fine restaurants and museums, but as he got to know her, she would've been just fine holding his hand while they waited in line for the Ferris Wheel or a roller coaster.

He laughed at the pleasant thought, imagining her giving him a hard time while he bought everything he encountered. Rob had a soft spot for corn dogs and cotton candy. They were just as important as bacon in terms of a man's list of food groups.

He continued his stroll, taking his time to reach his final destination. At the end of Jones Walk, he reached what he considered the best location for the warlocks' hangout, the freak show exhibit. The outside had all the decorations the curious human population craved: pictures of bearded ladies and mermaids on the wall, a machine that engraved your initials on a penny, and even more ways to suck the cash from your pockets.

The man who sold tickets for the show offered Rob a nod and let him pass. Rob hadn't been here in a while. The guy at the ticket counter appeared new and looked as thrilled as the last chap who had to warm the seat. A job was a job these days.

The hallways weaved and curved, but he didn't have any trouble following the path to the hidden rooms. As Rob got closer to the main clubhouse, his jaw tightened. The faces he passed in the hallway were either uncaring, or even worse, straight up freaking pissed. One guy even gave him a rude gesture, a past repo gig gone wrong when the man showed up as Rob carried away the goods. Not a single friendly face looked at him as he crossed the threshold into a large room with a bar and tables. The majority of the warlocks either nursed a drink at the bar or played some kind of card game at the tables.

A momentary hush came over the boisterous room the minute he walked in. Somebody in here had to be powerful—that was what he had to watch out for. Damn it all to hell, why was he doing this again? Playing the wizards' game to right the wrongs and keep warlocks in line?

As he strolled through the room, he reminded himself of why he joined the military. Why he spent years training and working with his team. Wasn't this situation the same? To protect innocents from those who had the means to harm them?

"You have a lot of nerve coming here, Shin."

Rob hid his smile. He wasn't exactly happy to be here either. The voice was familiar so Rob turned to look at the source. Flannery hadn't changed much since Rob had taken his rabbit's foot away. The dude had probably stolen another one.

"He stinks like wizards," Flannery's cohort at his table said. The two men shifted so they could smirk at Rob better.

"I've seen crusty *gisaengs* in broken-down brothels who smell better than they do," Harabeuji whispered with a snort.

Rob shrugged, pushing the pair into howls. The laughs were easy to brush off. During his first few days in SEAL training, the officers had barked all sorts of orders, breaking down the recruits until their bodies and minds hardened. A few jokes from a bunch of warlocks didn't amount to jack shit.

"Just turn around and march on outta here," the other man said. He tilted his black hat back to reveal a receding hairline.

Rob leaned on their table. "I'm thirsty, gentlemen."

"The bar don't serve your kind here," Flannery spat.

"And what kind is that?"

"The kind that will sell out another warlock brother."

Rob chuckled. He'd heard many others give him the same excuse to keep him from repossessing their shit.

"Why are you so intense?" Rob's eyebrows lowered. "You got something to hide?"

"Why d-don't you come check me?" Flannery's balls had apparently grown bigger while he was here among other spellcasters. He'd shown less spunk when Rob was in his backyard.

"I'll pass. I'm here looking for someone and I'm too busy to give you a pat down."

"You'll never find Dagger," Flannery said slowly. "He doesn't want to be found."

Rob didn't react to Flannery's words, although he was a bit surprised word had gotten out somehow.

"Soon enough, people like you won't matter when we bring down the wizards. Dagger will see to that."

"Uh huh. We've been saying that for thousands of years." Rob snagged some peanuts from the cup on the table. Neither man stopped him.

"He's more powerful than you can imagine. Dagger's the real deal."

Rob resisted grinning. The groupie stench was strong with this one. "I'm sure he is, but Dagger doesn't have the means to create his own dimension or even use a magician kit to hide a bunch of rabbits."

"Who the hell are you to speak? Can you waltz in and out of Limbo? Do you have the means to do it?"

Rob shrugged and feigned a step back. This part of his mission had gone quicker than expected. It was always the big mouths that felt the need to open widest in the end.

Rob took another handful of peanuts. Flannery opened his mouth to speak, but Rob turned away and marched right out with a definite destination in mind.

He had prey to hunt and didn't have time to waste on small fry.

There was only one way for Rob to reach his final destination at just the *right* place—even if that meant giving a few jobs to the competition.

"You'll give me what?" the other warlock asked at the end of cellphone line. The guy's voice was hoarse with a tinge of fatigue. He'd probably spent all morning working at a regular job after spending the night doing repo work.

"I'll give you a shot at every single gig I'd get assigned at Clive's place." He didn't work for Clive anymore so it was a win-win for both parties. "All you have to do is find something for me. A house in Limbo."

Ten calls later he was done. Not a single spellcaster turned him down. His former employer didn't exactly have the most attractive digs, but Clive got fed the bigger fish in the pond. Mostly due to Rob's efforts.

Now all he had to do was wait.

An hour later, a text message arrived with good news: *You got 9 min to get your ass to 10648 W 55th.*

Traveling from Brooklyn to Manhattan with jump points helped him get there with seconds to spare. He appeared before the caller who pointed where Rob needed to go.

"If you look to the far right, there's this structure that leans kinda weird," the man said.

Rob peered into the familiar pink haze at what could be described as a home. Someone, with apparently a lot of time on their hands, had used magic to construct a shelter from whatever materials he could procure: random slabs of wood and metal for the walls, along with a colorful satyr's blanket for the door.

For a guy hiding out from the wizards, Dagger didn't exactly have the nicest place compared to the beach house where Rob and Tessa fought him.

Rob slowly approached the place, careful to keep an eye out. With one hand under the flap of his satchel for easy weapon retrieval, he reached the doorway and peered inside. There wasn't much, just a bed of quilts and a lantern in the corner for light. Not that one needed to worry about the elements in Limbo, but you never knew what roamed around here.

A rustling of junk drew Rob outside. He found Dagger sitting on a nymph's enchanted bench with a fresh cigarette trailing smoke into the air.

"Why, if it isn't Mr. Shin," Dagger said after a long drag. "Have you returned to Limbo for a longer stay?"

"You know why I'm here."

Dagger sighed. "You never were one for chit-chat first."

"I came here to take care of business, even if that means taking you out."

Dagger's little smile grew. "You're cocky. That's growing on me, actually. I could kill you now, but that would be a waste, wouldn't it? Most of the brothers let the darkness within seep inside until their judgment is clouded. But you, on the other hand, are far sharper." Dagger flicked the glowing ash at the end of the cigarette on the bench. "The warlocks could use a man like you when the war comes."

Rob rolled his eyes. More war talk that would go nowhere. "Not interested. You should know by now I don't choose sides." He immediately changed the subject. The last thing he needed was more diatribe about how the warlocks planned to bring the wizards down. "Even if you've managed to create a means to blacken magical weapons, what makes you think you'll manage to take out all the wizards' arsenal?"

"Wouldn't you love to know that? Let's just say this place is the key." Dagger left the bench and strolled around a mound of tattered books and discarded clothes. "Contrary to popular belief, not everything stays here. The dwarves have been working with the Supernatural

Council to return all the weapons back into the world. Ever since I've gathered my cursed goodies — thanks in part to you — I've blackened most of the wizard weapons in Limbo. You did a lot of the work pushing most of what I needed through the portal. You need a particular amulet for cursed goods, which I don't possess. Thanks to you, once I figure out a way to get my tool, a lot more wizard wands are gonna bleed black."

Rob's jaw twitched. *You dirty piece of shit.*

Time to wipe that smirk off his face. He shifted to advance on Dagger, then paused. There was no way Dagger would be able to blacken *all* wizard weapons in the world. They'd have to be in close proximity to the cursed items he gathered.

So what the hell was he up to?

No time for Q&A right now, might as well get to the ass-kicking part. Rob opened his satchel.

"Wield it well, *Doryeonim*," the bag spirit implored. From within the folds he pulled out a long onyx staff. Black thorns jutted from the end. Sparks from its power heated the palms of his hands. A thrill pulsed through him as he gripped it.

"I guess this means you've decided to turn your back on us?" Dagger spat.

"I haven't done a damn thing to our kind other than return property to the original owners. What I will do is put my foot up your ass so far you're gonna taste the cotton candy I stepped on not too long ago."

"Show me what you got then." Dagger took a few steps back, then brushed his fingertips along the top of a metal block on the end of an antique bookcase. The dark metal came to life, wobbling a bit before it fell into an old wooden bucket with a loud clatter.

Rob held his staff steady, unsure what move Dagger would make. A mahogany fire wand sprouted from his palm. He pointed it in Rob's direction.

Rob raised his staff in a defensive pose, drawing on its power until it mingled with his own, building to a crescendo that roared in his ears like ocean waves crashing into the rocks. His body vibrated as he prepared to release the power gathering in the staff, sweat beading on his brow from the effort it took to control the magic. From the corner of his eye, he caught sight of the bucket. It shuddered before sinking into the junk and Rob stilled, his palms burning from the unspent magic in the staff. His focus wavered, the need to investigate nagged at him. Especially when a sinkhole began to form.

Maybe sinkhole wasn't an accurate term.

The contents of the ten-foot radius sunk in, only to rise again as something jerked and spasmed from the ground. A tiny head with glowing red eyes came first, it's bulky mass shuddering as it tried to find its footing. A set of metallic shoulders covered with old oiled leather armor rose through the junk, along with a set of large hands. A strong stench of iron shot from the creature. Rob held his ground, trying to swallow away any apprehension from the humanoid thing that flexed its massive hands.

The satchel on his hip quivered and spat out words Rob didn't recognize. Maybe he vocalized the curse words Rob held in.

Dagger must've paid a pretty penny for the iron brick he dropped into the bucket. Summoned golems were dangerous in the magical realm. Far too unstable, they were known to turn on those who called on them if the spellcaster wasn't powerful enough to keep them from taking them out after their target had been brought down.

Rob took a step forward, his torso vibrating with pressure like a volcano about to blow. The best offense was a full on attack in this case. He aimed the staff at the golem. The power circling in his stomach jumped into the end of the weapon and raced to the other side. He held tight as an arch of blindingly white lightning shot the golem point blank in the chest. The creature screeched as it flew backwards into Dagger's house. The wooden walls splintered into tiny bits as debris scattered wide.

Rob aimed again, feeling the heat in the staff writhing to be set free. He was unprepared for how fast the golem sprinted in his direction. His hands tightened on the staff as he fired again in quick bursts, but the golem quickly reached his side and swung wide. Rob brought the staff upwards, managing to block the blow. His teeth jarred from the impact. What little defensive magic the staff had, it wasn't worth shit.

The creature laughed, a choppy sound, as it raised its meaty fists high in the air to slam downward. Rob's block didn't come fast enough and the golem struck him on the left shoulder. The crunch of broken bones forced all the air out of his lungs. Rob let out a long curse as the blow struck.

"*Doryeonim*, stay sharp!" the satchel growled.

Pain radiated through his left arm. It was now hanging shattered at his side. Rob staggered backward, quickly reaching into his bag with his good right arm, for another weapon. Another swing came hard, but he sidestepped the blow.

Where is it? Where is it? Only once in his life had he gone through the whole inventory of his father's satchel, barely understanding most of it, but only one weapon in his father's arsenal would save his ass now: The *haetai*'s stick.

He stretched his fingers until he encountered a heavy twitching baton, no longer than his forearm. He yanked upwards, pulling until the stick emerged from the bag, lit as if on fire. With a mighty heave, he tossed the flaming weapon into the air, hoping and praying what his father told him held true. *"The haetai defends against evil when you need it, but use it wisely."*

The iron golem stormed at him again. Rob glanced around him and spotted a charmed Aegean shield. He gritted his teeth, dodging and weaving to avoid a giant fist to the head. Pain ripped through him as he held his left arm against his body with his right, only to let go so he could reach out to retrieve the shield.

The golem snarled and swung again.

Instead of feeling the jarring effect of the swing, the golem's hand fell into the shield. The golem roared, pulling back a corroded and sizzling limb.

The golem swung wider to catch Rob's legs as a blur came from the left and slammed into them. The *haetai* growled deep in its throat. He jerked his gaze in its direction, taking in a massive, yet beautiful beast from Korean legend. The *haetai*'s long incisors locked around the golem's shoulder, digging deep into the metal. The beast's lion-like form shook its head to deepen the wound, its scaly limbs twisting and claws the length of blades cleaving at the golem. Dagger's soldier tried to snatch its attacker off its back, but the *haetai* held fast and they tumbled away. Rob dug the balls of his feet into the uneven floor beneath him and scrambled away just as two grappling beasts cut a swath through the debris not a foot from where he had stood.

The two duked it out, the *haetai* clawing and scratching while the golem punched and bashed. The *haetai* was faster, far more vicious and managed to wrestle the iron golem to ground. With a loud screech, the *haetai* ripped off the golem's head like a forgotten rag doll. Another limb flew away, then a leg.

The *haetai* was no joke.

Instead of poking at its kill, the beast glanced at Rob and vanished into a flash of light. The stick around its collar fell to the ground for Rob to pick up. His arm burned as he held it, but he had bigger problems now.

"Rather handy," Dagger said from behind him. He closed in quickly from the left.

He tried to lift his right arm to block Dagger's forward stab, but he didn't twist around fast enough. Dagger grinned as he extended his fire wand with a blade at the end. The tip pressed against Rob's Adam's apple.

"Go ahead. Show me how fast you are," Dagger whispered. "Give me a reason to make you swallow this knife."

When Rob slightly shifted, Dagger grabbed his injured shoulder and squeezed. Tight. Pain coursed through him, spreading from his shoulder into his mouth. Rob grunted, refusing to give that piece of garbage warlock the satisfaction of hearing him cry out.

He pushed forward, holding tight to Rob's wound. "Start walking, Shin."

They shuffled away from the ruins of Dagger's house over a hill. No more than a hundred feet away, Rob spotted where Limbo disappeared into endless canyons of emptiness. The blackness had no end. When they reached the edge, Dagger laughed at his side.

"Do you know what's down there?" Dagger pressed the wand-blade closer until the tip cut into Rob's neck. "Limbo's architects needed powerful magic to hold countless magical things inside—and to keep others out. In order to do that, they trapped a demon down there."

Rob had heard enough. Ignoring the pain in his shoulder, he twisted out of the grip and threw a right hook, ready to block his vulnerable left side. Dagger was quick to respond, thrusting the blade forward with a dance of fire in its wake. Rob managed to dodge the heat searing across his chest, growing ever more pissed off, to throw a combination right hook, followed by a swift uppercut, then a right jab. Pain be fucking damned.

With a roar, Rob slammed into Dagger, shoulder to chin, as hard as he could, and drove the warlock toward the edge of the cliff. Dagger lunged toward him and rolled onto Rob, trying to bring the wand-blade close to his neck. "Do you want to meet what lives down there?" Dagger hissed. "It eats blackened magic."

"Not today, but you're more than welcome to check it out for me." Rob thrust one of his legs upward and placed his shoe in Dagger's chest. With a hard kick, he flipped Dagger over his body beyond the edge. Rob turned to watch Dagger fall through the mist and plunge into the chasm.

"Have a nice trip," Rob murmured. With satisfaction, he hoped Dagger enjoyed his stay in Limbo as much as he did.

"Well done, *Doryeonim!*" If the satchel had a face, Rob suspected the old spirit would be beaming.

"Don't congratulate me yet." Exhaustion settled into his shoulders and pain continued to stab at him from his shattered bones. Far too quickly the reality of the situation hit. He was injured and lost. How the hell was he supposed to get out of here? His thoughts went to Tessa, somewhere beyond the haze, and he hoped she got his message and she pulled through to save her business.

Dagger's final words bothered him. *"It eats blackened magic."* Did he have plans for the demon? Plans beyond bringing down the wizards? A creature powerful enough to hold the fabric of Limbo together had staggering power. Unimaginable strength.

Dagger was out of the way now, but what door might he have opened with his actions?

With no working wizard wands among the junk along the ground, Rob had no choice but to use a binding spell, which barely did enough to keep the pain at bay when his ribs were jacked up, and hope the bindings held while he searched for a way home.

Nothing stirred as he walked east. He'd keep going until a portal opened. If he got out once before, he could do it again.

By noon that same day, Tessa worked with Ursula and the event planner to make sure everything was in place for the evening festivities. She never expected the party to be so beautiful. Lionel and Amelia had converted their grand cathedral-like dining room into a party space. The twenty-seater dining room table was removed so a quartet could play and the guests could dance and eat food. Quincy had made arrangements with the event planner to have the food delivered by three this afternoon.

Even with the positive outlook, she couldn't help but feel disappointed. She had her wish, the party would happen and Cramer would be there. But the most important person she wanted here was likely somewhere far away.

The man who'd come through as her hero.

Tessa smiled. Of course, it would be Rob to bail her out of a mess again. Even if he couldn't be there, she wouldn't let him down after his efforts. This party would succeed and her business would rise from the fire unscathed — well, maybe a bit charred on the edges.

Everything was in place. Danielle had contacted Cramer and he said he'd show up promptly at 7 p.m.

Her client arrived as expected, appearing before her in a dazzle of white and gold.

"Miss Dandridge." He assessed the dining room and nodded. "This is unexpected, yet pleasing. When I learned from an associate of mine that you lost your scroll, I was quite surprised." He accepted a drink from a waiter. "That didn't sound like the woman I signed a contract with all those months ago."

"I've had some problems, but as you can see from today, I know how to bounce back and succeed."

He nodded. "Before I meet the women, did you have any problems finding anyone?"

She leaned forward to offer a sly smile. "You'll be more than pleased with them. One or two may catch you off-guard. Now all you have to do is act like the gentleman I know you can be. You might be rough around the edges, but I've learned that shouldn't hold you back from finding the right woman."

A few minutes later, Tessa and Cramer arrived to a party in full swing. The quartet played a lively tune and waiters served appetizers of calamari, roasted clams, and quiche squares. The culinary students had done a fantastic job. Twelve ladies waited anxiously as Cramer entered.

Tessa addressed them. "Ladies, thank you for coming this evening, even under such last-minute circumstances. I appreciate the efforts made for you to come out across the river and spend time with a valued client. For those of you who haven't met him…" She pointed to Cramer. "This is Archibald Cramer, distinguished member of the Supernatural Council and elder warlock. I hope you all have a delightful time."

Tessa stepped back from the deluge of bodies. The magic-magnets came at him first, asking questions and throwing out their hands for introductions. Cramer took everything in with a smug calm. He offered smiles all around. A welcome change. She left the group to check on the party.

Danielle tried to shoo her away. "Everything's fine. Stop worrying."

"I know, but I want everything to be perfect."

Danielle smiled. "It will be and Cramer's having a great time."

Tessa glanced at the entrance *again*. She wished everyone, including herself, could enjoy the festivities. Last night she'd had a foolish fantasy. A quick daydream where a man showed up in jeans and a black T-shirt. Even though he was underdressed in the dream, the grin he wore was all she needed. She tried to smile but failed.

Rob wasn't coming.

She had to face these kinds of situations and move on. Wasn't that a part of life?

The party continued with Cramer offering the ladies dances while the music played. She clapped her hands with everyone else as he swung his partners around the room.

Her eyes darted to the doorway as someone in a uniform appeared at the door. She glanced away, hoping the illusion would disappear. Her gut clenched. *Don't look, it won't be Rob — he's somewhere else.*

Slowly, she checked again and there was Rob, tall and dashing in his white uniform. She took one step and then another. Heels and all, she ran to the door where he lifted her and planted a long kiss on her lips. The music in the room faded away as she hung in the air supported by his strong arms. There were only his intoxicating lips and the feeling they evoked in her heart.

They separated, and she turned her head, embarrassed to have her guests see her swept up in the arms of a man only a few of them knew. But they didn't seem to mind and the moment was met with three or four whistles from the crowd, and a wink from Cramer. An older witch sat next to him grinning from ear-to-ear. Cramer leaned closer his date for a private conversation.

"What are you doing here?" Tessa asked as he put her down. "You should be out to sea at Bora Bora or something."

He chuckled, pulling her close. "I had an important mission to handle first." He sighed. "I had to move heaven and earth to get to you though. Somehow I made it thanks to Harry and a few of his wizard friends who patched me up. I've never been so glad to see biker wizards before."

"Are you all right?" She touched his face. The warm skin along his rough cheek felt so good.

"I will be. I got a new job. You're looking at the newest hire for a *special* branch of the United States Armed Forces."

"Special, huh? Sounds interesting. You'll have to tell me more later."

His hand stroked her back as he snuck in a quick peck. "To be honest, I wondered if you'd be happy to see me."

She shrugged. "Oh, stop it. After everything that's happened, I thought I'd never see you again." She kissed his lips again, lingering long enough to run her hands down his waist. "No, you're not a ghost. A flesh and blood man."

His eyes smoldered. "I'm not going anywhere, Tee. I plan to be around for a long time—right where you need me to be. Especially since we have some catching up to do."

"I agree." She suddenly felt shy. Even a few days had been far too long without him.

"I missed you, Tee."

She sucked in a breath. No man had ever said that to her before. Not a single boyfriend.

"Do you want a drink?" she managed. "Maybe sit down and have something to eat?"

He shook his head, his eyes still stormy. He had other ideas.

"I've been thinking about you, too. About us." She sighed softly. "But I do have a party to finish."

"Do you think a party is gonna stop me from what I want do to you?"

"No, probably not." Her breath hitched as the words she wanted to say burst forth. She had to let it out. "I was so hurt the last time we were together—I didn't get a chance to tell you how I really feel about you." She swallowed. "How I love you, Minho."

"You should never need to say it. We both already know how we feel." Rob smiled, the look on his face filling her with endless joy.

He leaned into her ear, whispering something dirty about a large linen closet he passed on the way into the dining room. *Another closet.* Her breath caught in anticipation.

She searched for Danielle in the crowd. The blonde had witnessed the whole encounter with the biggest grin.

Tessa mouthed the words, "You're on point now."

Danielle squealed and jumped. It was about time Tessa let her close out an event. Why not start with a client as important as Archibald Cramer?

She turned to Rob and fingered his uniform. Damn, he looked good. "Danielle and Ursula can handle the party. But there's one small thing I want."

"And that would be?"

A Cheshire cat grin spread across her face. "I wouldn't mind a reenactment of the end of that movie — *An Officer and a Gentlemen*."

Rob grinned and slowly picked her up. "You're worth the trouble this time."

THE END

DARK MAGIC DECEPTION

WARLOCK REPO MAN CHRONICLES #2

WILL YOU BE READY FOR HIS NEXT MISSION?

As dark forces lurk in the northeast, Rob must collect property from deadly targets. With Tessa pulled in deep into the ongoing battle, can she escape the coming threat?

Did you love REPOSSESSED?

Check out Natalya Stravinsky's series in the Coveted universe!

Available now from Ballantine Books!

SOMETIMES WHAT YOU COVET IS IMPOSSIBLE TO KEEP.

For werewolf Natalya Stravinsky, the supernatural is nothing extraordinary. What *does* seem strange is that she's stuck in her hometown of South Toms River, New Jersey, the outcast of her pack, selling antiques to finicky magical creatures. Restless and recovering from her split with gorgeous ex-boyfriend, Thorn, Nat finds comfort in an unusual place: her obsessively collected stash of holiday trinkets. But complications pile up faster than her ornaments when Thorn returns home — and the two discover that the spark between them remains intense.

Before Nat can sort out their relationship, she must face a more immediate and dangerous problem. Her pack is under attack from the savage Long Island werewolves — and Nat is their first target in a turf war. Toss in a handsome wizard vying for her affection, a therapy group for the anxious and enchanted, and the South Toms River pack leader ready to throw her to the wolves, and it's enough to give anybody a panic attack. With the stakes as high as the full moon, Nat must summon all of her strength to save her pack and, ultimately, herself.

ABOUT THE AUTHOR

Shawntelle Madison is a Web developer who loves to weave words as well as code. She'd be reluctant to admit it, but if pressed, she'd say that she covets and collects source code. After losing her first summer job detasseling corn, Madison performed various jobs, from fast-food clerk to grunt programmer to university webmaster. Writing eccentric characters is her favorite job of all. On any given day when she's not surgically attached to her computer, she can be found watching cheesy horror movies or the latest action-packed anime. Shawntelle Madison lives in Missouri with her husband and children.

31195705R00174

Made in the USA
Charleston, SC
09 July 2014